GUARDIANS
OF
THE ANCIENT ONE

The Parallel Time Trilogy (book two) expanding adventure unveils the ever more revealing nature of the mysterious Master Adepts of The Ancient One and their involvement with Admiral Starland and the space fleet of The Galactic Interdimensional Alliance of Free Worlds. Sen Dar gains control of the previously unknown space-faring Zon race living in a parallel dimension and sets them on a course to attack present day Earth. Witness the ever-deepening love affair between Captain Kalem and Mayleena, Etta's courageous antics, and their ongoing struggle to achieve self-mastery - so that one day they can return to The Ancient One's far higher mystic realm of sublime Sound and Light. Along the way, they must endure a very rare training to somehow survive Sen Dar's growing occult powers that he wields with unremitting effort to destroy them and rule over Earth.

GUARDIANS
OF
THE ANCIENT ONE

R. SCOTT LEMRIEL

ACKNOWLEDGMENTS

I acknowledge the basic proofing that editors assigned by Excel Book Writing did for Guardians of The Ancient One and Journey to the Center of the Universe (books two and three of the trilogy). When asked, a few kind fans, that benefited from this work, volunteered to do the final needed proofing that made it possible to bring the second two trilogy books to worldwide awareness. This is just FYI (for your information)—provided for the benefit of anyone who does not yet know.

My gratitude is expressed here for the fine work that book cover artist/designer Michel Bohbot brought to these two sequel book covers. He was previously hired to work with me to create the latest original book covers for The Seres Agenda and The Emerald Doorway (book one of The Parallel Time Trilogy) with spectacular results.

Much appreciation is sent as well to the many magnificent Master Teachers and fellow beings that are referred to as Silent Mentors. They are, for the most part, not yet known on Earth. The highly evolved space-faring races out among the stars respectfully acknowledge them as the Master Mechanics of the wondrous multidimensional creation. They hold in place all that exists in the multiverse, supported by the one living omnipresent non-nuclear or non-atomic energy simply known off-world as HU – derived from the first half of the word human hidden in plain sight. All galaxies and worlds literally float in the vast realms of outer space: including countless inter-dimensional doorways that exist between the many parallel dimensions of the physical universe; higher dimensions; and those far higher realms beyond time and space. Certain esoteric groups on Earth refer to the energy barrier that exists between the lower and higher world realities as the 'Void.' The majestic Silent Mentors do not reside on planet Earth. They are from very far out of town, so to speak, or from a lofty radiant realm that exists many dimensions above the mysterious 'Void.' Their home is located just above what is referred to as the Ocean of Sound and Light – known as the 'Source' or 'Prime Creator'. I constantly remain in awe of their capabilities and awareness.

Space Transporter shot straight upward at tremendous speed to abruptly stop at 10,000 feet.

At that moment, a lightly elongated triangular extraterrestrial spaceship twenty feet long with a slight batwing-like curved haul was radiating a thin luminous red aura around its surface. It came into view of the Space Transporter from hiding behind one of the moving tall dome-shaped clouds. A curved opaque cockpit window was positioned above and behind the curved apex of the elongated triangular hull. Three semispherical pods were set in an equidistant triangular formation pointed several feet down from the hull's curved bottom.

The alien ship began to emit a deep pulsating *hum*, as the glow around the hull intensified. Then it changed to violet light and a narrow energy beam shot from the alien ship's prow and hit the triangular hull of the Space Transporter. Just as the Space Transporter reached the level of the mysterious alien ship, its luminous red triangular hull pulsed and it darted into the distant background sky. A moment later, the Transporter exploded into billowing flames just as the sound of a Russian military anthem became audible, growing in prominence over the dissipating fiery debris.

Somewhere in Russia at that same moment, with fresh snow on the ground surrounding one large background hangar, was the Russian turbo-fanjet and rocket-powered prototype space vehicle. The distant sun was beginning to rise over the horizon in the crisp early morning air. Sunlight was reflecting off the snow on the ground behind the silvery-gray hull of the new elongated sixty-foot Russian Space Transporter. In the rear, six jet engines positioned between four huge rocket nozzles were fired-up in preparation for the first test flight. The sleek silver-gray metallic hull glistening from reflected morning sunlight down the elongated triangular hull flashed off the opaque glass-like curved cockpit window, positioned behind and above the pointed triangular front end of the ship. The brakes released, and the craft roared a short way down a long runway before it lifted upward at almost a ninety-degree angle, and darted swiftly upward to disappear high in the early morning sky.

Russian technicians inside their main control console, other launch personnel, several Generals, and the Russian President were watching the ascending atmospheric and space-worthy craft through a wide observation window. The President, in his late fifties with thick white hair, combed back and his slightly shorter, bald, top-ranking Russian General were gleefully smiling as they slapped each other on the back and confidently shook their fists toward the ascending rocket. The Russian anthem swelled in intensity just as the rocket exploded into a tremendous blinding fireball. The President and everyone else in the control room covered their faces from the subsequent blinding light. A moment later, the control room violently shook and everyone grabbed onto chairs, various instrument consoles, or anything else nearby to steady themselves.

As the exploding debris and flames continued to dissipate through the atmosphere, an opening in the flames appeared, revealing another hovering elongated, slightly bat-wing shaped hull of another alien ship, luminous with pale-red light. It moved further into view from behind a dome-shaped cloud, the light around the hull pulsed, and the ship darted away at incredible speed into the distant background sky.

Down below in the control room, the Russian President angrily barked an order to a nearby Aide. A moment later, the Aide brought a special phone up to the console and placed it in front of the leader. The President picked up the receiver and yelled a command into it.

Around the world, a hand picked up another special phone in a cradle on top of a highly polished teakwood desk and placed it next to his ear. The frowning President of The United States listened to an angry slur of Russian dialogue from the Russian President through the receiver.

Then he heard the Russian President say in English with a strong, angry Russian accent, "President Stockwell, we lost good men today! My Generals think your country has done this vial thing. A strange craft was seen near our prototype test spaceplane before the explosion. Who else could have such technology but the United States?"

"Vladimir, calm down," gently replied Sam. "I'm deeply sorry to hear about your men, but I don't care what your Generals say. We had nothing to do with it. Listen to me, Vladimir, something very dangerous is going on here. This morning, we launched one of our new unmanned Space Transporters to test a prototype escape device. It blew up shortly after launch before we could test the damned thing.

An unidentified craft shot some kind of beam at the hull, then sped away at such incredible speed, we couldn't even track it. Fortunately, as I said, this test Transporter was unmanned; but my Generals insist your military must be behind it. I don't believe my Generals are right, so don't jump to any conclusions until we know who or what destroyed both prototype ships."

Sam could hear several other subdued, angry voices speaking in Russian in the background behind the Russian President, and then Vladimir came back on the line - still a little miffed.

"My advisors say we should cancel our meeting in Geneva and our plans for more joint space ventures beyond the International Space Station."

"If you want to cancel Geneva, Vladimir, that's your choice," shot back Sam. "If we start to believe we're lying to each other now by telling cock-n'-bull stories to cover up covert attacks, it could put us right back into a dangerous cold war."

The Russian President asked a question in Russian, ending the sentence with the word "...cock-n'-bull?"

"I'm not going to explain cock-n'-bull to you. Ask your damned advisors what it means!" sharply continued Sam; but he controlled himself and cordially added, "Vladimir, let's both calm down. I'll get back in touch with you later today and please don't jump to any conclusions until we both know more."

Sam slammed down the phone as his Personal Aide in a blue suit - a trim fortyish, white-haired man with glasses, cautiously turned to head back out of the Oval Office; but the President stopped him with a sense of urgency.

"Get me General Faldwell on the phone immediately. No, wait a minute! Just tell him to meet me here as soon as possible and tell him to bring that crystal sphere he said he was given at Mount Shasta. There may be a connection."

The Aide chuckled and said, "You were right about him having gone off the deep end when he called with that ludicrous story about doorways to parallel dimensions and..." he winked, pointing his finger upward, "...aliens from... out there! Mr. President, in my opinion, Faldwell hasn't just lost a few marbles, he's on permanent vacation in the Twilight Zone."

"I didn't ask for your opinion, Mister!" shot back Sam. "If this situation escalates, this whole planet will be in serious trouble. Now... just get him!"

The Aide cleared his throat, solemnly turned, and walked in a hurry out of the oval office.

In the atmosphere above Mt. Shasta in northern California, a lone Galactic Scout Class spaceship was descending through several low dome-shaped cloud layers that encircled the backside of the mountain summit. It continued to spiral down past the clouds in a long swift arc, then suddenly stopped forty feet above the ground and a thousand yards away from the sixty by one hundred-twenty-foot sheer, gray rock wall. As the Scout ship slowly lowered closer to the ground, it began to emit a low-frequency *hum* and the thin blue layer of light enshrouding the hull began to pulse softly. A wavering rumble and pale-blue light a few feet across appeared on the center of the rock wall and steadily grew in size. It formed into a whirling galaxy of star-like lights surrounding a widening opening, revealing the lighted tunnel entrance to the Guardian's secret base inside Mt. Shasta. The whirling light expanded to one-hundred-twenty feet across and flashed several strobe-like donut-shaped lights across the valley, accompanied by several thunderous BOOMS. The Scout ship's hull brightly pulsed and it moved into the opening to disappear deep inside the mountain. The whirling stars spiraled closed and vanished to once again leave behind only a flat, gray rock wall.

The ship settled down inside the mountain base and gently touched down between two parallel rows (three in each row) of already landed Scout ships. The humming and light enveloping the hull ceased. A moment later, Captain Kalem climbed down from a spiraling open hatch in the bottom of the ship's hull. Appearing quite serious, he hurried up thirty feet of perfectly carved blue granite steps and stopped at a triangular opening, leading into a long level hallway that headed deep into the mountain's interior. He thoughtfully looked down and then walked inside.

Back in Washington D.C., a large window behind the President's desk overlooked the lawn of the inner grounds that surrounded the White House. President Sam Stockwell was sitting behind his desk, reading an official-looking paper. He began to sign it, just then, a knock at the door interrupted him. He looked up to see his Personal

Aide enter the oval office a little out of breath.

"Mr. President, General Faldwell has arrived. I have him waiting in the outer office," announced the Aide.

"Well, don't just stand there, man, show him in!" impatiently shot back Sam.

The Aide walked out of the oval office and closed the door behind him. Sam got up from behind the desk and walked around to the front of it. He nervously began to pace back and forth with his hand held to his chin. A moment later, there was another knock on the door. It opened and the Aide entered.

He began to announce, "General Harry Faldwell is... hey!"

But he was rudely interrupted by Harry pushing him aside to enter the room and he walked right up to the President's desk, removed his hat, and tucked it under his left arm.

"Mr. President... Sam, it's about time you called me here."

"General, I called you here on an urgent matter of State. We've got serious problems!" replied Sam, ignoring his remark.

"Of course, you know about our Space Transporter explosion and the destruction of the Russian prototype Transporter today."

"Naturally, I know, and I know who's behind it!" shot back Harry. "That's what I've been trying to tell you ever since my return from Mt. Shasta."

President Stockwell hesitantly gazed at Harry, and then cautiously continued, "I've got to admit, your story didn't sit well with me at first, but now I've got cause to give it some credibility. Reports of identical unidentified craft seen near both prototype Space Transporter disasters came in to me from NASA and the Russian President himself. Can you shed some light on this before it gets out of hand?"

Harry's eyes lit up, "You bet your ass I can, Mr. President."

The Aide frowned at Harry's remark, but the President ignored him as Harry continued unabated.

"As I told you, I've wanted you to look at something very special since I got back… something damned extraordinary!"

Harry reached into his pocket and pulled out the crystal sphere that Master Ra Mu gave him, and then handed it to the President.

Sam carefully looked it over as he held it up to the light coming through the window. He briefly gazed through it and nonchalantly handed it back to Harry.

"What does that have to do with the tea in China, General?" shot back the President. "There's an international crisis on my hands and you show me a damned crystal ball!"

"Look, Mr. President… Sam, it's a device," patiently replied Harry. "Give me a few minutes and I promise, you'll never again question the validity of the report I sent you after my return from the mountain. But…" and Harry nodded behind him toward the President's Aide, who forced a snide grin back at him before Harry finished under his breath, "we've got to be alone."

"Okay, I know when I'm not wanted," stated the Aide, as he turned and left the oval office, closing the door behind him.

Harry squatted down and placed the clear crystal ball with the faceted red ruby center on the carpet. Then, he stepped back a few feet and closed his eyes, while the President solemnly looked on, shaking his head; doubting the General's sanity.

Then Harry respectfully began to softly chant, "Ra-a-a-a-a Mu-u-u-u-u…" on his outgoing breath until the sound faded away. He repeated, "Ra-a-a-a Mu-u-u-u…" the same way and then chanted, "Ra-a-a-a Mu-u-u-u…" the third time, drawing out the sound longer on his exhaled breath.

A low fluctuating pulsing sound and a red ruby light began to emanate from the faceted ruby crystal, and the entire crystal sphere began to glow with a golden halo. The President was astonished by the phenomena and he gazed at Harry for his assurance they were safe.

"You mean... it's all true?" hesitantly stated the President.

"As I said, Mr. President, you bet your ass it is!" replied Harry with a cocky grin.

He grabbed a cigar from his pocket, proudly stuffed it into the corner of his mouth, and bit down, just as a holographic beam of blue light shot from the crystal sphere straight up to eye level in the center of the room. A round three-foot-wide light began to form, as the deep, resonant voice of Master Ra Mu could be heard coming from the ruby center within the crystal sphere; pulsing with each word spoken.

"Mr. President, I am known as Ra Mu. By now, you must begin to realize the validity of General Faldwell's story. You are about to witness the exact record log of events that culminate with General

Faldwell being in your office at this moment. What you see and the course of action you may choose to follow concerning what you discover may very well determine the survival or destruction of Earth as you know it."

Aghast, Sam felt for the desk behind him, clasped it, and then sat down against the edge. The Ancient One's humming Spirit sound and its hauntingly beautiful high flute melody began floating through the air. Then, a montage of images from Harry's journey beyond Mt. Shasta began to form within the holographic light sphere projection and the images cleared. Sen Dar had just shot Master Nim with the clear crystal laser pistol and he was stealing The Ancient One's parchment map-half and the Emerald Doorway Crystal from his body. While he looked on, Sam heard a sound like a cork being popped from a bottle and he delightfully discovered he was curiously unafraid as he began to experience his true inner Atma or spherical energy Soul-self move up and out of his physical body. Then his true radiant Atma-self darted across the desk and entered the light sphere projection, just as forming images whirled around him.

THE GUARDIANS SUSPECT A VILLAIN

Meanwhile, on the other side of the United States in northern California, inside a forty by one-hundred-foot oval room, nine men and three women: including Master Ra Mu; and Mayleena, seated at Ra Mu's side; with Etta resting on the table next to her, were seated around a large oval table made of a highly polished stone resembling black obsidian. Gold esoteric designs were etched into the circumference table's outer edge. Triangular doorway openings ten feet high were positioned at each end of the chamber. Two men and one woman were wearing parkas with a Guardian's Research Foundation patch on them. The other men and remaining women were wearing robes of various colors: each with slight design variations befitting the members of the mysterious, mystical order of The Ancient One's Master Adepts. Various conversations were taking place among different individuals when Captain Kalem walked into view through the triangular opening at the near side of the room. He walked around the left side of the table to approach Master Ra Mu, who was standing up at the far end of the table. As Ra Mu turned to greet him, Kalem whispered in his ear, then walked around him and over to Mayleena, seated at Ra Mu's right side. As he stood behind her chair, he fondly placed his hands on her shoulders, and she lovingly placed her right hand on top of his left hand.

"Captain Kalem has just informed me," somberly began Master Ra Mu, "that Admiral Starland's flagship has monitored alien craft exiting and reentering several interdimensional transit windows: one at the South Pole; and the other over Siberia in Russia. These same unidentified space ships were seen near both the United States and Russia's recent test vehicle launch sites and their subsequent explosions. They are not from any member of the Galactic Interdimensional Alliance of Free Worlds." He thoughtfully looked away, then turned back and added, "From what Kalem just told me, I am now convinced Sen Dar is behind this."

A surprised elder Guardian Council member said, "But we thought he was killed in the fight at the Peruvian volcano."

"Unfortunately, he is very much alive," continued Ra Mu, disappointed. "The Ancient One's stolen Emerald Doorway Crystal he now possesses has once again safely carried him into an uncharted parallel dimension on this planet Earth, and we must find out which one."

"It will be my pleasure, Master Ra Mu, to discover what garbage pile he's burrowed under this time," confidently stated Kalem. "It's clear to me that my destiny has always been to permanently stop him."

Mayleena looked up, deeply concerned, as she squeezed his hand resting on her shoulder. Kalem glanced down at her and smiled; then, he looked back at Master Ra Mu, who was gently shaking his head.

"Captain, there is something you must understand. Occult powers rapidly grow stronger in Sen Dar the longer he wears any of The Ancient One's mystic crystals. You need special training to fight the psychic illusions I've foreseen he is now capable of throwing at you."

"I don't quiver with fear when you mention that twisted madman's name!" boldly stated Kalem.

Mayleena reached up to Kalem's forearm with her slender, feminine, subtle blue-hued fingers and tugged on his sleeve.

Kalem patiently looked down at her.

"Listen to Master Ra Mu, Kalem. You know what he says is true."

Realizing the truth of her statement, he smiled his reassurance down at her, then gazed back at Ra Mu.

"Right! Of course, you know what's best. What do you want me to do?"

Ra Mu's gentle expression became deadly serious as he gazed back into Kalem's eyes.

"First, you must control your unruly emotions, Captain! Your anger could blind your ability to reason sensibly. Sen Dar would instantly use your lack of self-discipline to his advantage and your harm. Second, you, Mayleena, and Etta must agree to be trained following my instruction exactly."

Both Etta and Mayleena perked up with a keen interest in his statement.

"Third," continued Ra Mu, "you must be tested by this Council before confronting Sen Dar or attempting any further conflict with him."

"Now, wait just a minute! Why put Mayleena and Etta through this?" protested Kalem.

"One day, Captain, you will discover that the bond of love underlying and supporting all life is greater than any power," he mysteriously answered.

Puzzled, Kalem, Mayleena, and Etta glanced at each other, then turned their gaze toward Ra Mu, who was gazing at them with an inscrutable knowing grin and a twinkle in his eyes.

"Agreed! But first, I could find out where Sen Dar is hiding," replied Kalem, upbeat. "Etta could sniff him out. Right, Etta?"

Kalem grinned at his courageous Dren friend, and Etta's eyes widened with childlike enthusiasm. He immediately flew off the table next to Mayleena to hover up to Kalem, saluted him, then began to excitedly chatter away in Dren.

"I knew you'd be interested, my friend," chuckled Kalem, and he looked to Ra Mu. "With Etta's telekinetic ability to see what happened to someone just by touching an object that belonged to them, we'll find him." He confidently looked at Etta and asked, "Right, Etta?"

Etta excitedly flew around Kalem's shoulders several times and then landed on the table directly in front of Master Ra Mu. His eyes widened with anticipation as he nervously wiggled his fingers and chattered a few exuberant pleading Dren words.

"Depla, depla, depla, Master Ra Mu?" ("Please, please, please, Master Ra Mu?")

"Alright, Etta, you can go," replied Ra Mu, holding back laughter. "But I want clear pictures returned here from your photographic memory.

Etta hovered up in front of Ra Mu, raised his hand, and saluted him with his closed fist across his chest (just like a valiant human soldier would to his General), and then he flew back over to Mayleena and stopped to hover, grinning six inches in front of her face.

"Now you take care of Captain Kalem, Etta, and keep a low profile," she affectionately insisted.

Etta grinned back at her, briefly rubbed his nose with her nose, then spun around to face Master Ra Mu with eager anticipation of his next words.

"Captain, be very cautious!" seriously commanded Ra Mu. "If Sen Dar discovers you, you may not be able to escape. It remains difficult to determine just how strong his powers have become since you last tangled with him."

"I'll be cautious," replied Kalem, shrugging off the warning.

"Besides, I'll have Etta with me, and quite a warrior he is. Right, my friend?"

"Quibb!" ("Right!"), replied Etta, proudly grinning.

Gazing back at both of them, Ra Mu somberly commanded, "Once you two discover his whereabouts, return to this Council room immediately. Very specialized training will then begin for you, Etta and Mayleena. And Captain, under no circumstances should you and Etta engage in combat with him at this time. Is that clear?"

Etta flew up to Kalem's side just as Kalem cheerfully replied, "Got it!"

"Sop tep!" smartly replied Etta simultaneously in Dren.

"Oh, what swelled up boneheads!" indignantly blurted out Mayleena. "I have just as much ability as you two. I could just as easily..."

"Mayleena," gently interrupted Ra Mu, "it would be far more helpful if you remain here for now. You can better assist Kalem at a distance from Sen Dar than by his side. The risk is too high to place both of you too near him; but you may want to see them off. When they return, I will explain my meaning more clearly."

His friendly gaze then turned toward Kalem and Etta as he stated, "Captain, you and Etta had better get moving. I don't want the training delayed any longer than is absolutely necessary."

"I don't like this one bit, and I want you all to know it!" remarked Mayleena fuming.

Ra Mu looked compassionately at her and then gazed around the room at the other members gathered around the table.

"Does anyone else have anything to add before we all return to our duties?"

Kalem's lifelong Norbrian friend, Lieutenant Moreau, was wearing a Guardian's Research Foundation parka with the coat open, revealing his Galactic Alliance uniform underneath it, as he stood up concerned to address Master Ra Mu.

"If Sen Dar managed to access an unknown parallel dimension on Earth, then gain control of an entire space-faring race, Kalem could be walking into a trap. He should have a Scout squadron escort."

"Moreau, old friend, a fighter escort would be like yelling out loud at Sen Dar that we are on to him," interjected Kalem. "But with Etta along, we can locate him like a thief in the night."

"Sounds like Sen Dar's own famous last words to me," dubiously replied Moreau.

"Will you stop worrying?" snapped back Kalem.

Master Ra Mu remained patiently smiling at them as he continued, "The Ancient One's Spirit presence: its omnipresent Sound and Light will go with you and Etta; but it works best through the conscious man. Be aware and stay very alert!"

The rest of the Council members stood as Kalem gave Mayleena a hand to help her stand up from her chair. At that precise moment, the Ancient One's Living sound, like a million bees mixed with a low-frequency humming and crashing ocean waves, began to fill the room.

Several other people gathered around the table glanced around the room for the source; except Ra Mu and the other Adepts of The Ancient One, who were already respectfully smiling. The hauntingly beautiful melody of a single high-pitched flute from far away began to penetrate the underlying sounds. Kalem, Mayleena, and Etta raised their eyebrows with pleasure, noticing the flute melody, but Lieutenant Moreau didn't appear to be aware of it. Kalem's grin widened as if he had just understood something of vast importance for the first time, and he turned toward Lieutenant Moreau sitting at Mayleena's right side.

"Did you hear that uplifting sound?" he asked.

"What sound?" replied Moreau, puzzled.

His eyes followed Kalem's glance as he looked back toward Master Ra Mu and Kalem blinked several times as a new realization entered his awareness. Then Kalem shrugged off the effect.

"Oh-h-h... now I understand!" he whispered under his breath.

"Huh?" inquired Mayleena.

"Never mind. Come and see us off," he lovingly replied.

Etta hovered over to Kalem's side as Kalem wrapped his arm around Mayleena's slender waist. Then Etta lowered to his feet, his tail stopped glowing, and they walked together side by side out of the Council chambers through the triangular entryway on the far side of the room.

"Something isn't right about this!" stated Moreau voicing his concern at Ra Mu. "I can sense it! Kalem is about to walk into a trap!"

"Some things, Lieutenant," mysteriously replied Master Ra Mu, "we must trust to the omnipresent living energy or The Ancient One's wise care."

AN UNEXPECTED MYSTIC JOURNEY

It was nighttime back in Washington, DC. The city lights glittered through the window behind President Sam Stockwell, who was sitting in his chair behind the desk. Harry was sitting in a comfortable chair opposite the President. The holographic light-sphere being projected from the crystal sphere on the floor was showing General Faldwell reaching for the red phone just inside the open door to his Air Force helicopter that had landed nearby the flat, gray rock wall on the backside of Mt. Shasta.

A quick series of scenes followed in the projection before them: 1.) Ra Mu levitated off the black sand beach and flew through the air past the snowcapped mountain with the domed city nestled at its base. 2.) Bending to one knee before The Ancient One, Master Ra Mu transformed into his true luminous Atma or Soul-sphere surrounded with a pale gold halo, then merged inside The Ancient One's much larger luminous spherical presence hovering above him. They flew as one up through the vortex that opened into The Ancient One's far higher dimensional realm. The vortex closed and vanished. 3.) The President and Harry meeting in the Oval Office appeared next, just as Harry placed the crystal sphere on the carpet, then turned it on by chanting Ra Mu's name three times. The holographic light projection shut off, and President Stockwell experienced his Soul-sphere reenter his body. His eyes widened with amazement as Harry slowly rose to his feet, also appearing surprised.

"I'll be damned! I didn't even see that part of it before. Master Ra Mu dissolved and merged into that... whatever it was!"

"Then it must be true!" stuttered back Sam. "Everything that I just experienced really happened to you."

"As I said before," began Harry as he cockily stuffed his cigar back into the corner of his mouth and bit down, "you bet your ass it did!"

President Stockwell got up and walked around the desk to confront Harry, poised as if he was about to reach a firm decision. Harry stiffened his chin, nervously chewed on the cigar in the corner of his mouth, then took it back out.

"Mr. President, it's past time we moved into high gear," stated Harry. "As I suggested in my memo, we should ask for the help of the Guardians, especially Ra Mu. Well, what do you have to say now?"

"Harry, this situation must take top priority, and not a word of it is to get out," commanded the President. "This goes way beyond top secret!"

Harry grinned, took in a deep breath, and confidently stated, "Right! We'll go by the code word "GUIDED.""

"GUIDED?" asked the President.

"Exactly!" replied Harry - "Guided Universal Impact, Development, Engagement, and Defense."

Sam grinned back at him and shook his head.

"How do you guys come up with that stuff?"

Harry stuffed the cigar back into the corner of his mouth and proudly stated, "Years of field practice, Mr. President. Years of field practice."

"Can you reach this, Ra Mu?" inquired Sam concerned. "I must be certain that what I've seen and experienced here today is real before we act."

With a shrug and a hand gesture, Harry replied, "I don't know how to reach him. He works in mysterious ways. I guess I'll have to take another trip back to Mt. Shasta."

Harry nervously bit down on his cigar and stared at Sam for permission. Sam rubbed his chin with a hand in wonder, just as Ra Mu's voice began to be heard, growing louder as if it was swiftly coming toward them from a great distance. President Sam Stockwell and Harry gazed around the room to try and locate the source, and then their eyes simultaneously focused upon the crystal sphere resting on the floor. The red crystal embedded in the clear sphere's center began to pulse red light with each word spoken by Ra Mu's friendly voice.

"Good evening, Mr. President and General Faldwell. Pardon me if I startled you, but it's imperative, Mr. President, that you understand and come to know that what you witnessed from the crystal record log is true. Your space program and the security of this planet now depend on this. Therefore, I'll honor your request to personally meet with you."

"He heard me?" whispered to Sam under his breath.

Harry raised an eyebrow as a grin spread across his face.

"I told you he works in mysterious ways."

The sphere started to cast out a pale-yellow light, and it swiftly levitated to eye level in front of Harry and Sam. The faceted ruby in its center began to glow steadily, and the sphere began to spin as it swiftly dissolved into whirling golden light molecules. The light brightened as it formed into a three-foot-wide luminous sphere made of concentric layers of different colored teardrop lights: leading from a white core through the color spectrum to a violet exterior; surrounded by a pale gold light aura. Then the sphere enlarged as it slowly materialized into Master Ra Mu holding his six-foot-tall, clear quartz Master Crystal staff, crested with the Ankh and etched with mystical symbols. Harry and Sam were now shielding their eyes from the intense light coming from his transformation. Harry recovered first as he lowered his hand. Then he stuffed the cigar back into the corner of his mouth and bit down. President Stockwell very cautiously lowered his hand while he stared at Ra Mu with stunned fascination; mixed with a very cautious, respectful fear of the unknown.

"This..." respectfully stated Harry with a wave of his right hand, "is Master Ra Mu!"

Sam forced a weak smile and nodded toward Ra Mu.

"Thank you, Mr. President, for trusting your instincts this far. I'm certain you won't be disappointed," continued Ra Mu, and he grinned.

"How on God's Earth did you do that?" blurted out Sam, amazed. "That was... well… I don't know what to say that was."

"The experiences that you have had so far in this lifetime," calmly replied Ra Mu, "make it quite impossible for me to explain to you in words how I move around."

Sam gazed disbelieving back at Ra Mu, then at Harry, and he slowly began to reach behind himself for a set of buttons on the underside of the edge of the desktop.

Watching him, Ra Mu chuckled, "Mr. President, I'm not a Russian or Chinese spy, and they did not discover a breakthrough in science to create new espionage weapons."

"How do I know that Harry isn't brainwashed or that this isn't some kind of conspiracy or plot?" apprehensively replied Sam.

"Look, Sam," interjected Harry, "we've known each other for many years. You know I'm a hard-headed direct son-of-a-bitch! I didn't believe it myself at first, until after my own experience opened my eyes to the truth of all this. Damn it, Mr. President, Master Ra Mu is telling you the truth."

Harry confidently put his hands on his hips and sternly stared back at the President.

"I can see this will be difficult any other way," thoughtfully continued Ra Mu. "Mr. President, do I have permission to prove it to you?"

President Stockwell apprehensively nodded his approval and Harry relaxed, proudly grinning back at Sam. Ra Mu's eyes lit up, and he smiled back at the President.

"You have chosen wisely. Behold!"

Ra Mu held his crystal staff at arm's length as he closed his eyes. His body began to shimmer like heat waves on a hot desert plane, and brilliant light rays began to emanate in all directions from the center of his chest. Separate rays of white light touched this same spot on both Harry's and Sam's chests. Harry was standing with his arms at his side, calmly accepting what was about to happen but Sam was fearfully shielding his face with both hands from the light intensity.

A beam of white light, the thickness of Ra Mu's head, burst into the room from the ceiling and radiated down through Ra Mu's body, completely enshrouding it. Then it extended to both Harry and Sam, enveloping each of them in an aura of white light. The bodies of Sam and Harry began to dematerialize, slowly dissolving into their true Atma or Soul-light spheres hovering in midair. The room began to fill with an unseen chorus of a thousand male and female singers chanting the first half of the word human or Hu-u-u-u-u-u-u-u… hidden in plain sight: the oldest and most ancient name for The Ancient One used to make contact with its pure omnipresent living Light and Sound Spirit presence underlying and supporting all life. Their voices were mixed with a humming like a million bees, ocean waves, and an overriding hauntingly beautiful high flute melody.

Master Ra Mu's friendly voice continued, "Mr. President, your subconscious fears, aberrations, and emotional drives have been temporarily suspended. In this pure state of being, the truth cannot elude you."

President Stockwell's amazed, stuttering voice came from the pulsing center of his light sphere, "Uh... w-w-what... w-w-what's happening to me? This sound I hear...I know this. It seems so familiar; but... but I just can't quite remember."

"If your desire is sincere," remarked Ra Mu's voice softly, chuckling, "in time, you will remember your true self. Now you know what General Faldwell and I have revealed to you is true. You can no longer deny this."

"It seems so strange to me that I didn't see it before," replied Sam's voice in awe. "Yes... of course, you're right. Somehow, now I know it without doubt, but how? How is it possible?"

"That isn't important now," calmly replied Ra Mu's voice. "What is important is the safety of your space program and this planet. The Guardians adhere to one overriding universal law, which is 'Love and do as you will.' The freedom of individuals to choose their own destiny is held most sacred by us. Would you like our help, Mr. President, that is the help of the Guardians?"

At that moment, President Sam Stockwell, General Harry Faldwell, and Master Ra Mu re-materialized from their true Atma or Soul-self spheres back into their physical forms. The white light aura surrounding them withdrew back through Master Ra Mu's body and up through the ceiling. The unseen chorus, *humming sound*, ocean, and flute melody withdrawing with it faded to a faint echo and then vanished. The two rays touching the chests of Harry and Sam withdrew back to Ra Mu and then disappeared as he opened his eyes.

Harry promptly stuffed the cigar into his mouth, bit down, and assumed his tough outer military composure.

Dazed, the President slowly lowered his hands and said, "Everything is happening so fast... I don't know what to do."

"I apologize for having to put you through such an experience before you were properly prepared for it," calmly remarked Ra Mu, "but time grows short if you're to have the Guardian's assistance and protection. Trust what you know to be true with your own inner senses."

"Mr. President, Sam, I know it all seems overwhelming," encouraged Harry. "The same thing happened to me the first time Master Ra Mu gave me this experience. But the truth is truth, and I'm convinced he's here to help us. We've got to act fast before we lose another Transporter to that madman."

The President looked at Harry, then Ra Mu, trying to make a very difficult decision, and then he appeared decisive.

"All right then, as the President of the United States, I officially request the Guardian's assistance. The security of this country, our space program, and the world must be guarded at all costs. I'll arrange a meeting with the Joint Chiefs."

As the President reached for the set of buttons on his desk again, Ra Mu candidly interrupted him, "Mr. President, it would be far better if I remained anonymous to everyone else other than you and General Faldwell. I don't think the Joint Chiefs are quite ready for the experience you just had."

Sam visualized the thought, frowned, and said, "R-right! Of course, you're right. What do you suggest?"

Ra Mu grinned and replied, "General Faldwell could coordinate between your office and the Guardians. I'll be in touch with him when necessary."

Sam took a deep breath and let out a long sigh.

Then he gazed at Harry and confidently stated, "General Faldwell, you have my permission to get started; everything is to be kept above top secret."

Harry nodded and stuffed the cigar back into his mouth.

Sam looked at Ra Mu and inquired, "But I still have one question. What about the Russian and the Chinese space programs and their leaders? If any more rockets are destroyed, they'll surely conclude we're behind it, that is the United States."

Ra Mu curiously replied, "I assure you; the Russian President and the Chinese President will soon be going through their own experience with the Sound and Light of The Ancient One to confront the truth.

They will certainly understand the United States is not at fault. For now, Mr. President, farewell and thank you for the benefit of all life on this planet."

He smiled and respectfully nodded, raising his staff a few inches off the ground. Then he cheerfully grinned at Harry, and the staff began to glow with an intensifying golden light. Sam shielded his eyes as Ra Mu's body and staff dematerialized back into whirling particles of brilliant golden-white light. This time, Harry also shielded his own eyes from the brilliant luminosity, as the light formed back into Master Ra Mu's true Atma or Soul-sphere, surrounded by the pale-gold aura.

"Will you wait a minute? I have a couple of a million questions to ask you!" blurted out Sam.

As the light sphere slowly began to diminish in size, Master Ra Mu's kind voice remarked, "In the course of time, all of your questions will be answered. For now, Mr. President, farewell!"

The sphere dwindled to a small brilliant blue six-pointed star, brightly flashed, and harmlessly darted right through the White House Oval Office window.

ROMANCE AND MISCHIEF

$\mathcal{B}$ack at the secret Mt. Shasta Guardians' base, Kalem and Mayleena were walking together holding hands, headed toward Kalem's Galactic Scout ship parked twenty yards away. Etta was moving forward with them, hovering with his tail aglow next to Mayleena's left side. The thirty carved rock steps leading up to the triangular opening entrance to the base were in the background distance behind them as they walked up to the outer edge of the ship and stopped. Kalem let go of Mayleena's hand as he turned around to confront her, gently placing his hands on her shoulders. Passionately gazing into each other's eyes, gradually moving closer to kiss, Etta noticed what they were about to do. An uncontrollable grin spread around the crease of his mouth as his brows raised and his eyes opened wide with anticipation.

"Uh oh," he softly said to himself, embarrassed as his green cheeks flushed slightly red.

His tail glowed more intensely opalescent, and he widely circled them several times before he stopped upright between them and Kalem's ship to playfully cover his eyes with his hands. While he peeked through his fingers again, Kalem and Mayleena began laughing at his antics, and Kalem faked a disapproving frown.

"Take a hike! Scram!" he commanded, closing his fist with a thumb pointing behind him, just managing to suppress laughter.

"Give us a couple of minutes, Etta," chuckled Mayleena. "You know, vanish into the distance."

With cheeks now red with embarrassment, Etta jerked open the closed fingers covering his eyes to take another quick peek at them. Then he darted under Kalem's ship and up inside it through the open hatch under the hull. Mayleena grabbed Kalem's bodysuit at the chest to draw him closer, and he affectionately threw his hands around her slender waist, drawing her into his caressing arms.

"Please... be very careful," began Mayleena with worry etched across her brow. "If anything happened to you, I would..."

Kalem suddenly kissed her long and deeply passionate, and she surrendered in his arms.

Meanwhile, Etta appeared upside-down, moving his head and upper torso into view below the open hatch with his hands and closed fingers covering his eyes. He slowly moved his fingers aside to peek at them, kissing again. Mayleena's back was to him, and Kalem's head was cocked to one side toward him. Kalem opened his right eye, catching Etta peeking at them while he continued to kiss the swooning Mayleena. Surprised, Etta dropped his hands, and his eyes sprang wide open as his green cheeks now flushed deep rose-red with embarrassment again.

"Oops!" he softly murmured with puckered lips, and he darted out of sight back up inside the ship with a *whoosh*, leaving a brief light trail behind him from his glowing tail.

In rapid succession, Kalem and Mayleena heard thrashing sounds inside the ship, then BONG... THUMP, BABONG... THRUMP-BUBONK-CONK... a pause and then a loud... CLANG-G-G.

"Ow-w-w!" came Etta's muffled pained expression and then an angry, "Gr-r-r!" This was immediately followed by a quick succession of the fiery Dren swear words, "Chet... Edt oit chilba kal-rata... finda stab-o-rabid daubit... gr-r-r-r!

Kalem and Mayleena broke off kissing with uncontrollable laughter. In a few moments, they slowly looked at each other to try and control themselves, taking in big breaths together. But their grins uncontrollably widened again, and they broke out laughing as more thrashing sounds inside the ship came from a mad-as-a-hornet Etta.

"W-w-what's he doing in there?" queried Mayleena giggling, and she yelled out, "Etta, are you alright?"

Etta flew out of the open hatch and hovered upright a few feet away from the ship's hull with a beet-red face, rubbing the top of his head where he obviously bumped it. He cussed several more times in Dren, put up his dukes, took a few swings at the ship, then kicked the underside of the hull hard with a foot. Of course, this immediately caused him more pain, and he grabbed his aching foot with both hands, appearing to hop on his other foot in circles in the middle of the air with his tail brightly glowing. Then he continued to mumble out another angry round of very special fiery Dren cuss words.

"Oh-h-h-h... oh-h-h-h... daubit... shet chi a doi mocha stockus chui nock roso-riso... et cropit dabit sniggits... shrig stubochis snermf... oh-umpfa... gr-r-r-r."

Etta stopped in midair, facing Kalem and Mayleena. He slowly looked up to behold them holding cupped hands across their mouths, desperately trying to repress more uncontrollable laughter. He forced a big embarrassed grin at them, then wildly raced back up inside the ship. Mayleena and Kalem began more uproarious laughter until they had to hold onto each other to keep from falling over. As they began to control themselves, they started to again passionately gaze into each other's eyes. Then they turned around, clasped hands, and walked hand-in-hand under the ship. They paused directly under the open hatch, tightly embraced, tenderly kissed again, and then parted.

"My heart goes with you, my Captain, so bring it safely back to me," said Mayleena with a mischievous grin.

"And mine goes with you, so if I lose your heart along the way... you can keep mine," smartly stated Kalem, mischievously grinning back at her, and her grin dropped.

"Why you..."

But Kalem grabbed her and passionately kissed her again. She briefly struggled to free herself from his tight grip, then swooned again in his arms. Moments later, they parted, and Kalem began to climb up the ladder leading inside the ship. He stopped halfway to gaze down at her affectionately.

"Don't worry, Etta and I will be back soon."

Mayleena gazed worried back up at him.

"Be very careful and remember what Master Ra Mu told both of you. Stay away from that madman."

Kalem disappeared inside the ship, and Etta pocked his head back down through the hatch, confidently grinning.

"Cheob et ot om," ("Goodbye for now,") he cheerfully said.

Mayleena's Spirit immediately perked up.

"And goodbye to you too, dear Etta! Take care of yourself and look out for Captain Kalem."

Etta proudly grinned down at her and then darted back up inside the ship. The ladder withdrew, and the circular hatch opening spiraled closed like a camera shutter as Mayleena backed away from the ship's hull. She stoically watched the ship's hull light up, softly pulsing blue light and emanating a familiar low-frequency oscillating hum. The ship lifted four feet off the landing pad and momentarily hovered. Mayleena gradually receded into the distance as the ship moved over the top of several other landed Scout class ships. Then it gradually curved upward toward the back cavern wall and entered the lighted oval tunnel. As the ship approached the inside of the flat gray rock wall, a blue energy dot appeared at its center, and it began to spiral open. It widened into the whirling galaxy-like energy doorway, revealing the thickly forested countryside on the backside of Mt. Shasta below a clear blue sky. Bright sunlight was now streaming past the ship back into the oval tunnel.

The Galactic Scout stopped to hover a hundred yards further away from the secret entrance leading into the Guardians' base hidden within the mountain. The vortex whirled closed behind it and vanished, leaving behind the flat gray rock wall. The ship pulsed blue light and swiftly flew in a graceful curve up into the clear blue sky high above the mountain summit. It darted toward the west out of view.

ETTA PEERS INTO A MYSTERY

*K*alem was seated behind the ship's semicircular crystalline control console, observing the ocean far below on his viewscreen and clouds racing by outside the ship's hull. His hands, palms down, were depressed into the rose quartz palm guidance controls. Etta was perched atop the head of the console, intently watching the viewscreen with him.

"Etta, my friend," enthusiastically began Kalem as Etta looked around to hear him with wide-eyed attention, "we must be cautious, but with you along, I know we'll outwit Sen Dar - the demented pile of space rubbish!" And he winked at Etta.

"Quibb! Etu orbit cril ob pakt reel." ("Right! The demented pile of space rubbish!"), mimicked Etta, paused, then curiously asked,

"Che boa quo talam as enda Sen Dar?" (But how are we going to find Sen Dar?)

Kalem enthusiastically replied, "We'll go to his ship's old crash site in that Peruvian volcano. Then you can use your telekinetic ability to find out where he went and what happened to him."

Very pleased, Etta flew off the console to hover a few feet above it. Then he circled Kalem and stopped upright a few feet in front of his face, confidently grinning.

"Ob ab. Qum toi kemta." ("Of course. I'm very accurate.")

"Indeed, you are," chuckled Kalem. "You are quite extraordinary, and us warriors must stick together, right?"

"Ob aba!" ("Of course!"), replied Etta, puffing out his chest.

They slapped their palms together, then Etta proudly grinned and excitedly flew around the room.

"Alright already! Don't let it go to your head," commanded Kalem with a smirk. "We have real work to do."

Etta flew over to the console and landed. Frowning, he appeared hurt as he placed a hand on top of his head.

"Come on, Etta my friend, you know I was only joking," cheerfully encouraged Kalem.

Etta immediately perked up, grinning, and he extended a dexterous hand to his Captain. Kalem vigorously shook it and then saluted Etta with a closed fist held across his chest. Etta sat upright with his tail balanced straight out behind him and seriously saluted Kalem back.

A flashing crystal on the console signaled Kalem to touch several other faceted crystals. They began to glow respectively green and blue as the viewscreen changed scenes. Kalem was now observing his ship swiftly traveling over the last bit of ocean headed over a rugged mountainous shoreline.

He confidently announced, "Etta, we're coming up on the Peruvian coast in South America. Now we'll find out where that madman is hiding."

The ship passed through several clouds against a clear blue-sky background and continued in an arc over the tops of the rugged mountain range toward a wide distant jungle valley. Then it began to slow as it hovered down to continue its flight above the treetops, headed toward an extinct volcano that rose high above the jungle floor several more miles away on the far side of the valley.

Etta was lying on top of the console, looking up at Kalem - who was gazing at the viewscreen, watching his ship abruptly slow as it approached the top of the volcano's wide throat.

"First, we'll locate his wrecked ship," stated Kalem as he passed a hand over several faceted crystals, and they began to pulse.

A panel containing another viewscreen moved up from under the central control console and turned on as it stopped at a forty-five-degree angle to Kalem for clear observation. It revealed a three-dimensional computer graphics display of the inside of the bottom of the volcano. Three huge cavernous tunnels horizontally trailed away from the bottom of the shaft in different directions. Far down the two-hundred-foot-wide left tunnel, a small silver light flashed off the top of a fifty-foot-wide ledge that extended fifty-feet out from the right sidewall.

"That's it, Etta. We're going in," announced Kalem.

Etta's tail brightly lit up, and he hovered above the console at eye level with Kalem. He saluted his Captain again and darted out of view toward the back of the ship.

"Hmm... where could he have gone? What could he be up to now?" silently mused Kalem.

The ship stopped to hover above the open throat of the extinct volcano, and the hull brightly pulsed. Then it slowly descended into the deepening darkness. Light coming into the bottom of the volcanic shaft from the opening far above reflected off the dark obsidian-like lava walls to partially illuminate the beginning of the three huge natural tunnels as they horizontally trailed away in different directions from the bottom of the shaft. Kalem's ship hovered down the shaft into view as it made a curved ninety-degree turn into the foreground horizontal tunnel to continue down its length. The other two tunnels trailed away in different horizontal directions, before they disappeared in the far background.

As the Scout ship rapidly receded into the distance further down the tunnel, the entire length of the chamber appeared to go on for many miles, evenly illuminated from a blue-violet phosphorescent mineral embedded in the volcanic rock.

Half the hull of Sen Dar's ship was smashed into the extended ledge one-hundred-feet up the curved cavern wall, and a gaping hole with burn marks around the jagged edge was on its exposed side. Kalem's ship approached the ledge and slowly landed next to Sen Dar's ship.

Etta's was enthusiastically grinning as he hovered above the spiraling open hatch in the middle of the floor behind the control console. He was wearing a thin gold curved wire headset across his head with a faceted diamond on each end that was stuck into each ear hole.

"All right, my friend, the time has come," cheerfully stated Kalem.

With an impish grin, Etta comically bowed, sweeping his right arm across his chest. Then he darted out of the ship through the open floor hatch, and Kalem grinned, shaking his head.

Etta appeared quite small as he flew out from underneath Kalem's ship in a big arc and stopped, leaving a brief fading light trail behind him from his glowing tail. He darted over to Sen Dar's wrecked ship, stopped in front of the gaping hole in its side, and then cautiously flew through the jagged opening.

The control console was burned, bent over, and twisted. Etta was hovering from one area over much-wrecked debris to another in search of something. Then he stopped above the smashed console and looked down at the floor to see a partially exposed bodysuit lying beneath it. He carefully pulled it from under the wreckage, laid it out flat across the top of the console, hovered close to inspect Sen Dar's symbol embossed on the left chest area, then ran his fingers over its surface to carefully feel the texture.

The symbol revealed the apex of an upside-down pyramid suspended above a red world. The tip of a vertical sword above it touched the center of the pyramid's flat bottom. Two snakes wound around the blade above the handle, and their heads pointed toward one another with their extended forked tongues touching. Then Etta became motionless as if he was going into a trance-like state, and his eyes widened open, becoming glassy. He closed them, and his tail dimmed to a soft glowing pale-pink light just as the headset's diamond crystals stuck into each of his ears began to sparkle like a pair of diamonds in bright sunlight. A pinpoint of light between Etta's brows began to appear that slowly expanded into an ever-widening circle.

Inside himself, Etta was using his telekinetic ability to see the white light with his inner vision as it began to form into blurred images that quickly cleared to become a rapid series of historical scenes. He beheld Sen Dar frantically manipulating controls in a panicked attempt to keep his ship from being hit by the firepower coming from two pursuing Galactic Alliance Scout ships visible on his viewscreen. And they were rapidly gaining on his ship.

Outside the ship, the two Galactic Scout pursuers shot Mazon fireballs in quick succession from their hulls, headed toward Sen Dar's destruction.

Meanwhile, Kalem was intently watching the quick succession of telekinetic images on the smaller viewscreen being sent to him from

Etta's headset. He observed Sen Dar grab onto his control console to brace himself as the two fireballs exploded in rapid succession to each side of his ship, badly shaking it and knocking him to the floor; but he quickly jumped to his feet. He frantically glanced around himself, looking for a way out as sweat beaded upon his brow. Then his eyes darted to the viewscreen to discover two more fireballs had already been fired from the two Galactic Scout pursuers, and they were already near impact with his ship. He jammed his palms hard into the guidance controls to turn his ship; but it was too late.

One fireball exploded against the bottom hull, destroying one of the three pods extended downward, leaving electro-static lighting discharges arcing between the destroyed pod and the two remaining pods.

Inside the ship, Sen Dar was knocked to the floor again; but he jumped back up and lunged for the console only to stop himself as he suddenly remembered something vital. He grabbed The Ancient One's green Emerald Doorway Crystal hung on its gold chain from inside his shirt, then reached inside his shirt with his other hand. He pulled out The Ancient One's parchment, shook it open, quickly read something on the back, stuffed it back into his shirt, then quickly whispered something inaudible under his breath.

Outside, the ship was severely tilting to one side, and an explosion left a gaping hole in its side. Then the ship began to slowly plummet toward an impact with the ledge below and certain death.

Inside the sharply tilted wobbling ship, the gaping hole in the hull behind Sen Dar revealed that his ship was falling downward past the cavern wall with increased speed, and it was only moments away from impacting the ledge. Sweating profusely, Sen Dar gritted his teeth, closed his eyes, and mumbled something again, barely audible under his breath, and the green crystal lit up shining light out into the control room through his tightly clenched fingers. The crystal began to emanate silver-gold light that quickly spread over his entire body. He screamed in pain as his entire body turned silver-gold and quickly dissolved into his true Atma or Soul-self sphere of light a-foot-across with several black splotches on its surface. A spiral of starlight instantly appeared in front of his light sphere. It whirled open like a galaxy of stars revolving around a four-foot-wide interdimensional opening leading into a violet light tunnel. His light sphere darted through the whirling opening into the violet tunnel and disappeared. The opening spiraled closed and vanished just as flames engulfed the control room.

The ship impacted the ledge and partially exploded, sending a violet plume of fire out of the gaping hole in its side that soon cleared. The ship was now half-crumpled into the side of the ledge at a sharp angle as the two Galactic Alliance Scouts flew down beside it to hover above the smoldering wreckage.

Kalem continued for a moment to watch the two Galactic Scouts hovering above Sen Dar's wrecked ship on the smaller viewscreen, and then he sighed relief and grinned as he touched the transceiver crystal control to speak with Etta through the crystal headset.

"Good, Etta! Well done, my friend! The pictures are coming in loud and clear. At least we know he's definitely still alive. Now concentrate and dig deeper."

Etta's slightly muffled reply came back through the transceiver, "Quibb! Talam ne troypa." ("Right! Going in deeper.")

"Etta, you've earned your pay for a lifetime!" continued Kalem back through the transceiver with a confident grin. "Now concentrate and see if you can find out where he went."

He began to pay rapt attention to the small viewscreen, and Sen Dar's Atma or Soul-sphere with several small black splotches on its surface, appeared on it, moving at tremendous speed along a whirling tunnel made of violet and silver-gold light particles. He continued to stare at the screen ever more intently.

Inside Sen Dar's crashed ship, Etta suddenly began to experience the images zoom toward him until he began to witness what had happened to Sen Dar as if he had actually personally been there.

STUMBLING INTO GOOD FORTUNE

The image of Sen Dar's Atma or Soul-sphere darting down the violet tunnel suddenly changed to forty alien soldiers standing in three concentric circles around a red-robed Priest holding a staff. He was standing in front of a four-foot-high by a two-foot-wide black obsidian pedestal. Atop the pedestal was the bronzed bust of a man's head wearing a golden sun crown that looked remarkably like Sen Dar. Dusk light filtered down over them while they gathered near the center of a huge flat-topped ceremonial pyramid. They were humanoid with dark tanned skin; but they had larger foreheads with higher cheekbones and slightly larger oval eyes with deep-blue pupils. Their foot-long braided sideburns had various warrior symbolic jewelry woven into them, and except for the Priest, they were all dressed in violet-colored tunics with a laser-type silver metallic handgun belted at their sides. The black lava rock-strewn valley below the left side of the pyramid was laced with semitropical plants, twisted green pine trees, charcoal-colored spiraling minaret towers, and small dome-shaped dwellings lit from many windows. Nearby in the opposite direction, was tier after tier of a dark blue stone fortress built at the base and partially up the side of a tall black volcanic mountain topped by a caldera opening and glacial snows.

Several charcoal-colored, slightly bat-wing shaped anti-gravity Scout Class sized spacecraft were flying low over the city across the background sky. An oval cockpit window was positioned at the front top of the apex of their distinctive sharp-edged, elongated triangular bat wing-shaped tailing wings. Three semispheric pods were set in a triangular position on the bottom of their hulls, and a thin pale-red aura encompassed the hull of each ship. The Priest was standing next to the pedestal wearing a rich red ceremonial robe with dark-blue arcane symbols embossed upon the surface. A gold headband with gold feathers spread upward out of the top like a fan sat on his forehead. Gripped in his right fist was an odd-looking spiral gray metal rod with a large ruby crystal set on top.

Amazingly, as Kalem watched events unfold on the smaller viewscreen, he could hear the Priest begin to authoritatively address the gathered assembly in English with a strange accent.

"It was vowed he would return with great magic, as he did when he left our ancient ancestors by dissolving into a whirling fire before their astonished eyes. He foretold our destiny was to rule the world, even unto realms as yet unknown to us. Now, my brethren, the Zon race rules several other world systems, and the prophecy has been fulfilled."

For effect, the Priest raised the rod up toward the dark churning clouds high overhead. The red crystal brilliantly lit up, and a red static lightning discharge was shot from it toward the heavens.

He continued with gusto, "This world and many others are finally ours! There may be many more worlds and places yet to conquer with our new ships. Even the entire galaxy can be our home. Now is the time for a great celebration!"

The warriors began to scream wild cheers of victory in tumultuous celebration, but they were interrupted by the instant appearance - above the marble floor between them and the Priest - by an eight-foot-wide, vertical whirling interdimensional opening made of brilliant blue stars that hummed like a million bees. It widened, and Sen Dar's Atma-self with the small black splotches on its surface was thrown out of it to momentarily hover a few feet right in front of the Priest standing with his back to the bust of Zol Yul upon the pedestal. The Zon warriors were stunned into fear as their High Priest backed up against the altar, and the warriors fell to their knees. They began to rock on their heels with their hands held above their heads, chanting over and over again the name Zol Yul.

Sen Dar materialized from the radiant sphere from a bright flash of silver-gold light with a totally stunned expression on his face. He nervously glanced around while the crystal hung around his neck continued to glow through his clenched fingers. Then he let it go, and the crystal stopped glowing as it fell on the chain against his chest. The High Priest regained some courage as he became increasingly angry. Sen Dar frantically looked around again to find a way out; then, he controlled his emotions. As he turned to confront the Priest, he particularly noticed the bust on the pedestal looked remarkably just like him.

The Priest angry barked out, "Zon warriors, grab him! He has invaded the sanctity of Zol Yul's high altar."

The Zon warriors started to rise to their feet, still cowering before Sen Dar's miraculous appearance.

"Seize him!" forcefully cried the Priest as he pointed his staff at Sen Dar.

A bolt of red static electricity shot from the staff and enveloped Sen Dar in a web of light, but he had already managed to grab The Ancient One's crystal again, instantly causing it to glow green, and he vanished, only to reappear directly behind the Priest's back and the Priest was outraged.

"You fools, kill him," yelled the Priest to all the Zon warriors, "Kill him now!"

The Zon warrior soldiers began to draw their laser weapons to point them at Sen Dar, as Sen Dar grabbed his own crystal laser pistol from inside his shirt and fired it at the Priest. The Priest screamed as searing laser light melted him into a puff of vapor that quickly dissipated in the evening breeze. Tightly clutching The Ancient One's glowing crystal, Sen Dar fearfully grimaced as he gazed upon the stunned faces of the Zon warriors, and he slowly began to back up against the pedestal with his own head near the bust of Zol Yul. The three concentric circles of Zon warriors started to slowly advance inward around him as he pointed his laser weapon in their direction. The highest-ranking officer nearest Sen Dar suddenly bowed to one knee before him, and the other Zon warriors immediately followed his example.

"Oh… mighty Zol Yul," humbly began the high-ranking Officer, "you have finally returned to us. You have appeared before us as if from the fire itself, just as the legend foretold.

Sen Dar was briefly shocked by this turn of events and his incredibly good fortune as he noticed the Zon warriors glancing back and forth at the bust of Zol Yul and him. Then he gazed at the bust more closely to discover the resemblance was uncannily identical with his own face - as if he were an identical twin. Quickly gathering his sharp wits about himself, he lowered his crystal laser gun, grabbed the arm of the Zon Officer, and then pulled him to his feet.

"Rise!" he confidently commanded, poised like a King while the Zon warriors looked on amazed.

"What is your name?" asked Sen Dar, with a friendly but superior air. The Officer took a deep breath, then humbly stated, "I am General Luboc, in charge of the Imperial space battle fleet.

"You have done well, General Luboc," proudly stated Sen Dar, mocking-up friendliness. Then he commanded, "You may all rise!"

Sen Dar looked at the bust again, then back at Luboc with a cunning smile as the other Zon warriors rose to their feet.

"Who do you say that I am? Your answer will determine if you live as Supreme Commander of all my forces or you die instantly. Reply!" commanded Sen Dar with intimidating power.

Luboc fearfully stammered out, "You-u-u are our Zol Yul, our Supreme Lord, now returned to us after so many generations. My eyes are unworthy to behold you, Lord."

Sen Dar picked up the dead High Priest's staff from the ground and pointed it toward the heavens.

"Who do you all say that I am?" he forcefully asked.

All the Zon warriors began to yell Zol Yul over and over again while Sen Dar steadily gazed into Luboc's eyes.

A devious smirk rose at one side of his mouth as Sen Dar commanded, "Be sure you do not let your new position of honor go to your head as did my foolish and unfaithful Priest. I have removed his from existence. You are now Supreme Commander Luboc.

"My Lord, I am yours to command," humbly stated Luboc and he bowed his head.

Sen Dar put his arm around Luboc's shoulder, and they started to walk away together. The Zon warriors parted to let them through, bowing to Sen Dar as he passed by them. They formed into two disciplined lines, and they started to closely; but respectfully follow behind them.

Sen Dar mocked-up affection and softly said to Luboc, "Come, Supreme Commander and tell me all about your space ships and the city. Then tell me what you have done with my conquered worlds and their people. It must have been a long time since I was here among your ancient ancestors."

"Yes, Lord!" replied Luboc. "Twenty generations have passed. According to our ancient scrolls, when you left us in light and fire, our ancestors had not even learned how to build with metal.

Now, since the discovery of anti-gravity power, we have been able to travel to other worlds and bring them under our rule."

"Then I am very pleased with what your people have done with what I left them," said Sen Dar's, and his devious grin widened.

"Tell me, have the scientists yet discovered other dimensions parallel to this one?"

Luboc was blank-faced, then he appeared puzzled as they stopped walking.

"Uh... n-n-no, my Lord!" he stammered out, then cautiously asked, "What are dimensions?"

Sen Dar gazed at Luboc in a fatherly manner and answered, "I will teach our scientists about them. Now take me up in one of your starships. I may have need of one soon, and I wish to know how well they are constructed. I may want to make some modifications to them myself."

"As you wish, Lord Zol Yul," loyally replied Luboc.

Supreme Commander Luboc graciously waved his arm toward a

waiting Zon Scout Class Demon ship that landed twenty yards in the background on a slightly lower level of the landing pyramid.

At the ship, Sen Dar paused to look over the craft. He soon appeared quite pleased with himself, as he and Luboc boarded the ship by climbing up a ladder that was extended to the ground from an oval opening in the ship's side just below the cockpit window.

The ship soon started to emit a high-pitched wavering hum as a pulsing pale-red light enshrouded the hull. It lifted off straight up and stopped to hover high above the ceremonial landing pyramid. Scattered dark clouds rapidly passing by high above the ship were headed beyond the nearby black volcanic snow-capped mountain and the multiple-tiered dark blue stone fortress that had been built at its base and partially up the side.

Far below, the strange city encircling the pyramid between the mountain continued to spread out from the pyramid's three other sides until it gradually thinned out into a wild countryside of more semitropical plants and twisted green pine trees. Several wide rivers wound like snakes through the landscape strewn with black lava rock formations, and in the distance, high plateaus tapered one behind the other across the horizon.

EARTH'S SECRET TRANSIT WINDOWS

*K*alem thoughtfully gazed at the picture on the small viewscreen that was swung out from underneath the console. The newly designed and acquired Zon Demon Scout fighter Sen Dar demanded the Zon general provide, continued to hover above the ceremonial pyramid a moment longer, then it darted at high speed up into the dark cloud cover moving in over the surrounding countryside.

"So... the evil bastard is back in business again!" angrily mused Kalem to himself. He touched the crystal transceiver control linked to Etta's headset and started grinning, "That's perfect, Etta. Everything has been recorded. Come on back aboard." Then he looked away with a grimace as he thought to himself, "With ships like that, he must be planning something big... very big!"

A moment later, Etta flew into the ship through the open round floor hatch carrying Sen Dar's bodysuit. He flew over to Kalem and dropped it in his hands.

"Good work, my friend!" exuberantly remarked Kalem. "You'll receive a commendation for this."

Etta puffed up his chest and saluted his Captain. Kalem smartly saluted him back and gave him a hearty handshake.

Then he seriously stated, "We must find him, Etta. His power will keep growing the longer he wears The Ancient One's stolen crystal. Are you with me?"

"Ka chet cump tet as pak met gon nulie?" ("Do you want me to bite him into submission?") answered Etta, and he grinned wide, showing his large, tightly gritted white teeth.

"No-o...no-o!" chuckled Kalem. "I don't want you biting him into anything," And he pointed with his index finger to emphasize, "He's deadly dangerous, Etta, remember? No heroics, understood?"

Etta frowned, disappointed.

"I want you to quietly steal The Ancient One's stolen crystal from his self-appointed royal swelled-head and return it to me before he even knows what happened," added Kalem, and he winked.

Etta's courage swelled, and he twirled around in several circles before he hovered in the air to very seriously gaze back at Kalem for further instructions. Kalem laid Sen Dar's bodysuit across the top of the control console to his left, then reached over and ran the palm of his hand over the top of another blue crystal control, lighting it up. The large viewscreen against the inner wall of the ship, opposite the control console, came to life, showing a transparent three-dimensional image of Earth laid out flat. Both Kalem and Etta began to intently study the planet's land masses and the poles. They soon noticed that various locations were marked off at different points around the globe. The title across the top of the map projection in gold read...

EARTH'S NATURAL INTERDIMENSIONAL TRANSIT WINDOWS

They could see seven concentric circles surrounding each dot that had been placed at twelve locations with a title above each dot. One dot respectively positioned over the North, and South poles read - North Pole Transit Window and South Pole Transit Window: another one over the Bermuda Triangle area was marked - Bermuda Triangle Transit Window; another one marked over Mt. Shasta in northern California was titled - Parallel Lemuria Transit Window (Highly Restricted Access Only); one over the big island of Hawaii was labeled - Galactic Interdimensional Transit Window; another one over Siberia in Russia was clearly marked - Inter-planetary Jump Window; and another was marked - Multi-Parallel Time Dimension Transit Window, just above an indicated extinct volcano in Peru's interior; another one situated between Mississauga near Toronto, Canada, and Niagara Falls in the United States over Lake Ontario was marked - Deep Space Transit Window; and one situated near Sedona, Arizona in the United Stated was titled - Direct Causal Plane Transit Window

(Highly Restricted Access Only); one over the Himalayas Mountains near Lhasa Tibet read - Parallel Time Dimension Transducer Window; another one over the Gobi Desert in the remote part of eastern China was labeled - Trans-dimensional Bypass Window; and one more in the Pyrenees Mountains between Spain and France was titled - Inter-dimension Grid-Point Transfer Window.

Kalem excitedly said, "Etta, look over here! This is where his ship was wrecked in the Peruvian volcano, but he didn't go through the interdimensional transit window there. It's not far from Cusco and that's nowhere near the volcano. Admiral Starland has already verified that from the flagship. The Ancient One's crystal must have thrown him through another transit window and we must find out which one."

Etta flew in front of Kalem to begin closely looking at the map; but Kalem anxiously commanded, "Etta, touch Sen Dar's clothes again and try to find the location of the interdimensional doorway that he went through."

Etta hovered over to the console and landed on Sen Dar's bodysuit. He touched Sen Dar's symbol on the suit with the fingers of one hand, then looked wide-eyed at the viewscreen as if he was going into a trance-like state. He closed his eyes, and the headset's diamond crystals in each of his ears sparkled to life.

Kalem looked down at the smaller computer graphics viewscreen swung out from under the main console, and blurred images began to form.

An image appeared of a horizontally whirling interdimensional opening high in the atmosphere above the vast alien terrain and city surrounding the black ceremonial pyramid near the base of the snow-crowned volcanic mountain. The energy vortex was fading in and out of visibility as if it were breathing.

"Good job, Etta! You've done it again! Now which one is it?" excitedly asked Kalem.

Etta continued to concentrate, and the image on the smaller viewscreen changed to an identical view of the world map on the large viewscreen with the area marked - South Pole Transit Window, greatly enlarged. The concentric circles around the dot marking this location were pulsing with light. Kalem touched another crystal control on the console, and the entire large world map on the main viewscreen changed to a full view of the - South Pole Transit Window.

"Now it's our turn, Etta," stated Kalem. "We're going to this planet's South Pole. You can take off the headset."

Etta snapped out of the trance as he grabbed the headset and lifted it off his head. The glowing diamond crystals on each end, stopped glowing, as he laid the headset on the console. He hovered above the console, then landed on its edge, sitting upright. Kalem grabbed the bodysuit and stuffed it underneath the console. Then he placed his hands palms-down into the rose quartz palm impressions, lighting them up with a soft pink glow.

The ship lit up next to Sen Dar's wrecked ship and lifted off the ledge. It slowly moved out into the center of the cavern and momentarily hovered, then sped down the length of the tunnel toward the volcanic shaft. A few moments later, it darted at a curved ninety-degree angle up the throat of the extinct volcano toward the surface.

Master Ra Mu, with the Master Crystal staff gripped in his hand, was standing next to Mayleena inside the secret hidden Guardians' Mt. Shasta base. They were standing halfway across a semicircular thirty-foot extended flat ledge next to carved blue marble steps that lead several feet down to a transparent, convex bubble-shaped thirty-foot-high and twenty-foot-wide wavering energy shield. The clear view beyond the shield revealed that winter snow covered the backside of Mt. Shasta and the surrounding thickly forested countryside valley. Behind them, a triangular entryway and long hallway were cut into a thirty-foot-high and twenty-foot-across green granite wall.

"Master Ra Mu," began Mayleena, very worried, "Kalem has been gone too long. It would be just like him to boldly challenge Sen Dar and walk right into a trap.

"This time, I have to agree with you," replied Ra Mu with a thoughtful chagrin.

She frowned as she glanced away, then abruptly looked back, surprised he actually agreed with her. Ra Mu was smiling with encouragement.

"Kalem is very capable and courageous," he assured her. "He'll return to you. For now, you must trust with all your heart in The Ancient One's Omnipresent Spirit Sound."

"Master, will you walk with me through the shield to the open ledge?" she asked, distressed, gazing through the shield. "The fresh air and cool breeze always make me feel better."

With a father's kindness, he placed an arm around her shoulder, and they walked down the few steps. They briefly paused in front of the transparent shield, then stepped together through it to harmlessly pass to the other side as the shield's wavering energy silhouetted itself around their bodies.

On the other side, they appeared to pass right out of solid rock as the energy field briefly silhouetting their bodies closed together behind them. They had stepped onto a horizontal flat rock ledge that extended another fifteen feet out from a steep snow-covered mountainside. The triangular hallway and marble steps leading a few steps down to the shield on the other side remained briefly visible through the wavering energy field before it transformed back into the appearance of a steep snow-covered slope. They walked to the edge of the ledge, and Mayleena took a relieving breath of cold mountain air as they both stared wide-eyed at the majestic panoramic view that stretched out for hundreds of miles far below. The thickly forested valley floor was covered with a foot of the first winter snow, and the lightly frosted trees sparkled in the bright sunlight like an enchanted fairyland. A slight breeze blowing through their hair whistled around them as Mayleena sadly glanced down. Ra Mu noticed her somber mood and lifted her head up by her chin with his hand so that their eyes met, just as tears began to well up in her eyes.

Pouting, she sadly pleaded, "There must be something I can do to help him.

Ra Mu smiled and confidently encouraged, "You can come with me and contemplate on The Ancient One's Spirit Sound. It's been referred to many times on Earth as "The Music of the Spheres," and when you learn how, you can clearly hear it anytime you wish. It comes from the higher realities beyond this physical world, and it's very uplifting. For now, you can help Kalem more in this way than any other. Your inner strength will one day be added to his but this test he must pass through on his own."

She forced a courageous smile as she brushed away tears from her cheeks with her hands. They turned and walked together back through the appearance of a steep snow-covered embankment as the energy shield momentarily lit up, silhouetted around their bodies again, before it closed back together to appear as a steep snow-covered rocky slope high up on the backside of Mt. Shasta.

CAUGHT LIKE RATS IN A TRAP

Kalem's ship flew into view from the east high over the ocean on a beautifully clear day. It sped downward in a long arc, abruptly slowed, and stopped to hover above the beginning of vast snow and ice-covered landscape that reached into the far northeastern horizon background in every direction. The sun's rays were glittering like fine diamonds off the frozen wilderness five thousand feet below the ship along a wide curved cliff shoreline.

The large viewscreen was turned on inside the ship, revealing the ocean and snow-covered landscape stretching below it into the distant horizon. Kalem was standing up in front of the console as he touched a crystal control - while Etta hovered in front of him wearing the crystal headset.

"Okay, Etta, this is it," stated Kalem. "When we come out of this adventure, even the Adepts will acknowledge you are a brave warrior. The Ancient One will guide us to success, right?"

"Quibb!" ("Right!") Qui talta tam kistalm yop." ("I'll be right back.") confidently replied Etta.

"I know you will, my friend, but go with stealth and be very cautious. I have the transport energy sphere tuned to your headset so you can see through it with your great Dren sixth sense. Ready?"

"Qua ba cheta bolums q um!" ("You bet your ass I am!") smartly replied Etta grinning wide.

Kalem chuckled as he touched a violet spherically faceted crystal on the console next to the left palm guidance control, lighting it up, and the transparent golden energy sphere formed around Etta, sealing him inside it. Then it turned opaque and shrank to a foot in diameter. Kalem touched the transceiver crystal twice, and it changed from red to blue, and he began to speak to Etta via the intercom mode linked to Etta's headset.

"Can you hear me alright, Etta?"

Etta's enthusiastic voice came back, "Quibb, q mia feep! Feep!" ("Yes, I hear fine! Fine!")

Kalem reached down and touched a crystal control on the side of the smaller computer graphics viewscreen that was swung out from under the main console. The representation of a spinning energy vortex doorway flashed on the screen made of millions of light molecules whirling around an energy tunnel opening high in the atmosphere. It appeared to lead into another parallel dimension on Earth.

"The mockup perfectly shows the vortex," confidently stated Kalem through the transceiver. "I'm locking you onto the opening now to send you through it to the other side."

He touched the faceted violet crystal again, and the golden sphere containing Etta turned transparent, then faded from view.

The transparent sphere materialized twenty feet out in front of the ship, and it again became opaque. Then it darted in a long arc several thousand yards away, momentarily stopped, and proceeded slowly to gradually vanish from view as it moved through an invisible vortex opening in the sky.

Kalem looked more closely down at the small viewscreen, and he could see the whirling vortex spinning in a clockwise spiral in the air - while Etta's gold sphere slowly moved through toward the other side and nighttime. In the further distance, Kalem could faintly make out many lights coming from hundreds of dwellings that surrounded the base of a black flat-topped pyramid structure. A huge citadel with tall sinister-looking charcoal-colored metal spires was spread out like a murky shadow across the farther background that was silhouetted against the base of a tall glacial snow-crowned black volcanic mountain.

"You're doing just fine, Etta," encouraged Kalem through the transceiver. "After they see you as I do now, my courageous friend, no one will ever disrespect you again."

Kalem touched another crystal on the side of the small viewscreen, and the images coming from Etta's headset were instantly transferred to the main viewscreen. Clearly visible in every detail were thousands of tiny light molecules whirling inward toward a center point between each end of a twelve-foot-long by six-foot-wide clear parallel time dimension tunnel opening. Rapidly vibrating blue light molecules were spinning counterclockwise at a slightly faster time rate on the far side of the vortex opening, and whirling green molecules were spinning clockwise at a slightly slower rate on Kalem's side of the opening. The two whirling energy fields rapidly slowed their differing pulsing vibrations as they spun inward toward each other to join together, creating the twelve-foot-long spinning energy tunnel.

As Etta's protective transport sphere slowly passed the halfway point on its journey through the vortex tunnel, it brightly excited the whirling luminous tunnel walls around it but not enough to obscure the clear daylight sky behind it with Kalem's ship hovering nearby the opening.

The sphere passed out of the tunnel into the unknown parallel time dimensional on Earth and continued several hundred yards further into the night sky under its own luminosity, as the vortex tunnel far behind swiftly vanished from view. A rich tapestry of brightly twinkling stars around and behind Etta's radiant golden transport sphere now adorning the surrounding sky.

Aboard the ship, Kalem saw images from Etta's point of view

coming to him from the headset. Etta looked up through the transparent wall of the surrounding energy transport sphere to gaze at the splendor of the star-filled night sky. Then his gaze turned to the city lights coming from the many dwellings surrounding the bottom of the landing pyramid. In the further background beyond them, he could see the sinister-looking citadel nestled at the base of the snow-crowned black volcanic mountain. Kalem reached over and touched the transceiver crystal control.

"Etta, my friend, you're now on your own, okay?" he inquired.

"Quibb!" ("Right!") replied Etta's excited voice back through the transceiver.

"Be very stealthy. Sen Dar is insane, but he's no fool!" cautiously added Kalem with a concerned grin. "Attempt to get the crystal from him only if it appears safe to proceed. Otherwise, beat a path back to the ship. Understood?"

"Stoobock!" ("Understood!") replied Etta's voice.

"Contact me again when you reach the citadel," ordered Kalem. "I want to see everything and good hunting, my friend."

"Tak! Chom ba na comrond." ("Thanks! This is an adventure.") cheerfully replied Etta's voice.

Kalem reached down and touched the faceted spherical crystal again, and the gold energy sphere enveloping Etta faded and vanished from around him, leaving him hovering in the night sky with his tail glowing in brilliant opalescent colors. Etta smiled wide with anticipation as he pretended to roll up shirtsleeves he didn't have.

Then his glowing tail intensified, and he darted off into the distance like a firefly, leaving a swiftly fading light tracer trail behind him as he began to zigzag ever downward in a long arc toward the citadel at the mountain's base.

Back in the Guardians' council room, Master Ra Mu and Mayleena were now standing at the head of the black obsidian oval table. Ra Mu reached down and touched a small blue faceted crystal control at the table's edge, lighting it up, and a faint low-pitched humming motor engaged. Part of the oval ceiling slid back, and a large oval viewscreen was lowered down, stopping above the table in front of them. Then a blurred image began to appear on the screen.

"Admiral Starland has been monitoring Kalem's ship," Ra Mu said to Mayleena with an encouraging grin. "Perhaps he can give us an update on their progress."

Worried, Mayleena stated, "It's been too long. He should have reported in by now. Something may have gone wrong."

"There's no need to worry, young one," encouraged Ra Mu. "Kalem will return to you. Now perk up. You wouldn't want to worry, Admiral Starland."

She forced a weak smile, and they both looked at the oval viewscreen, just as Admiral Starland's image came into focus. He appeared cheerful as he stood in front of the main console closer to the main viewscreen, with Lieutenant Marin seated at the console directly behind him. In the background, several other bridge personnel were busy monitoring many glowing multicolored, faceted crystal instrument banks that lined a gradually curved wall.

"Hello, Master Ra Mu, my old friend, and Mayleena, you are just as lovely as ever!"

Her Spirit lifted with an impish smile, and she replied, "And if you were twenty years younger, I would be worried about you instead of your son." Then her smile dropped, and she stated, "I'm very concerned about him, Admiral. I've been told his ship is being tracked."

"Oh, don't worry, young lady," chuckled back the Admiral. "Kalem has gotten himself into and out of worse scrapes than you can imagine, and yes, we've tracked his Scout ship to the South Pole Transit Window. As we speak, it's hovering at a safe distance from the interdimensional vortex opening."

Aboard the flagship, Starland was observing Master Ra Mu and Mayleena on the main viewscreen, standing at the back of the black obsidian table inside the Guardians' Mt. Shasta base.

He calmly continued, "Etta was sent through the vortex a short time ago to investigate."

"Can you contact Kalem?" inquired Ra Mu. "It's very important that he does not engage in battle with Sen Dar under any circumstances until after he receives more training."

"No doubt, you have already told him this yourself," replied Starland with a smirk. "Knowing my son's overly courageous hardheadedness, they could get into trouble. I'll have him patched through to us in a moment." He looked at Marin and softly ordered,

"Lieutenant, contact Kalem and put him on the split-screen mode with Ra Mu and Mayleena."

Her nimble fingers touched several small faceted crystals, and she looked up smiling, "He's coming on the screen now, Admiral."

"Kalem's image within his ship formed on the left side of the viewscreen's vertical split mode, opposite the framed images of Ra Mu and Mayleena inside the Guardians' base.

It won't be long now, Admiral. What happened to Sen Dar has already been recorded," reported Kalem, and he more seriously continued, "Admiral, not only is he still very much alive; but The Ancient One's crystal projected him through the South Pole Transit Window into an uncharted parallel dimension not yet explored by the Galactic Alliance. He now has complete control of another entire space-faring people called the Imperial Zon race, and he may have provided them with the means to cross between parallel realities. As we speak, Etta is taking pictures inside their citadel." He added disappointment, "It looks like he's gathered together another team of unwitting pawns to do his dirty work for him."

"Captain, listen closely, and this is a direct order!" commanded Starland. "Under no circumstances are you or Etta to engage in conflict of any type with Sen Dar until after both of you have completed more training with Master Ra Mu. Is that perfectly clear?"

"Perfectly! Master Ra Mu said the same thing to us before we left the base," answered Kalem.

Starland turned to Lieutenant Marin, "Patch Kalem through to Ra

Mu now."

Inside the secret base in Mt. Shasta, Master Ra Mu and Mayleena were watching the oval viewscreen suspended above the black obsidian oval table as Admiral Starland's image switched to Captain Kalem aboard his Scout ship.

"Greetings, Master Ra Mu," cheerfully stated Kalem, and then he delightfully gazed at her and gasped, "Mayleena!"

She leaned forward to seriously gaze back at Kalem, and she insisted, "Kalem, you listen to Ra Mu. Come back to me, or I will be so..." but she stopped herself by putting a hand over her mouth as tears welled up in her eyes.

Ra Mu placed a consoling hand on her shoulder and sternly stated, gazing at Kalem on the viewscreen, "Captain, stay clear of Sen Dar no matter what may happen. Her future, your future, and Etta's future depend upon this."

"Come on, you two," began Kalem with cocky confidence, "give a guy the benefit of the doubt. I'm nowhere near him. Etta will return soon, and we'll both be back at the base before morning. Stop worrying."

He momentarily looked away to monitor several instruments and then turned his gaze back to them.

"I've got to go now," he impatiently stated. "Etta's telepathic pictures are coming in again. I'll contact you when he's back aboard, and don't worry."

The oval viewscreen switched back to Admiral Starland. He

smiled at Ra Mu and Mayleena and said, "We will continue to track him from here."

"Thank you, Admiral," replied Ra Mu, and he nodded his head.

Mayleena lowered her worried gaze as the viewscreen in front of them went blank. Ra Mu compassionately gazed at her, and then he gently picked her head up with his fingers under her chin as several tears ran down her cheek.

"Now more than ever, you must trust in what you know to be true from your own experience. The Ancient One's Spirit Sound is with him now."

"I know, but will you watch over him anyway with your Spiritual powers?" she hopefully asked.

"Mayleena," he replied like a father, "if I interfered with Kalem every time danger lurked, he would never gain the experiences and meet the challenges that are necessary to awaken his own inner potential for self-mastery. It's you, Mayleena, who can help him most now."

"Me?" she shot back, puzzled. "I don't understand."

"In time with the training, you will," he kindly replied. "Stay trusting in what you know within about The Ancient One's omnipresent living sound and send Kalem all your love and confidence.

Come on now, cheer up."

He gently took her hand, and together they turned around and slowly walked out of the Council room through the triangular doorway opening at the far end of the room.

In the Zon domain, a huge palace made of blocks of dark blue stone had been built that tapered inward and upward one level after another (tier after tier) at the base and partially up the side of the dark volcanic mountainside. High walls surrounded each tier with tall-spiraled guard towers set along the wall perimeters. The top tier was crowned with a large ivory-colored dome that rose to a sharp point upon which was attached the imperial Zon symbol: a blue-green planet similar to Earth with different continental landmasses and the image of their huge citadel superimposed across the planet's equator; and now crested atop the Zon symbol was Sen Dar's own personal symbol – a red world set just above the square base of an upside-down pyramid with the vertical point of a sword touching the top of the red world; and two snakes wrapped around the blade that spiraled above the handle until their heads turned inward with their forked tongues touching.

A series of circular maroon-colored stained-glass windows surrounded the base of the ivory dome, and a donut-shaped flat landing platform encircled the circumference of the dome's base below the windows. Two Zon Scout Class fighters parked on the landing platform lit up pulsing pale red and emanating a course high-pitched hum. The ships lifted off the platform and darted away to disappear in the background night sky.

A moment later, Etta flew into view from the foreground sky, headed down toward the base of the ivory dome. He stopped to hover above the surrounding ledge, then landed by an open horizontally pivoted circular window, and his tail stopped glowing. He cautiously peeked in through the window, and then slowly crawled through the opening.

A tall statue of Zol Yul that looked just like Sen Dar was in the center of a two-hundred-foot-long oval-shaped room under the ivory domed ceiling. To the right of the statue in the back of the room was a carved marble throne chair raised two steps above the floor on its own marble platform. Sen Dar had one foot on the top step and one on the floor next to the throne. He was addressing several dozen Zon officers and warriors that were standing in a semicircle around him. Etta stealthily poked his head into view from behind a marble column on the far side of the room to watch events unfold.

"When this United States or Russia launches another prototype space vehicle, you will cause them to self-destruct as before by cutting into their energy storage cells," sternly commanded Sen Dar, and he angrily added, "I want them at each other's throats! Is that clear?"

They were too afraid to answer as he stepped off the platform by the throne chair and stopped on the next step just above the Zon warriors. He reached forward and grabbed a junior officer by the lapels, who was standing next to Supreme Commander Luboc. The junior officer trembled as Sen Dar drew him up close to his own face so he could gloat down at him.

"Is that clearly understood?" he asked again with a nasty sneer.

"Ye... ye... yes, Divine One!" stuttered the terrified shaking warrior.

Sen Dar released him and looked at Commander Luboc, who bowed humbly compliant.

"I will see to it personally, my Lord," he proudly stated as he lifted his head.

Sen Dar relaxed as he stepped back up onto the platform to stand next to the throne chair. He turned around and gazed with regal arrogance at all the Zon warriors.

"After destroying their next rocket launches, it will be much easier to rule over them." He paused for effect and continued, "The Zon fleet will then travel to other worlds in their parallel dimension as I taught you." And he forcefully declared, "The new Zon destiny is to conquer the entire multidimensional universe."

He maliciously grinned as he gazed over his new obedient space-faring warrior race, and he arrogantly stated, "You all have my Divine blessings." He held his closed fist high over his head and yelled, "Now go... to victory!"

The Zon warriors screamed with battle lust as they raised their polished silver laser guns high above their heads. Then they crossed both arms over their chests with the clenched fist of their other hand and bowed their heads to their new Emperor. Sen Dar duplicated the gesture in return, and the Zon warriors began to file out of the room. He held his superior posture until the last warrior left, and then he suddenly appeared exhausted as he stepped up to the throne chair and sat down in it, slumped over. He breathed out a relieved sigh, then slowly got back up to sluggishly walk to his right behind the throne chair and into a long corridor.

Walking upright, Etta cautiously came into view from his hiding position behind the marble column and stealthily trailed behind Sen Dar down the same corridor.

Later that night, Sen Dar was asleep stretched out on his back on the right side of a plush oval bed with his head resting upon a blue satin pillow. A five-foot-tall twisted wooden structure similar to driftwood with barren branches jutting out from the main trunk in many directions was standing up in a wooden stand next to him. The Ancient One's Emerald Matrix Crystal was hanging from its gold chain on a branch near his head. The entire fifty-foot square room was covered with a plush deep-red carpet. Heavy purple satin drapes hanging from the surrounding walls were embossed with Sen Dar's symbol over the top of the Zon world symbol. The same symbol was also mounted on a plaque placed above the opening in the parted drapes that led from the palace hallway into his private sleeping chambers.

Etta quietly scurried into the room from the hallway and ducked behind the wide folds of the left parted curtain. He stealthily continued to make his way behind the curtains that draped the entire room until he approached Sen Dar's bed. Then he cautiously parted a fold in the curtains with his fingers, peeked through it to see Sen Dar sleeping, and closed it again. He touched a crystal in his left ear on the side of the headset he was wearing with a finger. It pulsed once, and he quietly whispered in Dren, "Tem baleeta." ("He's sleeping.")

Aboard his ship, Kalem was watching events unfold on the computer graphics viewscreen from Etta's perspective. Etta's hand came into view as it parted the fold in the curtain again, revealing Sen Dar apparently still fast asleep.

"I see him, Etta," whispered back Kalem in the transceiver. "I wish I were there myself..." and he gritted his teeth... "to strangle him with my bare hands!"

"Tal amba tam kistalm?" ("What about the crystal?") whispered back Etta's voice.

Kalem hesitated, then whispered, "Grab it, then get the hell out of there and be very, very cautious."

Back inside the sleeping chambers, Etta slipped out from behind the curtain, cautiously walking on all four limbs. He slowly crept over to the edge of Sen Dar's bed just in front of the driftwood tree, then darted behind the branches around its backside. He popped his head up above the edge of the bed between several branches just inches away from Sen Dar's open hand resting by his head. Etta's eyes nervously widened as he stared unblinking at Sen Dar's face. A drop of sweat ran down his brow as he slowly stretched out his slightly shaking fingers to reach for the crystal hanging from the gold chain on the branch just above Sen Dar's head. He glanced up at the crystal for only a moment to grasp the chain and lift the crystal off the branch just as Sen Dar barely opened his left eye. It slowly turned in the socket, and pale-red light reflected from the depth of his pupil like a cat's eye in the moonlight before he snapped his eye shut again. Etta jerked his head back down to intently gaze at Sen Dar, who appeared to still be very much asleep, and he placed the chained crystal around his own neck. He triumphantly grinned at Sen Dar and carefully turned to walk away. With unexpected lightning speed, Sen Dar's hand thrust out from the side of the bed and firmly grasped Etta around his back just behind his armpits so Etta couldn't turn his head to bite him. Etta's immediate squeals of terror were followed by Sen Dar's hideous laughter as he rose out of bed. Still firmly holding Etta's body, he lifted him off the ground and held him at arm's length.

Furiously defiant, Etta tried to turn his head around to try and bite Sen Dar's hand, ineffectively snapping his jaws in empty air, and he soon began to cuss instead, using every conceivable Dren swear word.

"Stabba risa, nachit dabba rabbits, sinks, snorple packal daggit," and he angrily growled, baring his gritted white teeth.

"Hah-hah," sadistically chuckled Sen Dar. "Going somewhere with my property, rodent? On no, no, my little pet, you're all mine now!" And he yelled out, "Guards!"

Two Zon Guards rushed into the room carrying a rectangular four-foot-long by a two-foot-square steel wire cage. One of them opened the latched door as Sen Dar reached behind Etta's neck with his other hand, grasped the chained crystal with his fingers, then the headset, and he yanked both off his head.

"I was expecting you, little lizard," he stated with vicious delight. "You will deliver a crystal all right but not the way Kalem thinks."

Sen Dar threw Etta into the cage hard, smashing him into the back wire mesh wall, and the Guard snapped the door shut. Etta staggered semiconscious to his feet as Sen Dar pulled a piece of cloth from inside his shirt. He tightly wrapped the crystal headset inside it, stuffed it back inside his shirt, and then placed the gold-chained Emerald Doorway Crystal around his own neck. Then he grabbed the green crystal in his right hand, and it instantly glowed through his clenched fingers as he walked up the cage bars, hypnotically staring maliciously wide-eyed at Etta. Etta shook his head to try and clear his mind, but a moment later, he started to stare hypnotized back into the glowing light as he began to hear Sen Dar's telepathic thought projection.

"Now... you will do my bidding!" firmly commanded Sen Dar's sadistically delighted voice.

Glaring back blank-faced in a wide-eyed trance, Etta compliantly nodded his head. Sen Dar waved his left hand, and another identical gold-chained crystal appeared clutched in his fingers. He let go of the real crystal in his right hand and the glow shut off as it dropped on the chain to his chest. He lifted the chained crystal over his head and tucked it inside his shirt. Then he placed the false duplicate chained crystal around his neck, just as Etta shook his head to snap out of the trance and angrily growled up at him. Sen Dar reached inside his shirt again and took out the cloth wrapped around the crystal headset. He unwrapped it and then stuffed it into the cage through the narrow space between the thin steel wire bars.

"Now put it on, lizard!" he angrily commanded, sneering. "Then call your precious Captain Kalem."

Sen Dar reached over and grabbed a laser gun from the nearest Guard and menacingly pointed it at Etta's head as he leaned forward, scowling through the thin wire mesh bars.

"Do it now, rodent, or die!" he forcefully commanded.

Etta scowled back at him as he slowly put the headset back over his head and reluctantly touched the diamond crystal set in his left ear hole.

Kalem appeared worried as he gazed down at the blank computer graphics viewscreen, and he touched the transceiver crystal control.

"Etta! Etta! Answer me, Etta! Damn it, where is that little Dren. Come in, Etta!"

The viewscreen suddenly flashed on, revealing Etta's point of view back through the headset. Kalem could see Etta's hands clutching the thin wire bars of the cage and Sen Dar's close-up face maliciously glaring back at him.

"Etta, are you alright?" anxiously asked Kalem.

Sen Dar was looking down at Etta through the steel wire bars as he heard Kalem's slightly muted defiant voice coming through Etta's headset. The tiny diamond crystals in Etta's ears glittered with each word Kalem was speaking.

"What have you done to him?"

"Why nothing... yet!" replied Sen Dar with a sneer. "In a moment, I will state my demands."

He menacingly pointed the laser gun at Etta's head through the thin wire bars as his eyes widened to hypnotically stare again into Etta's eyes.

"Now... turn off the headset!" he commanded.

Etta's face went blank as he slowly reached up to touch the left headset crystal again.

Kalem could see Etta's hand as it reached up to touch the left crystal of the headset and the screen suddenly went blank.

"Damn it!" he shouted with angry frustration. "Wait till I get my hands around your evil neck." He touched the transceiver crystal again and urgently called, "Etta! Etta, come in!" But there was no response, and he slammed his fist on the console.

Sen Dar's hypnotic eyes remained wide open while he continued to point the laser gun at Etta's head, and Etta began to hear his telepathic thoughts.

"You are now under my control again!" his voice commanded.

The false crystal duplicate around Sen Dar's neck began to glow just like the real one as Etta succumbed to Sen Dar's control, resuming his glassy-eyed blank stare. Sen Dar let go of the glowing crystal in his right hand, and it dropped on the chain to his chest; but it remained glowing. He stuffed the laser gun in his left hand into his pants pocket, opened the cage door, then firmly grabbed the back of Etta's neck with his right hand and pulled him out of the cage, keeping him at arm's length. With his left hand, he lifted the duplicate glowing chained crystal over his head and placed it around Etta's neck. Then he took the laser gun back out of his pants pocket, pointed it at Etta's head, walked over to the curtain draping the center of the wall, and pressed a spot. The curtain rolled back, revealing a large vertical oval mirror hung on a dark blue granite wall to the right of a horizontal open oval window.

He stepped back, concentrated on Etta again, and loudly commanded, "Awaken!"

The false crystal around Etta's neck stopped glowing, and Etta snapped out of the hypnotic trance only to discover a laser gun held in Sen Dar's left hand pointed at his temple and his other hand tightly gripping the back of his neck. Sen Dar positioned himself, so both he and Etta were facing the mirror to make it possible for Kalem to see them reflected in it when the image was transmitted back through Etta's headset.

"Now, Etta," ordered Sen Dar, "turn the headset back on."

Etta reached up, touched the headset crystal in his left ear, and both diamonds sparkled to life.

"As Lord Zol Yul, I challenge you to battle man to man!" arrogantly began Sen Dar. "It will be just the two of us in our two ships. Reply immediately, or Etta dies now!"

Kalem was now standing, gazing down at the spectacle displayed on the smaller computer graphics viewscreen. He sat down hard in the chair, then reluctantly touched the transceiver control crystal.

"Knock off the Zol Yul crap, Sen Dar!" he replied with disgust. "If I agree, will you let him go unharmed?"

Sen Dar pointed the laser gun away from Etta for a moment to aim it at the mirror so that Kalem could clearly see it pointed in his direction.

"He will return to you unharmed. It's you I want, dear Captain!" he insidiously stated.

Then he gazed up at the ceiling with malicious delight, intentionally waving the gun away from Etta.

Back inside Sen Dar's sleeping chambers, Etta's eyes carefully watched the laser gun move away from him as Sen Dar's fingers loosened around his neck, and he suddenly ripped free of his grip with his tail brightly glowing. He raced out of the room through the open oval window next to the mirror and darted into the night sky. Sen Dar intentionally fired the laser wide, blowing a hole in the wall on the left side of the window.

While watching Etta's point of view displayed on the viewscreen as he raced higher into the sky, Kalem yelled encouragement, "Etta, fly like a bolt of lightning. Fly as if the fires of Enos were behind you, and don't look back."

Several more Guards rushed into the Sen Dar's sleeping quarters, and one of them nervously asked, "What are your orders, Divine One?"

Appearing relaxed, Sen Dar arrogantly ordered, "Back to your posts, all of you."

"But Sire, the creature is escaping!" asked the other, even more puzzled Guard.

"Yes, I know," flatly stated Sen Dar. "Leave me!"

The mystified Guards humbly bowed, saluted Sen Dar, and walked out of the room. He took out the real chained crystal, placed it around his neck, sat down on the rug, and crossed his legs to sit upright. Then he grabbed the crystal in his right hand, and it sprang to life, radiating green light through his clenched fingers that partially illuminated the room as he closed his eyes to concentrate deeply.

AN ERRAND
OF VENGEANCE

*E*tta was flying in to the night sky away from the oval glass windows that surrounded the base of the ivory dome atop the fortress citadel, and he briefly stopped to look back over his shoulder. Then he darted away, leaving a vanishing light trail behind him as he passed high over the nearby ceremonial pyramid.

Kalem sighed relief as he lowered his head, then looked up and said to himself, "He got away. The little bugger actually got away." Then he touched the transceiver crystal again and asked, worried, "Etta, can you hear me? Are you alright?"

Etta's excited voice answered back, "Quibb! Quibb! Quma sob toi kistalm!" ("Yes! Yes! I have the crystal.")

"Incredible! Just damned incredible," excitedly shot back Kalem through the transceiver. "Hold on, my friend, I'm bringing you back through the transit window now."

And he touched the violet transport crystal, lighting it up.

A brilliant panorama of stars glittered in the background distance behind and above Etta as he hovered in the atmosphere. The Zon ceremonial pyramid and the citadel nestled at the base of the snowcapped volcanic mountain were in the far distance behind him. The transparent gold energy sphere appeared around him again and turned opaque. Then it pulsed twice and slowly moved back through the invisible vortex, temporarily lighting it up. As the golden sphere began to reappear coming out of the faint whirling vortex tunnel into daylight, the night sky on the other side remained briefly visible before the vortex completely vanished. The sphere pulsed twice again, then darted toward Kalem's ship, hovering a little further away.

Kalem was standing up several feet behind the control console when the glowing energy sphere materialized in the air above it. It expanded in size and then vanished from around Etta, leaving him hovering in the air with his tail glowing. He excitedly flew twice around Kalem, chattering away in Dren before he stopped to hover directly in front of him.

"Etta, my friend, you did it!" exclaimed Kalem with a cheerful grin. "You really did it! You can fly with me anytime and anywhere. I'm proud to have you fight at my side."

Etta hovered upright, appearing to stand in the air with his glowing tail extended out behind him. He saluted Kalem, and a salute was snapped back. Then Etta started to take the chained crystal off his neck, but Kalem stopped him.

"No, Etta, keep it on for now," he said, and he grinned. "You rescued it from that self-appointed royal scum ball."

Etta proudly flew over to the main console and landed on it as Kalem touched the main viewscreen control. The clear deep-blue midday sky outside the ship appeared on the screen as Kalem's concern began to show while he gazed at the empty sky.

"Something isn't right!" he said to himself. "Sen Dar would have sent ships after us by now. Let's high tail it out of here."

Meanwhile, Sen Dar was still sitting on the floor with his eyes closed, deep in concentration. The Ancient One's real crystal around his neck was still glowing green light through his clenched fist tightly held to his chest. He opened his eyes wide, appearing to look right through the walls of the room at something far off in the distance. His subtle light body or Astral-self that looked just like him; except it was made of thousands of tiny transparent points of light, appeared getting to its feet as it separated up and out of his physical body. With a sinister grin, his Astral-self sent out a telepathic command.

Etta, hear me now. You are again mine to control! His voice commanded as his Astral body floated standing upright to the wall beside the mirror, and it passed right through it.

Kalem was busy operating the ship and he didn't see the false chain around Etta's neck as it began to glow. Etta was once again in a wide-eyed trance state as he stealthily began to levitate behind Kalem, and he stopped several feet from his back. He began to hear Sen Dar's telepathic voice with a slight echo as if it was coming from deep inside a cavern; but Kalem didn't appear to hear anything.

Now, Etta, you will do my bidding, commanded Sen Dar's voice.

Etta affirmatively nodded his head, just as Kalem looked up at the blank viewscreen to become shocked by what only he was seeing displayed upon it.

"In the name of The Ancient One, where did they come from?" he asked himself, dismayed. "Etta, Zon ships just appeared out of nowhere. Hold on, my friend. We'll lose them!"

Kalem plunged his hands into the crystal palm controls, lighting them up, and the ship tilted on its side as if Kalem was trying to avoid something headed toward the ship.

From his point of view, Kalem was seeing two-dozen Zon Scout Class charcoal-colored, slightly batwing-shaped triangular fighters on his viewscreen. Several had already fired green oval energy bolts headed toward his ship. Kalem began to guide the ship one way and then another, as fireballs appeared to sail by each side of the viewscreen. Several explosions violently rocked the ship, and he grabbed the console with both hands to steady himself.

Etta remained floating upright behind him stiff as a board, apparently unaffected in any way, and Kalem plunged both hands back into the palm controls, then reached over with one hand and grabbed the octagon-shaped fired control crystal, lighting it up. He looked back at the viewscreen to see several blue Mazon fireballs shot from his ship, headed toward the approaching Zon fighters.

Moments later, both ships exploded from direct hits, and he shouted out encouraged, "Alright, you bastards want a fight? Bring it on!"

Then his jaw dropped when he saw a half dozen Zon warships materialize in place of the two he thought he just destroyed.

"What the hell is this?" he shouted and touched another lit faceted crystal control. "We'll lose them, Etta, if they can't see us," he shouted, determined over his shoulder toward Etta.

Outside, Kalem's ship was erratically flying, making ninety-degree turns, flying straight up, then veering left and right as if trying to avoid being hit, but there was nothing in the clear blue sky; except his Galactic Scout ship. Two more Blue Mazon fireballs shot from the ship darted into empty air, and the fiery energy balls disappeared in the distance as his ship faded from view. A moment later, it reappeared in the background a mile away.

Kalem could see on the viewscreen that the Zon fighters were now far away in the distance, encircling the empty space where his ship had just been.

He stated, relieved over his shoulder to Etta, "My friend, they can't catch up with us now."

As the words left his lips, two-dozen more Zon fighters appeared directly in front of his ship.

"What the... we'll outrun them."

Etta remained in a trance, hovering upright, staring at the viewscreen. From his perspective, absolutely nothing was on the viewscreen but the empty blue sky outside the ship. Yet, Kalem was still seeing dozens of Zon Scout fighters surrounding his ship, and they simultaneously fired at him from every direction.

"They won't hit us!" he shouted over his shoulder to Etta and grabbed the invisibility crystal control again, lighting it up.

Then he gazed at the viewscreen to watch his ship disappear from the surrounding Zon Scout ships, then reappear another mile away. More multiplying Zon ships immediately appeared closer to his ship, simultaneously firing dozens more of the oval green energy projectiles, and they were almost at impact with his ship. Kalem frantically touched several more crystal controls, and all the viewscreens surrounding the inside circumference of the control room lit up, revealing a three hundred sixty-degree view outside the ship. In the near distance, more Zon ships appeared out of thin air completely surrounding his ship, simultaneously firing hundreds more of the oval green energy weapons.

"Etta, I'm sorry I got you into this, but we'll take a bunch of those devils with us!" he courageously shouted.

And he grabbed the Mazon fire control as he looked up at the viewscreen to see four blue Mazon fireballs dart from his ship, headed in various directions. They hit several more Zon ships, exploding them into light particles, but he instantly experienced his own ship violently shake, and part of the hull to the side of him was blown in, knocking him to the floor. More explosions hit, and he looked up to the viewscreen to see vast numbers of the oval energy projectiles filling the entire screen, and they were almost at impact with his ship. He raised a hand to shield his face from impending doom.

"No-o-o, damn it!"

Inside the control room, everything appeared absolutely normal, calm, and quiet as Kalem crouched down, shielding his arms across his face. The crystal was still glowing around Etta's neck as he lowered directly behind Kalem. A quick beam of light shot from the false crystal hit Kalem in the back of the head, and as then, it spread around his torso. Kalem appeared to freeze in his tracks. Only an empty blue sky appeared on the viewscreen, and Sen Dar's soft hideous laughter echoing from a distance began to grow louder.

Well done, Etta! His voice arrogantly chuckled. ***Well done, indeed!***

Sen Dar's luminous transparent Astral-self appeared boldly walking right through the hull of Kalem's ship and up to Kalem's side. He was wearing an Astral-self version of the real Ancient One's crystal glowing green through the clenched fingers of his right hand. He was also holding another duplicate false chained crystal in his other hand, and he placed it over Kalem's neck. It turned on, glowing green. Sen Dar pointed at Etta, and the false crystal around his neck faded away.

"You have no need of that anymore," his voice delightedly stated. Etta nodded his head in complete compliance as Sen Dar's Astral-self backed up to stand ten feet behind Kalem to concentrate. A duplicate luminous transparent image of Kalem moved right out of Sen Dar's Astral-self form and walked up to Kalem's rigid physical body. Then it merged inside it and slowly dissolved from view.

"No, my dear Captain, I don't have to kill you when I can get you to do that for me," he stated toward Kalem with delight. "Did you think you could really fight me? Weakling Galactic Alliance human, you're now my servant, and I have very special plans for you. Now go and destroy the Guardians' base and be certain Master Ra Mu is inside the base with you. Do you clearly understand?"

Entranced, Kalem nodded his head as Sen Dar looked back and forth at him and Etta.

"You will both be rewarded in heaven by destroying yourselves in the explosion," he stated, grinning, and then commanded, "Now, my warriors, go to victory. Go!"

Smirking in satisfaction, Sen Dar's duplicate Astral-self walked back out of the ship right through the hull and his soft laughter echoed as it faded into the distance. Kalem was now firmly in a hypnotic daze and placed his hands in the palm controls as Etta flew over to his side. Devilishly determined, they grinned at each other and then slowly turned to look at the viewscreen. Outside, the pale-blue light enshrouding the ship's hull intensified, and it changed through the color spectrum, flashed a strobe-like white light, and the ship darted in an arc of light across the distant sky.

Sen Dar's Astral-self reappeared floating through the wall back into his Zon sleeping quarters, and it continued to walk several inches above the plush carpet toward his sitting physical body. It floated above the body and entered it through the top of the head, disappearing inside. Sen Dar opened his eyes and stood up in one swift move. He let go of The Ancient One's real Emerald Doorway Crystal, and it stopped glowing as it dropped on the gold chain to his chest.

He thought to himself with cunning delight, ***This is too easy!***

"Now, this Earth world will be mine in both dimensions, and if Kalem fails to do it, I'll command Ra Mu to destroy himself," he mused aloud. "Then I'll command Admiral Starland to destroy his own Galactic Alliance fleet."

A SPY
AND A THREAT

*A*dmiral Starland was standing beside Lieutenant Moreau on the bridge of his flagship, quietly discussing something. Communications Lieutenant Marin was sitting at the main control console gazing up at the viewscreen. Several bridge personnel were standing in various places around the room monitoring instruments. The viewscreen displayed a topographical representation of Florida and the area southeast in the Atlantic Ocean known as the Bermuda Triangle. A red spiral of whirling light appeared over a small part of this area, and Marin excitedly looked around at Starland to interrupt him.

"Admiral!" she urgently called out.

Admiral Starland turned around and moved behind her.

"Yes, Lieutenant?"

"A Zon ship just passed through the Bermuda Triangle Transit Window. It's headed on a vector for the United States launch facility at the southern tip of the state they call Florida."

"Switch the scanner to the Siberian Transit Window," commanded Starland, and he turned to Lieutenant Moreau. "If my hunch is correct, there should be another Zon ship coming into this dimension right about now."

"I don't get it!" remarked Moreau.

"Just watch this," replied Starland with a curious grin.

The viewscreen switched to an overview of Russia. Another red vortex energy spiral was over central Siberia, and a blue dot appeared coming out from the center of the spiral.

"Plot its course, Marin," ordered Starland. "We must know where it's headed."

Marin touched several crystal controls, and the blue dot at the head of an extended moving line of dots appeared on the viewscreen. It continued moving from the red spiral vortex in a gradual arc across Russia, and it stopped north of Moscow over an area clearly marked, "Russian Plesetsk Launch Facility."

"Sen Dar has to be behind this!" replied Starland, annoyed. "He must know the United States and the Russians both plan to launch another prototype space vehicle only minutes apart in just six hours."

"It doesn't make any sense," stated Moreau. "If Sen Dar controls ships like that, why would he destroy rockets that can't possibly threaten him?"

"He would know, as I do," replied Starland, concerned, "that if the two test vehicles are destroyed again, both countries would be at each other's throats before the day is over."

"What about Captain Kalem?" shot back Moreau, alarmed.

"He should be back at the Guardians' Mountain base by now," thoughtfully replied Starland.

"Admiral, let me go after those ships!" urgently requested Moreau.

"You may prepare your squadron, Lieutenant, but wait for my order before proceeding."

Moreau saluted the Admiral and walked away in a hurry. Starland looked at Marin, who was looking back at him, awaiting his orders.

"Contact Master Ra Mu and tell him the alien ships have moved into position over both launch sites. He'll want to notify the Presidents of both Governments. Then find out if Kalem has safely returned to the Guardians' base."

The Admiral stared intently at the viewscreen over Marin's head and humbly thought, *Ancient One, spare these Earth people from that madman's blind lust for power. So many on other worlds have already lost their physical bodies from his insanity.*

It was nighttime back in Washington D.C. and moonlight coming through the window softly bathed General Harry Faldwell and Senator Judith Cranston while they peacefully slept in their bed at home in the suburbs. Harry was lying on his back, loudly snoring with his left hand-held palm down on his chest, and Judith was lying on her side facing him with her left arm flung across his chest. A low-frequency humming began that started to pulse, and it slowly grew louder until it pervaded the room. A pale blue light just out of view began to appear and swiftly grew brighter. Master Ra Mu's voice began to be audible as if it was approaching from a great distance.

Wake up, General, his soft voice cordially requested. A moment passed, then he humorously stated, *Oh well, I guess I'll have to do this the hard way*.

A light instantly appeared coming out from under the covers on Harry's side of the bed. The top cover began to move, as if underneath it forty pairs of hands were simultaneously massaging every part of Harry's body, and he startled awake.

"Oh God, now what?" he nervously asked, and he backed up in one quick jerk against the headboard with his eyes fixed down at the light, watching multiple hand movements taking place under the covers over his entire body.

The effect suddenly vanished, and Harry apprehensively lifted his head to behold another source of light at the foot of his bed.

"Why can't you knock like anyone else?" he sarcastically inquired.

Master Ra Mu's Soul-sphere surrounded by a pale-gold aura was hovering just above the foot of the bed as Harry heard his amused voice again pulsing out of the white light core.

There's no time for that now, General. Your snoring is harder to get through than an earthquake, and I've been in some really big ones, and he chuckled.

"Big what?" shot back Harry, irritated.

Harry vigorously rubbed his face with both hands, then shook his head to fully awaken himself as Judith stirred awake and gazed up at her husband.

"Can't sleep, dear?" she lovingly asked.

Then she noticed light coming from the foot of the bed and slowly turned her head to see Master Ra Mu's hovering Atma or Soul-sphere. Her mouth dropped open, and her eyes bugged out as the luminous sphere transformed into Master Ra Mu's physical self with a pale-golden aura softly radiating around it. Harry's worried gaze flicked back and forth between Ra Mu and his astonished wife.

"Um... Judith, don't be frightened. He's a friend of mine."

Judith remained stiff as a statue in shock.

"Good evening, Senator Cranston," said Ra Mu with a friendly grin. "There is no need to be alarmed. Your husband is right. My name is Ra Mu, and we are friends."

Still in shock, Judith briefly looked at her husband, then back at Ra Mu, and she fainted into a deep sleep.

Ra Mu shrugged and said to Harry, "Well, she took that a little better than expected. But you must excuse me, General. My visit here is urgent. An alien ship has been detected hidden near your Area 51 launch site. A similar ship is also positioned near the Russian launch site. They intend to destroy both space prototype vehicles, and we have confirmed Sen Dar is the menace behind it all."

Surprised, Harry quickly checked his wristwatch and then looked up, worried at Ra Mu.

"But the second Space Transporter is scheduled to launch just two hours from now!"

"There must be a spy at both launch sites," seriously stated Ra Mu. "We've been monitoring both alien ships, and we've discovered a way to detect the alien presence. The occupants have a slightly faster heart rate than a human in your reality. Here, you'll need this."

A three-inch-long, faceted green crystal that tapered to a rounded point materialized on Harry's lap. He cautiously picked it up and looked it over.

Ra Mu continued, "This device will glow when you detect the spy with it."

Harry threw the covers off, revealing his boxer shorts and a sleeveless t-shirt as he sat on the edge of the bed and urgently stated, "I'd better get down there fast!"

"I'm aware of your plan to join forces with the Russians to use your new secret weapons together for the first time," stated Ra Mu. "It's a worthy plan; but just in case it fails, I'll have a squadron of Galactic Scouts standing by to assist you. At any rate, when Sen Dar discovers what you've done, you will need their help."

Harry breathed deep and replied, "And we're grateful for your help, but I'd like to see what the billions spent on advanced weapons research is worth after all these years. I just never thought we'd have to join military forces with the Russians to fight off a greater danger than we ever were to each other during the cold war days with the old Soviet Union."

Harry glanced down at Judith. She was now smiling, experiencing a peaceful dream. He bent down and kissed her forehead, then got up out of bed.

"I'll have a lot of explaining to do," he apprehensively said. "We were just married last month."

"Yes...I know!" chuckled Ra Mu. "But don't worry. Judith is very adaptable. In time, she'll be of great help to you with your um... diplomatic skills. Farewell!" And he grinned wide.

Puzzled by the remark, Harry opened his mouth to ask a question just as Master Ra Mu faded from view.

SAVED BY
A MAINTENANCE MAN

It was a beautiful sunny day with no snow on the ground at the backside of Mt. Shasta in northern California near the one-hundred-and-twenty-foot by sixty-foot gray rock wall. From high in the background sky, Kalem's ship appeared, flying down in an arc toward the backside of the mountain. It passed over the forest trees, slowed, and stopped to assume a hovering position thirty-feet above the ground and fifty yards away from the flat gray rock wall. The rock wall lit up, and the whirling tiny blue galaxy-like stars appeared and widened open, revealing the one hundred twenty-foot-wide by sixty-foot-high smooth oval lighted tunnel encircled by the rough-hewn cavern opening. And the whirling stars widened more, revealing the tunnel continued several hundred yards further to open into a landing bay carved out of the inside of the mountain. Six Galactic Scout ships were parked on the far side of the landing bay floor in two parallel rows. Another clear glass-like oval tunnel opening on the back wall above them continued deeper into the mountain's interior. Kalem's ship slowly moved into the opening, and it was soon hovering down out of view in the direction of the other parked ships. The whirling opening in the rock wall spiraled closed and vanished.

The ship hovered further down inside the launch bay and landed next to another Scout ship. In the background, a rock platform at the top of carved blue granite steps led up to the triangular hallway opening that headed deeper inside the mountain. Kalem dropped to the ground through the open hatch underneath the ship, wearing the false Emerald Doorway Crystal around his neck. Etta flew out of the bottom hatch and over to him, then hovered down to walk by his side. With deadly determination, they began to walk together in a hurry up the granite steps. Halfway up, Etta hovered up waist high and darted ahead of Kalem through the triangular entryway.

A short time later, Etta flew into view from the far end of a long triangular hallway. Kalem appeared behind him, walking at a brisk pace. Mayleena walked into view from the opposite end of the hallway, noticed them coming toward her, and she joyfully started jogging toward them. She reached the middle of the hallway and stopped just as Etta flew up to her.

"Dear Etta, I thank The Ancient One you're both back safe!" she very cheerfully remarked.

He completely ignored her and darted away while her surprised gaze followed him until he disappeared through another triangular opening at the far end of the hallway.

"Etta, what's wrong with you?" she yelled after him.

She turned back around just as Kalem reached her position, and she threw her arms around his neck and tried to kiss him, but he remained rigidly non-responsive, and she slowly backed away, deeply worried.

"What's wrong with you two?"

Kalem gazed back at her with a blank face and shrugged his shoulders. Then he looked past her right shoulder down the hallway and unemotionally answered, "I... I had to fight Sen Dar after all, and I'm stressed from the battle. He miscalculated when he fired at us, and I made the right choice. He is finally dead!"

Mayleena compassionately gazed up at him, took his head in her hands, pulled his head forward, and kissed him on the brow, but he remained emotionally unresponsive. She grabbed his hand and affectionately squeezed it with both her hands, but he still remained unmoved.

"What happened to you?" she asked, dismayed. "Something is very wrong!"

Kalem pulled his hand away and stiffly stated, "I'll explain it all later. First, I must give my report, and I need rest."

Then he forced a weak smile back at her, and she stared disbelieving back at him.

"Let's talk about it later," he added as he turned from her and continued to walk in a hurry down the hallway in Etta's direction.

Mayleena suspiciously stared after him, and then she placed her hands on her hips and thought, worried, *I must find Master Ra Mu fast!*

She hurried away in the opposite direction.

It was now early morning at the secret U.S. Strategic Space Command hidden somewhere below the highly classified Area 51 base in Nevada as Harry, in his four-star General's uniform, and Judith, in a complimentary tight-fitting blue dress, stood together near the back of the control room. Dozens of technicians, filling most of the seats in several rows across the room, were busy monitoring preparations for the second Space Transporter launch as a serious Air Force Colonel approached Harry.

"We're ready, General."

"Alright, Colonel, gather everyone together in the center of the room," commanded Harry.

The Colonel picked up the intercom phone on the wall behind them and smartly stated, "Attention, everyone. Listen up! I want everyone to move to the center of the room. This won't take long."

He waved a hand, and several dozen military police with guns drawn entered the room through the doors on both sides of the complex, sealing off all exits. Harry took the three-inch-long faceted green crystal Ra Mu gave him from his pocket, and Judith gazed surprised at it.

"What's that for? What are you going to do?"

"Don't be alarmed, Judith. You'll find out soon. We're going to catch a spy!"

He walked toward the personnel being gathered together in the center of the room, and Judith curiously followed behind him. He briefly pointed the crystal at each one of them until he reached the last man; but the crystal still did not light up. Frustrated, Harry took a cigar out of his jacket pocket, angrily bit down on it in the corner of his mouth, nervously yanked it back out, and threw it into a nearby trash can.

"Where is that rat?" he angrily asked himself. "He's here somewhere." Then he loudly barked out an order at the Colonel, "Search the corridor and the launch pad. Light up all of them. Did you completely secure the base?"

"Yes, Sir," confidently replied the Colonel. "No one's getting out of here."

"Well, don't just stand there, man, get cracking!" ordered Harry, fuming.

The Colonel saluted Harry and then hurried toward the closed doors on the far side of the control room. Several Guards opened the doors, and the Colonel walked through them just as another military policeman rushed up to him from the outer hallway and whispered in his ear. The Colonel blanched, then rushed back into the control room and over to Harry.

"We have him," he confidently stated.

"Where? Harry demanded.

"A coded transmission was detected being sent from outside this base to an alien ship hidden high in the atmosphere behind cloud cover. It was traced to a ground crewman at the launch runway. The MPS are bringing him in now."

A moment later, two big muscular military policemen pulled and half-dragged a defiant man in through the control room entrance doors. He was dressed in a ground crewman's garb with a knitted pullover ski cap covering his forehead and ears. They hauled him up to within a few feet of Harry, and one of the policemen handed Harry an alien-looking, silver-gray palm-sized communicator with several buttons on its smooth oval surface.

"You will not be able to stop us now!" angrily remarked the Zon prisoner, struggling to free himself, but the Guards firmly held him by the arms. "You cannot stop Lord Zol Yul or the Zon warriors from our destiny!"

"Lord Zol Yul, huh? You meant to say that lunatic, Sen Dar," sarcastically shot back Harry.

The prisoner arrogantly stuck out his chin and said, "I do not know this... Sen Dar! Zol Yul will destroy all of you for this! All of you!"

"So, this is a Zon warrior," remarked Harry giving him an intimidating gaze. "Kinda' puny, aren't they?"

Frowning, Judith poked a finger in his ribs.

"May I, General?" she politely encouraged as she boldly stepped in front of Harry, and he reluctantly stepped back as she gave a friendly smile to the Zon prisoner.

"How did this Zol Yul come to power?"

The prisoner hesitated and then defiantly replied, "He appeared before us on the High Altar and fulfilled the ancient prophecy. Lord Zol Yul is Lord overall! Each of you will regret your actions with me!"

And he fiercely lunged at Judith, but she quickly stood behind Harry, just as the two Guards forcefully yanked their prisoner back away from them. The prisoner angrily struggled to get free, but one of the Guards slapped him across the top of the head like a bad dog, knocking the knitted ski cap off, revealing his hidden long braided sideburns that dropped down the full length. His features now appeared obviously alien, with his larger forehead showing. Harry pointed the crystal device at him, and it instantly began to glow, pulsing radiant green energy. He handed the glowing crystal to Judith, and she reluctantly held it between two fingers at arm's length. Harry grabbed the Zon warrior by his shirt with one hand and pulled him close, face to face, while the two Guards firmly held his arms.

"What are you going to do with me?" asked the worried captive.

"First," Harry fiercely began, "you'll tell me all I want to know about your new fat-head leader. His real name is Sen Dar, and we'll deal with him soon enough."

Harry angrily put his nose right up to the Zon's nose like an angry drill Sergeant with a new recruit in boot camp and angrily yelled,

"Then we'll put you two maniacs away in some nice padded room for life!"

The prisoner was momentarily terrified, then he angrily yelled out, "Lord Zol Yul will bury you in ashes. You cannot stop... a God!"

Harry looked with pitiful disgust back at the Zon prisoner.

"You brainwashed fool! He's a fraud, a fake, and his real name is Sen Dar." He angrily yelled at the Guards, "Get him out of my sight!"

Harry nodded his head toward the doors, and the Guards dragged their struggling captive away. Then he put the alien communicator to his lips and pressed a button.

"Listen up, Zon warriors, and listen good. We captured your spy. Tell your fake fat head leader, Zol Yul; he's not fooling anyone. We know who he is. Now tell him General Harry Faldwell wants to talk with him. Do it now!

Judith slipped her hand over the alien communicator before Harry could utter another word, "Remember diplomacy, General. It's more powerful than angry threats and more effective."

"Alright! Alright already!" he shot back, irritated.

Unconvinced, Judith reluctantly took her hand away, and Harry impatiently spoke again into the device, "Well... where is this Zol Yul?"

A male voice answered Harry back through the communicator.

"Our Lord Zol Yul is linked through to you now," he arrogantly stated.

"We already have your spy, Sen Dar. I'll chase you to hell and back before I'll let you destroy another one of our Space Transporters."

Judith stood beside Harry grimacing at his questionable diplomatic skills as Sen Dar responded back through the communicator.

"I'm surprised you had the intelligence to discover him," he condescendingly began. "You are, after all, only the puny General of a little country with toy rockets. You will soon be doing my bidding if I let you live!"

Harry shot back, fuming, "Puny? Come and say that to my face, skinny bone-headed dirt ball!"

"Oh great!" remarked Judith, disappointed. "That's what you call diplomacy?"

Harry scowled at her as he took another unlit cigar from his shirt, stuffed it into the corner of his mouth, and angrily bit down. He nervously began to pace back and forth and suddenly stopped to address Sen Dar again through the alien device.

"We're not alone in this fight, Lord of nothing! You'll get your phony royal fanny fried before we're done with you!"

Judith angrily ribbed him with her elbow as she clapped her hand over the communicator.

"Harry, you're blowing it!"

Harry yanked the device away and then reluctantly gave in to her firm determination.

"Alright, damn it!" he softly whispered.

Sen Dar's arrogant voice came back through the device, "Your Capital city will fall next if you do not heed my demands," worthless General! Neither your pitiful Galactic Alliance friends nor your miserable excuse for an Air Force can stop my vastly superior Zon warriors or their vastly superior warships. Yes, I know about this Galactic Alliance."

"Warriors my ass," defiantly shot back Harry. "Come and get your well-deserved spanking. This communication is over!"

Harry turned around and looked at the Launch Control Director, that was now standing behind him.

"Proceed with the countdown," he angrily commanded, and he forcefully barked an order at the Colonel standing nearby, "Get me the President on the direct line, and I don't mean a minute from now!"

The Colonel turned and hurried away. A few moments later, he returned with a red wireless handset with a blinking green light on top, and Harry picked up the receiver.

"Mr. President, we've captured an alien spy on the base that was involved in our recent Transporter destruction. He says he's a Zon warrior, and Sen Dar is, in fact, their new ruler."

"I'm on my way over to the control center now," answered back the President's voice through the phone. "I can talk with the Russian President on a secure line from there."

Etta was now in a storage room inside the secret Mt. Shasta Guardians' base, jogging up to an open cabinet storage compartment with a six-inch-long by two-inch-wide polished chrome timed bomb device. His nimble fingers touched several crystal controls on the top of the cylinder, and they lit up, blinking. An LCD (liquid crystal display) window on its surface showed... 05:00 minutes, then... 04:59 as it began to count down rapidly. He opened the metal door and placed the device on the inside surface. It magnetically locked in place, and he closed the door as he began to hear Sen Dar's sadistic telepathic voice again directing him.

Good... good, Etta. You're doing exactly the right thing. Master Ra Mu will be very pleased.

Hypnotically glassy-eyed, Etta forced a bright sadistic smile of his own, and he ran over to the bag he had placed in the middle of the floor. He reached into it and took out another bomb device, then repeated the procedure by placing it underneath a countertop. He grabbed another bomb from the bag and hurried out of the storage room, headed around the corner down the triangular hallway. But he ran headfirst into a cart being pushed by a maintenance man and was knocked backward unconscious, head over heels to the floor.

The very concerned man ran to Etta's side, gently lifted his head, and asked, "Etta, are you alright?"

Etta's eyes started to open, and he shook his head, snapping out of the trance state. His eyes suddenly bugged out as he remembered what he had just done, and he rapidly began to chatter, very concerned in Dren up at the man as his tail lit up. Then he darted back into the storage room and up to the first cabinet door.

He yanked open the door and frantically yelled, "Quma doe tam bocks! Quemi bockum!" ("I've set the bombs! They'll explode!")

"What bombs, Etta?" asked the worried Maintenance Man as he ran into the storage room and up to Etta's side.

Etta touched the crystal controls on the bomb attached to the door, and the timer stopped at 00:05 seconds. Then he darted under the counter and disengaged the second bomb. The Maintenance Man hurried over to Etta just as Etta grinned relief up at him. Then Etta suddenly remembered Kalem, and shocked concern spread across his face.

"Captain Kalem!"

His tail brightened, and he raced out of the room and headed down the triangular hallway.

The dismayed Maintenance Man hesitated, then yelled after Etta with puzzled concern as he hurried out of the storage room, "Etta, wait up! Etta… wait!"

Kalem was hypnotically glassy-eyed, standing behind a curved control console in a brightly lit black obsidian walled room. Many faceted luminous crystal controls were symmetrically laid out across the top of the console. Several of the timed bomb devices on top of it were already blinking - counting down. Kalem reached into his shirt with his right hand and grabbed Sen Dar's already glowing fake duplicate crystal hung from the gold chain. He held it up to his face, and he began to hear Sen Dar's telepathic voice coming from the crystal that blinked with each word spoken.

Good! Good, Kalem! began Sen Dar's voice with vicious delight.

Now place the beneficial devices all over the console and set them for sixty seconds. You will have repaired all of the damage by then.

Kalem mechanically smiled and reached down behind the console to take two more bombs out of the bag at his feet. He started the timers and then attached one in the center of the main console and the other one to the wall directly behind him. Just then, Etta flew into the room and circled Kalem three times, rapidly chattering fiery Dren words at him. Sen Dar's telepathic voice again came through the crystal around Kalem's neck.

Stop him, you fool! fiercely yelled his angry voice.

Kalem angrily backhanded Etta, tossing him into the wall, instantly knocking him out cold. As Etta's body fell limp to the floor, Mayleena ran into the room and looked horrified down at Etta.

"Kalem no-o-o," she screamed, alarmed, "stop what you're doing. What's the matter with you?"

She bent down and picked up Etta in her arms, then cradled him to her chest. Completely unemotional, Kalem gruffly pushed past her, knocking her into the wall.

"Kalem, please snap out of it," she loudly pleaded. "I love you. Please… stop this!"

She noticed the crystal glowing around Kalem's neck and then the timed bomb devices on the console set to explode. Then she felt something touching the back of her head that was turning her head around, and she reached up with her hands behind her neck to feel it, but nothing was there. She slowly looked around to see a timed bomb device attached to the wall and looked closer at the display window that showed the device continuing to count down from 00:45 seconds.

She spun back around, shocked by Kalem's actions, and cried out, "Kalem, what have you done?"

She cradled Etta closer in her arms and ran past Kalem out of the control room. Kalem grabbed his laser gun from his holster and pointed it at the back of her head to fire just as the crystal around his neck blinked once and went out. He could hear Master Ra Mu's projected telepathic voice as The Ancient One's omnipresent energy filled the room with the sound of a vast ocean of crashing waves, a deep humming, and the hauntingly beautiful melody of a single high-pitched flute.

"Kalem, stop! Listen to The Ancient One's Sound and snap out of the trance. Do it now. Use your inner strength. Fight off Sen Dar's spell."

Kalem's glazed eyes brightened as he blinked to alertness. He slowly dropped the laser gun down to his side as he began to consciously recognize Master Ra Mu's firm voice.

"Ra Mu?" softly said Kalem, a little bewildered.

Mayleena ran back into the control room without Etta, and she stopped, noticing that Kalem appeared to have snapped out of the trance. She started to cautiously walk toward him, just as Sen Dar's voice came out of Kalem's mouth.

"Where are you, Ra Mu, you coward," he hotly demanded. "Come out and fight me."

Frightened, Mayleena started to slowly step back toward the doorway as Kalem raised the laser gun and pointed it at her head. Kalem was gazing at her with a twisted smile and a mad look of malice as he slowly advanced toward her. Horrified, Mayleena took another step back.

"Kalem, please stop this," she pleaded, terrified. "Why are you doing this to us? It's me, Mayleena. I love you!" And she began to cry as she pleaded again, "Please come back to us..."

The crystal momentarily blinked off and on, then off, and Kalem's expression instantly changed from a glassy hypnotic stare to one of instant, consciously aware concern.

"What... where am I?" he groggily asked, then became alert.

Mayleena breathed a sigh of relief and lovingly gazed back at him.

"My love, you are here with me!" she said as she threw her arms around him and kissed him. Then the crystal lit up again, and Kalem grabbed his head with both hands in intense pain, struggling to fight off Sen Dar's control over him, but quickly succumbed and slipped back into a trance. His face grimaced with Sen Dar's angry malice as he pointed the laser gun at Mayleena's head, grabbed the back of her hair, and yanked her head back to press the gun into her temple.

Mayleena stumbled backward a few feet and fearfully yelled, "Fight it, Kalem! Don't give in to it! It's me, Mayleena and I love you!"

He backed her right up to the wall by the timed bomb device that was now directly above her left shoulder. The LCD window was counting down from 00:15 seconds as Etta flew into the room with his mouth open. He darted past Kalem's chest and clamped his mouth onto the chained crystal as he passed by, ripping it off. The crystal went dark just as Kalem turned to fire, but he suddenly snapped out of the trance instead, with his arm stopping just short of pointing it at Etta. He lowered the gun. Etta flew to Mayleena's shoulder and landed, dropping the chained crystal into her open hands.

Etta very excitedly stated, "Et pod Sen Dar! Et pa u nas kistalm." ("It was Sen Dar! It's a false crystal.")

Mayleena walked up to Kalem and put a hand on his shoulder as he gazed back at her, a little groggy and very puzzled.

"The evil demon was controlling you... with this!" she very compassionately stated as she held up the false crystal.

Kalem looked at the chained crystal in her hand, and his eyes widened with alarm as he began to recall what he had just done.

"Oh my God, I've set the timers! This whole place is about to blow!" he stated with stunned urgency.

And he jumped into action, wildly racing around the room to disarm one device after another. Then he twirled around and leaped at the device still counting down on the wall right behind Mayleena and Etta, who was now perched on her shoulder with his glowing tail wrapped around her upper chest. The LCD window display was counting down 00:03...00:02...just as Kalem's forefinger touched a crystal control on the side of the device, stopping it at 00:01. Kalem dropped his shoulders in nervous exhaustion, let out a long-relieved sigh, rolled his eyes in the back of his head, and collapsed to the floor. Etta flew off Mayleena's shoulder and down to Kalem's side to compassionately gaze at his unconscious friend. He rubbed Kalem's brow with his fingers as Mayleena knelt down by Kalem's side and sat on the floor. She gently lifted Kalem's head and placed it in her lap, then leaned over and tenderly kissed his forehead.

She looked very concerned over at Etta as she held out her hand and said, "Dear friend, Etta, find Ra Mu. Tell him what happened and give him this phony crystal. Then bring him and some Council members here fast."

Etta gazed concerned down at Kalem, and then he grabbed the chained crystal from her open hand and darted out of the room.

A RENEWED COLD WAR TURNS WARM

$\mathcal{B}$ack at the secret U.S. Strategic Space Command Center, President Sam Stockwell was now standing by the large control console directly across from the main command viewscreen. He picked up a special red handset, just as General Harry Faldwell, with his usual unlit cigar stuffed into the corner of his mouth, and Senator Judith Cranston walked into the control room escorted by two Secret Service Agents in dark suits. The Agents quickly walked them up to the President, then one turned and walked away, and the other one stood behind Harry.

"Alright!" said the President into the phone and briefly paused, then continued, "Let me know when the Russian President is on the line." He hung up the phone, turned to greet them, and stated, relieved,

"I'm glad you're both here!"

"Mr. President, it's Sen Dar, alright!" Harry sternly replied. "I'd recognize the voice of that lunatic anywhere."

Judith grimaced and gently ribbed him.

"Brilliant words, Harry. Wow! Some diplomacy. If there was ever any place I'm really needed, it's by your side."

Harry scowled back at her and said, "Judith, you don't understand! That deranged madman has declared war on the United States and Russia. He intends to destroy our next Space Transporter and the next Russian prototype jet and rocket-powered space vehicle. We've got to move fast while we still can!"

Judith rolled her eyes and looked away, a little embarrassed for both of them as they stood in front of Sam, who appeared unmoved by their actions, patiently waiting for them to finish. The light on the red phone suddenly flashed yellow, buzzing three times, and Sam punched a button on the cradle to put it on speakerphone.

"Hello, Mr. President. This is President Sam Stockwell," he very cordially began. "Listen to me Vladimir, it looks like we'll have to work together on this one, and we better do it quickly."

The Russian President replied this time with a cordial Russian accent, "Moscow too was threatened by the madman Zol Yul. Then something remarkable happened - a miracle. This Master Ra Mu appeared before me and showed the truth. He said you had the same experience. He warned me that a spy was on the base, and that spy is now in chains."

Harry yanked the cigar from his mouth, cleared his throat to get Sam's attention, and placed his hand over the speaker on the phone cradle. Sam smirked at him, then reluctantly touched a button, putting the phone on hold.

"Excuse me, Mr. President, but I have a plan that can work!" he urgently stated to Sam. "We could combine forces with the Russian scientists to jointly use our laser cannon and scalar wave defensive satellites together for the first time. We can set up an energy mirror against any force Sen Dar may throw at us up there or on the ground."

President Stockwell's eyes lit up with the idea, and he nodded approval to Harry, and Judith also approvingly grinned at his plan as Sam touched the hold button again.

"Pardon me, Vladimir, I was momentarily detained. One of my Generals has suggested something that could very well work, but it will take real trust on both our parts to put it into action. Now please listen to what General Faldwell has to say."

"I will listen," somewhat apprehensively began Vladimir's voice through the handset speaker. "Under the circumstances, what other choice do we have?"

As Sam handed Harry the phone, Harry covered the receiver with his hand and whispered under his breath to the Secret Service Agent who approached from behind him, "Get Griswold! You know, that top NASA scientist nut on UFOs."

The Agent shrugged and looked puzzled back at Harry.

"Oh… damn it, what's his first name?" mused Harry frustrated to himself, then his eyes lit up. "Oh yeah... Hubert! Get Hubert Griswald down here pronto!"

The Agent nodded and walked off in a hurry as Harry continued to speak into the phone.

"Hello, President Vladimir. This is General Faldwell," respectfully began Harry.

"I am listening," cautiously responded Vladimir's voice through the speakerphone.

Harry cleared his throat and continued, "This is what we propose. We have the ability to connect our main command computer together with yours for the first time. Then we can link together both of our orbiting weapon platforms to create a defensive energy shield and combine our laser cannon targeting capabilities to defend ourselves to our mutual benefit."

Harry nervously stuffed the cigar into the corner of his mouth. While he anxiously waited for a response from the Russian leader, Hubert and Harry overheard muted conversations taking place between Vladimir and several of his Generals on the other end.

"Perhaps you assume too much, General Faldwell," Vladimir's defensive voice finally replied back. "Why do you think we have such weapons in space?"

Harry firmly shot back, "I didn't want to say it in this way, but we both know full well our two countries have had deployed and working defensive weapons platforms in space for quite some time. The people in our two countries don't know about their existence, but we both do. We don't have time for any political games of denial now if we want to survive what's coming."

There was a pause on the line, and then Vladimir sighed and said, "Continue, General Faldwell."

Harry blew out a relieved sigh and continued, "Well... we could link together our laser cannon and scalar wave defensive platforms in space to form a protective energy shield that could deflect any weapons the Zon ships may use against us. Utilizing - Direct Inverse Projection – we could reflect their firepower back upon them. Your top scientist will know what I mean."

In the President's office back in Moscow, Vladimir was standing behind a large antique desk holding a similar red phone in his hand. Two of his Generals and one bearded scientist type in his late sixties were standing behind Vladimir, intently listening to the speaker in the handset upon the President's desk.

"Yes, what a coincidence!" continued Vladimir on the phone with a slightly sarcastic grin. "As your saying goes in that ride I believe is in your Disneyland, 'It's a small world after all.' We have been working on just such devices ourselves... um... as you stated for a long time now!"

Harry's slightly defensive voice shot back through the speaker on the handset, "Yes, well, ours have been prototype tested, and they've been operational for years."

President Stockwell motioned for Harry to hand back the phone, and Harry handed over the receiver. Then Harry stood with a proud grin next to Judith and confidently stuffed the cigar back into the corner of his mouth.

"This is President Stockwell back on the line, Vladimir," very cordially stated Sam into the phone. "Let's arrange a conference call linkup between our top two scientists in one hour. Will that be agreeable?"

Vladimir's voice answered back, "Agreed!"

"Well then, for now, do svidaniya Vladimir," said Sam, very upbeat back in Russian.

"Ah-h... you say goodbye in Russian better than me!" delightedly shot back Vladimir's voice through the speaker on the handset. "Maybe you should work over here for a while. Yes?"

And a hearty laugh from Vladimir's with his Generals came back through the speaker.

Sam chuckled and replied, "I'll take a rain check on that, Vladimir. Goodbye for now."

"Yes, goodbye!" cheerfully answered back Vladimir.

Sam hung up the phone. He seriously gazed at Harry and Judith and then asked Harry,

"Launch is less than two hours away. Can we do it in time?"

Harry took the cigar from his mouth with a cocky grin and confidently stated, "Damn right, we can do it! I've got Hubert Griswald on his way here now. He could interface our defense computer system with their system before they'd even know he'd done it!"

President Stockwell confidently grinned at Harry and said upbeat, "Excellent!" Then he looked at Judith. "And I'd like you, Judith, to diplomatically assist us as an interpreter. Is your Russian up to snuff?"

"That's why I'm here!" she very enthusiastically shot back.

Sam looked thoughtful and said, "Well then, this may just work!"

MASTER LUMIERA'S MYSTERIOUS WARNING

*K*alem was now sitting in a chair toward the back of the right side of the oval black obsidian table in the main Council room at the Mt. Shasta Guardians' base. Mayleena was standing behind him, rubbing his shoulders. He appeared quite alert, having fully recovered from Sen Dar's psychic control over him, and Etta, paying strict attention, was calmly sitting upright in a chair directly opposite them with his two hands resting palms down on the tabletop. Master Ra Mu was standing a few feet further away at the head of the table with his crystal staff held in his right hand.

"That was too close!" he seriously stated, gazing concernedly at Kalem. "I warned you not to engage in combat with Sen Dar until after your training."

Kalem replied, a little embarrassed, "Well... uh... under the circumstances, it was quite unavoidable."

Ra Mu kindly smiled at him and stated, "This time we were all very lucky! If Etta hadn't run into the technician and snapped out of the trance, we wouldn't be having this conversation. To be safe in the future, you, Mayleena, and Etta will need training in the parallel Lemuria dimension on this Earth under the direct guidance of Master Lumiera and myself. We must leave immediately."

"But what about the next Space Transporter launch and the Zon threat?" asked Kalem, gazing concerned back at Ra Mu.

Mayleena enthusiastically jumped in, "The launch is scheduled to take place any minute. Maybe we could watch it on the viewscreen."

"There's no time left for that in this parallel reality, and Master Lumiera is already awaiting our arrival in the domed city of the Adepts."

"Well, may I inquire what precautions," continued Kalem raising an eyebrow, "have been taken for the Transporter's security?"

Calmly grinning back at him, Ra Mu replied, "I think the United States and Russia can hold off any initial attempts by the Zon ships to destroy both test Space Transporter vehicles. But after that, I'm certain they'll need our help. Admiral Starland has Lieutenant Moreau standing by in command of several fighter squadrons in case of any emergency. For now, you can let go of any concerns you may have, Captain. All three of you will have plenty of time to train where we're going. Each of you must remember that the molecular time rates flow at different rates of speed in the other parallel dimensions than what you are familiar with here. Nevertheless, Sen Dar is on the loose, and we have no time to waste. Well, Captain, do you feel up to piloting your ship again?"

Cracking a cocky grin, Kalem answered, "I'm a little tired, but I'm ready for anything!"

"Me too!" courageously chimed in Mayleena, just as Etta flew up and over the top of the table to cutely puff out his chest and proudly gaze at Ra Mu.

"Qum emtah ot omany!" ("I'm ready for anything!") he very courageously stated.

They cheerfully grinned at Etta's antics, and Ra Mu sighed, then warned, "Very well then but beware! Each of you will be tested to the limits of your awareness. Your very survival will depend upon the outcome, and with Sen Dar on the loose, there isn't a moment to lose."

He turned and walked in a hurry out of the room through the triangular entryway, closely followed behind by Kalem, Mayleena, and finally Etta, slowly hovering behind them.

It was early morning the next day back at Area 51 beside the very long launch runway, and a second prototype Space Transporter was ready for take-off, hovering a few feet above the runway. In the distant background, the morning sun was just appearing, rising above the horizon over the distant desert mountain range. Time mysteriously sped up, and the sun swiftly moved a little further into the sky until it was fully round in view above the horizon. Then time resumed its normal flow, just as several desert birds flew into view. They began to circle not far from the hovering anti-gravity-powered Space Transporter.

In Russia, it was now nighttime, and another one of their elongated triangular turbofan jet and rocket engine-powered prototype Space Transporters was on the long runway, ready for launch. It was clearly lit around the hull by a dozen ground-level floodlights.

High above Earth, Admiral Starland's massive mile-long oval Galactic Alliance Emerald Star flagship was slowly moving across the rich Milky Way star-filled background of space, surrounded by a familiar pale-blue antimagnetic aura. The moon was looming in the background beyond the ship as Earth came into view, while the ship assumed a geosynchronous orbit above the planet's equator. Two groups of Galactic Alliance Scout ships in V formations - one group with seven and the other group nearer the foreground with six - were hovering to each side of the front end of their massive flagship, slowly continuing to orbit high above Earth's atmosphere.

Aboard the flagship, Admiral Starland was standing behind the main control console on the command bridge looking at the large viewscreen, and Lieutenant Marin was seated at the console directly in front of him. Earth was filling the bottom half of the viewscreen beyond the visible front end of the flagship with the two Scout fighter squadrons hovering in V formations to each side of it as Lieutenant Moreau walked up to the Admiral.

"The Scout squadrons are in position now, Admiral," he respectfully stated.

"Very good, Lieutenant!" said Starland while he continued staring at the viewscreen. He turned to Moreau and sternly ordered, "But remember, Lieutenant, I don't want any Scouts to engage the Zon ships unless it becomes absolutely necessary. We cannot interfere with the Earth people unless things turn in Sen Dar's favor."

Moreau angrily replied, "I knew Sen Dar was behind this whole mess; I'm beginning to understand how Kalem feels about him. I'd like to get my own hands around his murderous neck!"

The Admiral replied with a wise, compassionate grin, "Some things, Lieutenant, even if they appear entirely destructive, can force long-standing opponents stuck in military and political competition, that neither really wants, to genuinely band together for the first time. The outcome can be very constructive in order to survive a greater threat."

"I just don't see the point of allowing any further destruction from those Zon devils when we could prevent it all from here," snapped back Moreau, obviously frustrated.

Starland calmly continued, "We must have the patience to see the purpose of The Ancient One's omnipresent living Sound working behind all things before we act rashly."

"Well... yes, I know you're right, Sir," concurred Moreau, and he sighed.

"Go and join your men," encouraged Starland. "Then move your squadron into an orbital position above the Area 51 and the Space Transporter launch runway as planned. Send the second squadron into position over the Russian launch runway facility. If the Zon ships begin to win, I want your squadron ready to chase them all back to their own parallel dimension on this planet. Sen Dar will think twice about attacking again if he knows Galactic Alliance ships are involved."

Moreau nodded his agreement and saluted the Admiral with his fist held across his chest. Then he walked out of the bridge control room, and Starland looked back at the viewscreen.

A single Scout ship appeared on it, flying out of the open launch bay at the front of the flagship, and it flew over to the group of six Scouts to take up the lead position at the apex of the V-shaped formation. A moment later, the blue glow around the hulls of both squadrons brightened, and both V formations darted away in opposite directions. Moreau's squadron flew toward the North American continent that was just coming into view on the left side of Earth and the second squadron flew toward Northern Asia to quickly vanish beyond Earth's northeastern hemisphere.

Meanwhile, Kalem was sitting at the control console of his Scout ship with his hands in the palm guidance controls, looking at the viewscreen. Mayleena was standing by his side. Etta was lying along the top of the console, also gazing at the viewscreen. Master Ra Mu was standing behind Kalem and Mayleena, holding his crystal staff in his right hand. The viewscreen was showing them the inside of the

Guardians' secret Mt. Shasta Scout launch bay. Five additional Scout ships were parked in two parallel rows beside his ship on the right side of the bay. Then his ship began to lift off.

The clear glass-like oval tube that continued above the other end of the launch bay headed deeper inside the mountain. It appeared to extend into the far distance toward an opening with faint daylight streaming down into it from the other side. A smaller clear glass-like crystal transport car tube built parallel to the larger tube led a little deeper inside the mountain. It veered away at a curved ninety-degree angle, traveling deeper into the mountain's interior. Kalem's ship moved up near the oval opening at the back of the launch bay and slowly flew into it. His ship dwindled to a tiny speck as it continued its flight to the other end of the tunnel and then passed out of it into the daylight streaming down into the opening. The ship was headed into Earth's secret parallel Lemuria dimension.

There was a beautiful clear deep-blue sky above the secret parallel dimension on Earth and the oval cavern opening two-thirds the way up the tall snow-capped mountainside. It was positioned just above the luminous blue-green waterfall cascading out of the cavern opening. Just below the waterfall, the smaller sealed transparent transportation tube exited the mountain and continued down the mountainside behind the waterfall to the mountain's base. It disappeared in the thick blue-green forest trees that lined the back of the huge transparent domed city, located on the western lower plateau of the mountain.

Kalem's ship appeared flying out of the large oval cavern opening above the waterfall and it stopped to hover high above the huge dome. Far below, the three very large gold-capped and quartz-tipped white alabaster pyramids towered in the far background of the mysterious city. The semicircular mountain range with waterfalls pouring down their sides to become rivers and then lakes adorned the backside of the huge dome's interior. Clear crystal and gold minaret-like towers that surrounded the pyramids continued into the lush countryside. Majestic palatial estates, partially made of multicolored crystals and variously colored granite, were also scattered throughout the lush countryside around several of the larger lakes.

One of the transport tubes led directly from the translucent oval ivory dome, surrounded by the three giant towering pyramids, into the countryside. Another one extended from a platform near the base of one of the three pyramids. Numerous other transport tubes snaked along the ground to various points all around the circumference of the dome's base. Several continued beyond it to disappear at various points within the background forest trees. Two of the double-terminated quartz crystal-like transport vehicles moving at high speed within two of the transport tubes were changing glowing colors at each end from blue, to red and to gold every few seconds. One Scout class ship like Kalem's ship and one huge Oceanan Spectrum Crystal ship were landed on individual pads built around the exterior half of the huge dome that faced the distant ocean. In the far distance, a broad grass-covered plateau extended several miles from the dome at the mountain's base to a wide half-moon-shaped black sand dune beachhead that stretched along a beautiful turquoise ocean coastline. The sky overhead was extraordinarily clear and bright as Kalem's ship slowly descended toward the domed city.

His ship soon landed at the dome's base on one remaining circular landing pad near the entrance leading into the city. A hundred-foot walkway connected to the pad led up to the semicircular archway opening that extended ten feet out from the dome's base. Fifteen-foot-high prehistoric ferns lining both sides of the walkway continued in lush growth between the other pads and around the dome to extend into the tall green fir forest that surrounded the backside of the dome in a semicircular pattern. One Scout ship was now landed on a pad to one side of Kalem's ship, and the huge Oceanan Spectrum ship was landed on a larger pad on the opposite side. Master Lumiera walked into view from the back of the archway wearing a saffron monks-type robe and simple sandals as the hatch on the underside of Kalem's ship opened. Even with his shiny bald head, he appeared trim and virile with smooth, wrinkle-free skin. A ladder extended to the ground from underneath the ship. Kalem stepped down a few rungs and then jumped to the ground. He turned around to help Mayleena as she climbed down the ladder, and Ra Mu followed behind her. Etta hovered down out of the hatch and passed by Mayleena's shoulder, while Master Lumiera, smiling, watched them. To the visitor's perceptions, Lumiera appeared to be emanating a faint gold aura around his entire body. He strolled over to the middle of the walkway to meet them, and Master Ra Mu respectfully nodded his head to the venerable elder Master Adept of The Ancient One. A respectful nod was given him in return.

"Welcome, travelers, to this sacred city!" jovially stated Master Lumiera.

"Thank you, Master Lumiera, for granting us entrance to the city of the Adepts and for your assistance with their training," respectfully replied Ra Mu.

Master Lumiera turned and seriously gazed with a respectful nod at Kalem, then at Mayleena, and finally at Etta, hovering between them. They each nodded in return; then, he cheerfully grinned at Master Ra Mu.

He stated in a warm brotherly manner, "When you were my student, you too were bold, daring, adventuresome, and just as headstrong as these eager young ones. Therefore, of course, it will be my pleasure to assist in any way with your students."

Ra Mu grinned back at him as he continued toward Mayleena and Etta, "Mayleena, you are still my favorite flower in the garden, and Etta, it's so good to see you again!"

Mayleena blushed as Kalem questioningly smiled at her, while Etta flew up beside Lumiera, then bowed very low.

Mayleena humbly said, "I am gratefully honored to learn anything from one so masterfully adept with the knowledge of The Ancient One and travel beyond the physical body."

Smiling, Lumiera replied in a fatherly fashion, "Child, one goes on and on into eternity in their personal discoveries about the vastness of The Ancient One's love and support of all life. The Sound and Light behind and supporting all things speaks to the inner ears and eyes of the childlike listener. None of us as true individuals or the Atma ever stops learning at any point during the ongoing adventure of our eternal lives."

"Master Lumiera," curiously inquired Kalem, "what exactly is this training with illusions we keep hearing about?"

"You'll know that soon enough, but I'll speak plainly," he benevolently replied. "You three must survive the coming tests if you are to be of any benefit to your people."

Forcing a grin, Kalem stated, "Now... just hold on a minute. What's this... if we survive stuff?"

Lumiera wisely grinned, "If you are to challenge Sen Dar, you will have to withstand the onslaught of all of your worst fears - your worst nightmares. He's very negative in nature now, so it's natural for him to use the worst of that sort of thing on all three of you. However, Master Ra Mu and I sense that each of you is strong enough to come through the tests in the end. We'll explain it all on the way. Please... follow me."

Kalem apprehensively gazed at Mayleena and Etta, and Etta gazed the same way back at him, but Mayleena appeared surprisingly cheerful as she strutted ahead of them behind Lumiera. Kalem turned to seek support from Master Ra Mu but was unexpectedly given a blank hard stare in return.

Lumiera stepped up to a glass-like oval door at the end of the semicircular archway that led inside the domed city, and it spiraled open. He stepped through the opening, and Mayleena cheerfully followed. Etta hovered through the opening behind her, and Kalem followed. They quickly disappeared within the city.

Ra Mu stopped to turn and gaze out over the top of the tropical jungle area into the distance toward the ocean shoreline and the rising sun. He closed his eyes for a moment, and then he began to hear The Ancient One's living omnipresent Sound pervading, and a golden glow momentarily appeared within his inner vision before it enshrouded his physical body. The Sound and Light instantly vanished as he opened his eyes to lovingly gaze again at the distant horizon over the turquoise ocean. Then he too turned to casually enter the city, and the glass-like oval door spiraled closed behind him.

THE WALLS OF IGNORANCE FALL

$\mathcal{B}$ack at the secret Area 51 U.S. Air Force underground base, in the launch control room hidden below the base hangars, Harry was studying the viewscreen with a cigar clamped down in the corner of his mouth. Judith was standing next to him, jotting down something on a notepad with a pencil. Dozens of technicians around the room were busily monitoring all aspects of the approaching Transporter launch take-off. An Air Force Lieutenant Colonel was sitting behind the center of the main control console talking on the phone.

Hubert Griswald, a balding and slightly rotund man in his forties wearing thick glasses, wrinkled old slacks, and a worn cardigan sweater, appeared quite irritated as he boldly walked up to Harry.

"General Faldwell, I don't like what I just heard! Not one word of it! You don't really want me to give away our whole defense computer secrets to the Russians... do you? This just can't be..."

"Oh, knock it off, Griswald!" barked Harry, cutting him off. "Shut up and listen! This isn't one of your simulation games. We've got real problems. We know what shot down our unmanned Space Transporter and the Russian manned Space Transporter, and they aren't from either country if you get my drift, Mr.!"

Puzzled, Hubert doesn't quite get his drift, and Harry disappointedly eyed him, then quickly glanced toward the ceiling to get his innuendo across. Hubert dropped his jaw in astonishment as the realization finally hit home,

"Oh... come on, Hubert! We went over this in-depth before, remember?" impatiently stated Harry.

Hubert self-righteously shot back, "Damn... damn and double damn! I told all of you that one day this would happen, but oh no... all you, warmongers, wouldn't listen to me... a mere scientist. Instead of wasting our technology on weapons to destroy each other, we should have been preparing for the inevitable. Didn't I say extraterrestrials should have been our priority all along?"

"Get a hold of yourself, man!" angrily demanded Harry. "We've got to link up our command computer and defensive platforms with the Russians, and we're running out of time. We can beat those alien devils with our own technology, but we can only pull it off together. You should like that. Can you do it?"

"Of course, I can do it, but I think you're all nuts!" cockily replied

Hubert, insulted that he'd even been asked the question.

Harry sternly eyed him, "Then get cracking, man," he barked out. "We don't have a moment to lose, and while you're at it, see if you can track those alien ships. One should be near the launch site by now, but you can forget about radar. It doesn't pick them up."

Hubert's eyes lit up, and he stated, "I'll try detecting them with infrared from one of our spy satellites. If there's anybody alive in those alien ships, we'll pick them up all right, but it'll take a few minutes to realign the satellite."

Hubert jumped at the control console and slammed himself down in a chair by the keyboard. Harry walked over and stood behind him to look up at the main viewscreen, while Hubert's fingers literally flew over the keyboard. A few moments later, the viewscreen changed to a 3-D widescreen computer image of a laser weapons satellite orbiting high above the colorful gem of planet Earth. A clearly apparent solar array extended from both sides of the long cylinder-shaped main body, a large dish antenna was mounted underneath the bottom pointed down toward Earth, and a sleek laser cannon was mounted on one side that extended to a long clear crystal point.

"Okay...that's it!" Hubert exuberantly stated. "We're aligned and locked onto ground tracking from here."

Then he typed something else on the keyboard, and the viewscreen changed to a computer graphics representation of a Zon ship approaching the state of Nevada at very high speed. The ship was glowing with various colors, indicating different levels of heat, and several distinct human-shaped red heat signatures were inside.

"I've got the bastards!" yelled out Hubert. "That can't be a conventional ship of ours or the Russians. They're moving way too fast. Wait a minute! Now they're slowing down at an unbelievable rate."

High in the distant sky outside the base, a Zon Demon Scout ship flew from the distant desert horizon and abruptly slowed. Then it stopped to hover behind a large cumulous cloud, pulsing with a faint red glow. Visible through a break in the cloud on the distant desert ground was the infamous Area 51 top-secret classified base. Another one of the newly designed Space Transporters was at the beginning of the long runway in the final take-off launch mode.

At the base, Harry appeared tensely worried and yanked the unlit cigar from his mouth.

"Damn them! Now that makes me really mad. The damned thing stopped in the atmosphere a mile from the launchpad. Those Zon devils will not get another one of our Transporters."

It was nighttime in the Russian Launch Command and Control Center. A Russian General was standing next to the command computer console looking at a large viewscreen on the back wall. It showed an infrared computer graphics representation of a Zon ship flying at high speed into Russian airspace near Plesetsk - the Russian Cosmodrome test launch facility north of Moscow, and the alien ship dramatically slowed as it neared the launch pad. The very worried General barked an order to a Lieutenant standing next to him, and the

Lieutenant hurried away. A thin, spectacled scientist type in his forties was sitting at the computer console keyboard in front of the General, much like Hubert Griswald was seated in front of Harry at that moment back at Mission Control in the secret base hidden within Area 51 in the Nevada desert.

The Russian General urgently looked at the scientist and ordered in broken English, "Vlasik, get Griswald online now. No time to lose!"

Vlasik nodded compliance, picked up a red handset, and pushed a button on the console.

The Air Force Lieutenant Colonel sitting at the console next to Hubert noticed a similar red phone handset light-up blinking on the console, and he quickly hung up the black handset he had to his ear to pick up the red phone. He listened for a moment, then urgently got up and approached Harry.

"General Faldwell, Sir, Plesetsk is online. One of their scientists has monitored another one of those alien ships on approach to their launch facility. They say their infrared instruments on a satellite picked it up."

Having overheard the conversation, Hubert jumped out of his chair to his feet.

"That's Vlasik!" he excitedly began. "He's their top computer expert and the only one in the world capable of linking their equipment with ours... that is... besides me, of course."

Harry dubiously stared at Hubert and asked, "How is it you're so familiar with this Russian, Vlasik, anyway?"

Having also overheard the ongoing conversation, Judith walked up to them and disappointedly looked up at Harry.

"Oh great!" she sarcastically began. "There you go again, Harry, with your usual fine diplomatic edge."

Harry smirked back at her and impatiently sighed, but it was Hubert who now appeared insulted as he stood up from sitting in the chair.

"Vlasik is a true scientist, not a politician, General. He and I play chess together twice a year at the International Scientists' Convention in Switzerland. Like me, he's been trying to get his President and his Generals to seriously work on protective shielding and defensive weapons technology aimed at any extraterrestrial threats for years. The cold war may be over, but some really bad attitudes still remain."

Harry impatiently shook his head and angrily commanded, "Well... don't just stand there gawking at me, man! Get on that damned line with him. I want us fire-ready in five minutes, or I'll have a couple of scientists for breakfast."

Hubert grimaced at Harry and reluctantly acquiesced, then quickly sat back down in the chair and picked up the red handset.

He cheerfully stated in Russian, "Zdrast-vui-te, Vlasik, kak de-la?" ("Hello, how are you, Vlasik?")

Back at the Russian Launch Command Center, Vlasik was holding a similar red handset to his ear, cheerfully grinning as he replied, "Ah... Hubert! Harosha, spaciba." ("Ah... Hubert! Good, thank you!")

Hubert's voice coming through the speakerphone on the desk, facetiously replied, "Looks like we have to save them from themselves. Now we finally get to play with our toys the way we always said we would have to one day."

Vlasik curiously replied in English, "Yes... it is a bit of a miracle, my friend. Are you ready to link computers?"

Hubert was still holding the red phone to his ear at the U.S. Space Command facility, while he kept typing on the keyboard and very jovially replied to Vlasik's question.

"You bet I am. I've been ready for years. I'll send the passcode first. We should be able to align our orbiting laser and scalar wave platforms at those alien ships in minutes. Good luck, my friend."

"We will need it, yes?" came back Vlasik's voice through the speakerphone on the console.

In space, a large Russian orbiting defensive satellite platform facing Earth was moving along its orbital pathway headed across the northern hemisphere toward the right and the night side of the planet. It had a large dish antenna mounted on one side of the tube-shaped main body that appeared similar to the United States defensive platform. An elongated laser cannon pointed toward Earth was mounted on the opposite side. Two small directional rockets fired to change their position, and it gradually turned until a Russian space agency symbol came into clear view on its side. As Russian defensive platform continued along its orbital pathway until it diminished in the distance, the U.S. defensive platform came into view from around the left side of Earth's northern hemisphere, moving along its orbital pathway. Several directional rockets fired, and it too adjusted its position to directly face the Russian satellite platform that was now just two miles further away.

THE CAVE
OF FEARS

In the parallel Lemuria, under the Adepts huge domed city, the closed end of a transparent transportation tube began at the beginning of a marble boarding platform stationed just outside the base of one of the three towering gold crowned and quartz capped pyramids centered in the city. The transport tube continued to run along the ground like a snake through the city and out into the countryside to end in the far background at the base of a huge dome. A set of marble steps near the beginning of the platform by the closed end of the tube led down to the ground, then up more steps to two large gold doors set in the base of the far-left pyramid. The sun was brightly beaming down through the clear dome from a blue sky, making colors appear more vibrantly alive than the parallel dimension where the United States existed. This was highlighted in the distance through the domed canopy by giant prehistoric-looking ferns and the tall blue-green fir forest that surrounded the dome's base just beyond several spacecraft parked on individual round landing pads. The large Oceana Spectrum Crystal ship was clearly visible beside Kalem's Scout ship landed on its circular landing pad near one of the clear arched entryways to the city. A transport car speeding within a luminous blue vacuum tube away from Kalem's landed ship headed into the city abruptly slowed. It passed nearby the translucent ivory dome centered between the towering pyramids, slowed again, and stopped near its base. The changing-colored lights on each end shut off.

At the loading platform, Master Ra Mu, Master Lumiera, Kalem, Mayleena, and Etta were all comfortably sitting inside the car as the tube end opened and swung upward. The car continued to slowly move forward out of the tube, and it stopped near the end of the platform by a four-foot-high marble stone control monolith and the four marble steps that led down from the platform. The curved top half of the car opened upward. Kalem, Mayleena, and Ra Mu holding his crystal staff, followed by Lumiera, stepped out of the car onto the loading platform. With his tail aglow, Etta flew out of the car and hovered next to Kalem. Lumiera and Ra Mu then headed down the four steps and continued to walk up the thirty steps toward the two gold doors, followed close behind by the others.

Lumiera reached the doors first and touched them. Both doors silently swung open toward them. Etta was the last to enter the pyramid, and the huge doors silently closed behind him.

The inner chamber of the pyramid was made of a polished white and blue granite stone, emitting pale light from a phosphorescent self-luminous gold mineral-laced throughout it. The room was completely bare; except for three chairs covered in soft white fabric placed back-to-back facing away from each other in a triangular pattern. They were resting on a lush, richly colored rug embroidered with ancient mystic symbols. The living primordial omnipresent Sound of The Ancient One was whirling around the room in the form of the high, lilting flute melody and soft rushing wind mixed with the subtle sound like a million bees and soft background crashing ocean waves. The sloping walls of the one-hundred-foot-wide square section of the pyramidal-shaped room gradually tapered upward out of view beyond the high ceiling toward the top of the pyramid. Two triangular archway entrances were positioned on opposite ends of the room. Ra Mu and Lumiera entered the room through the far-left archway and approached the chairs, followed by Kalem, Mayleena, and Etta hovering forward next to Kalem's side.

"Welcome to the inner sanctum," remarked Master Lumiera. "Each true individual Atma or what people on Earth call Soul awakens this nature of their true-self in this place when properly prepared. Only bold, daring, adventuresome, and enterprising beings dare cross this threshold. From here, you each enter the pit of darkness - the darkness each carries in their heart."

Master Ra Mu interjected, "You must each confront and conquer your worst fear or overcome it through attuning yourselves to the radiant omnipresent Sound of The Ancient One, also known among many world systems as the 'Source' or 'Prime Creator' behind and supporting all life. Your love for one another and absolute trust in this living Sound presence will result in your success."

"What happens if we don't overcome our worst fear?" hesitantly inquired Kalem.

"Then, Captain," seriously replied Master Ra Mu, "your fear becomes your Master, and you do not return from the pit of darkness. Only if all three of you succeed can you hope to challenge Sen Dar and defeat him with his own misuse of power. Do each one of you clearly understand this?"

And he carefully gazed into the surprised eyes of all three of them.

Kalem and Mayleena glanced at each other and then at Etta, who was poking his head up the backside of his chair to quite innocently gaze at Ra Mu. His little fingers were firmly grasping the top of the chair, and his beautiful large bulbous blue eyes were filled with wide-eyed concern.

Noticing his forlorn look, Lumiera cheerfully stated, "Don't worry, Etta! You're a courageous warrior Spirit. You will make it through all right."

Etta suddenly cheered up and proudly stated, "Chet obi qui dem tep rulm!" ("You bet I'll make it through!")

Ra Mu carefully studied each one of them again and then stated, "This chamber is one-third of the way up in the exact center of the pyramid. The quarts cap at its apex set above the gold sheath crown around the top acts as a conductor and collector of the omnipresent Sound and Light. This intensifies everything within the room for positive or negative results depending upon the self-disciplined control or lack of it that exists within each individual. In this way, an individual learns how to master fear. If each of you truly gives up fear in this lifetime, you'll never need to give up anything else ever again."

"If any of you wish to forego this training," interjected Master Lumiera, kindly smiling, "now is the time to bow out. There is an old Earth saying that states, 'This is your last chance!'"

Kalem, Mayleena, and Etta glanced at each other, and Kalem bolstered up the courage. He took a deep breath, lifting and lowering his shoulders, and confidently said, "Let's do it. I'll go through hell and back to permanently stop Sen Dar."

But he did not get the response he'd hoped for, and Ra Mu ominously added, "Oh, you will, Captain. I assure you... you will!"

None of the three trainees liked the sound of that last statement, but they each sat down in the chairs anyway with courageous caution to prepare for whatever may come next.

"Settle back in the chairs and close your eyes," began Lumiera in his soft melodic tone. "Gently place your inner attention on the spot just above and between your eyebrows where you each normally visualize images when your eyes are closed. Remember, only the Atma, the real you or spherical energy being, can imagine anything, not the brain in your head. Then inwardly, in silence, send out the telepathically connecting word known as… HU… drawn out to contact and experience The Ancient One's living omnipresent Sound. This is the first half of the word …human… hidden in plain sight before the unconscious awareness of most Earth human beings. It can no longer remain hidden from you three. When you behold the splendor of its light, let go and follow where its guidance leads. Ride the Sound into the depth of your imagination."

As Kalem, Mayleena, and Etta began to sink deeper and deeper into their inner imaginative worlds, Lumiera and Ra Mu stoically stood by with their arms out to their sides by their hips, and their open palms protectively pointed toward the three sitting trainees. A moment passed, and then a glowing golden light began to flow down from the ceiling through Lumiera and Ra Mu, then to and around the three in the chairs, surrounding all three occupants with particles of radiant whirling energy to form a transparent sphere of light around them. The Ancient One's Spirit Sound grew louder; then it transformed into a hauntingly beautiful uplifting melody of a high flute with woodwinds, full stringed harps, and a low-frequency hum like soft electricity. The three trainees began to hear Master Lumiera's softly whispered telepathic voice.

Just go with the Sound. Silently send it out like this... Hu-u-u-u-u-u-u... long and drawn out until it naturally fades. Then go with the sound's guidance.

And his voice began to echo as it swiftly faded away.

A mysterious force suddenly zoomed forward toward the three

chairs past Ra Mu and Lumiera and into the sphere of light surrounding the three sojourners. They gradually began to blur or fade in a whirl of fine molecular gold light.

The image quickly cleared, revealing the view of a thirty-foot-wide dimly-lit bottomless appearing cavern. Three-foot-wide steps carved out of black obsidian rock led in a downward spiral into the darkness around the circumference of the cavern wall. Thousands upon thousands of steps appeared to continue below until they faded into a seemingly endless depth. Kalem and Mayleena suddenly found themselves with their eyes closed on the top step that appeared to extend right out of the solid rock wall. No entrance remained behind them, and the only direction to go was ever downward. They both held each other with eyes tightly shut as Etta appeared flying out of the rock wall behind them with his brightly glowing tail. He stopped to hover next to them. They slowly opened their eyes and carefully gazed around themselves. Mayleena looked over Kalem's shoulder to see the vast fall that would occur if any of them slipped over the edge of the narrow steps, and she frightfully gasped. Kalem grabbed her and pulled her back toward the cavern wall. Etta confidently flew over the edge, then back and forth several times, appearing somewhat delighted, as caves and caverns were his natural habitat.

"Where are we?" asked Mayleena, mystified.

Kalem appeared puzzled, and then replied, "They mentioned something about us confronting our worst fears. I think we're supposed to head down the stairs since apparently there is no way up."

And he looked annoyed at Etta.

"What are you so damned cheerful about?"

"Remember, caves are like home to him," replied Mayleena grinning.

"Oh… that's just great!" Kalem remarked. "We're about to confront demons from hellfire, and the leaping flying lizard here is out for a joy ride!"

Etta immediately flew up to Kalem's face and put up his dukes to have it out and angrily spouted, "Quen chet zomlba u luzerbas? Talpa otb sim Covaulc?" ("Who are you calling a lizard? What's wrong with caves?")

Kalem put up his palms to kindly placate Etta and gently replied, "Okay… okay, Etta, don't take it personally. I was only kidding. Nothing is wrong with caves; except this one leads to the pit of darkness, remember? And we've got to find a way through this madness!"

Etta grimaced at Kalem and then flew behind them to cautiously peer over his shoulder down into the deepening darkness. Kalem and Mayleena looked at Etta, and his green face turned beet red with shame for hiding behind them. Then he immediately straightened up, confidently puffed up his chest, and courageously flew down the stairs ahead of them. Only Etta's tail was now lighting the way further down the steps, and every few seconds, he hovered back up toward them again to see if they were all right before he'd dart back down into the darkness.

Back at the Strategic Space Command Center, the second Space Transporter was being shown full length on the large control room viewscreen in launch mode readiness. President Sam Stockwell was standing behind Hubert Griswald, sitting at the control console wearing a headset with a mouthpiece curved around by his lips. Judith was standing to the left side of the President, and Harry was standing to Hubert's right side, chewing on an unlit cigar stuck in the corner of his mouth. Then he nervously began to pace back and forth behind them. The Launch Control Director, wearing a short-sleeved white shirt, striped tie, and a headset with a thin wire mouthpiece curved around in front of his lips, was standing in front of several monitors on the left side of the main control console watching the main viewscreen.

Concerned, President Stockwell looked down and asked, "Hubert, is everything aligned with the Russians, and will this work? We've only got one shot at this."

Sweat was beading down Hubert's forehead as he looked up at Sam and then quickly returned to continue frantically typing in more computer commands before he nervously replied, "Um...Vlasik and I are ready, Mr. President, but we've never done this before. You know the damn things weren't designed originally to shield anything. Since long before those space platforms were built, Vlasik and I have been trying to encourage or really recommend to you and the Russian President that they should be used as protective shields. Nothing, not even nuclear bombs, can get through such a shield. They could cover entire cities. They..."

"Damn it, Hubert," interrupted Sam, "I know all that, but will it work now?"

Hubert cockily grinned and stated, "You know we've been experimenting with massive low-frequency generators for some time. So have the Russians, since long before the old Soviet Union broke up. This type of frequency can be projected from two generators that have been placed at great distances from each other. Where these two beams intersect, a concentric energy generator or carrier field is created. Low-frequency beams of this nature can then be directed right through the center of the planet without any resistance, or they can be reflected off satellites to any point on Earth as defensive weapons."

Hubert's fingers rapidly ran over the computer keyboard, and the large viewscreen flashed on a computer graphics representation of what he was talking about. Then it changed to a close-up view. From high orbit, Earth was shown with a focus on the North Pole which was marked in the center of the viewscreen. The United States was marked across the North American continent, and Greenland appeared southwest of the depicted North Pole, trailing away into the southernmost hemispheres to Central and South America. Northeast of the North Polar Region was all of northern Russia, including Siberia, Europe, and the Scandinavian peninsulas. The symbol of a large dish antenna array was marked in a remote Arizona desert area, and another one was marked in the everglades area on Florida's southern tip. Two more were marked in Russia: one slightly northeast of Plesetsk - the Cosmodrome Russian missile launch test center north of Moscow; and the second was marked slightly north of Svobodniy - another Russian missile test launch site on the most southeastern Russian border coast just above China. Hubert continued to speak in the background over the images on the viewscreen.

"Okay now... watch closely!"

The viewscreen showed a computer graphics representation of the turbofan jet and rocket-powered Space Transporter on the Plesetsk runway in Russia. It quickly arced northeast up into orbit across Russia on a trajectory headed toward the United States, and it continued out across the Pacific Ocean past the Kamchatka peninsula. A red energy beam was suddenly emitted from the dish antennae marked in Arizona to a satellite marked with moving letters beside the satellite that read:

UNITED STATES MILITARY SATELLITE - TOP SECRET

The satellite was slowly moving from east to west, away from the North Pole over the sea between the Russian Kamchatka Peninsula and Alaska. A green energy beam was then instantly emitted from the dish antennae symbol marked north of Svobodniy, just as the beam from Arizona was reflected off the satellite toward the rocket and the two beams intersected, creating a halo of glowing light surrounding the rocket. The beams didn't appear to interfere with the rocket's progress as it passed far below the satellite. Both beams continued to track the satellite, keeping a constant shield around the speeding prototype.

Hubert very seriously commented, "As you've just seen in the simulation, where the two beams intersect over a target, a powerful self-generating energy force is created. Once that's done, we can direct, bend or use the energy to do practically anything we want without anyone even knowing it's there. We can bend or change the weather with it, transmit a destructive beam of energy along with it or send any kind of thought impulse to a person or to a whole city of enemy people for any reason. But... and this is the really exciting part, we discovered that energy created by the field could be so tightly woven that it is impenetrable. Nothing can get through it, not even a hydrogen thermonuclear explosion."

Another computer graphics image appeared of the United States anti-gravity powered, elongated-triangular, 2nd prototype Space Transporter taking off from the classified runway located inside Area 51 in the Nevada desert. It flew northeastward across the continental United States and quickly arced upward into orbit high over the Atlantic Ocean.

Suddenly, another green energy beam was emitted from a dish antennae symbol marked north of Plesetsk above Moscow. It reached the Russian satellite marked with moving letters beside it that read:

RUSSIAN MILITARY SATELLITE - TOP SECRET

The satellite was also moving from the east toward the west above the Atlantic Ocean equidistant between Northeastern Canada and the Scandinavian peninsulas. The green beam was reflected off the satellite toward the US Space Transporter, just as another blue beam suddenly emitted from the dish antennae marked in the Florida everglades headed up toward the Space Transporter. The two beams intersected at the luminous U.S. Space Transporter, creating an energy halo around it as it continued along its orbital trajectory. The two beams continued to track the rocket, keeping the protective energy shield in place.

Hubert continued, "The Russians have two huge frequency generators, and we have two more that are almost identical in size and power. As you've now seen, by aligning our scalar-wave generators together for the first time, two of the projected beams bounce off the orbiting satellite platforms that are aligned with two more beams which are focused on crossing in front of the U.S. Space Transporter and the Russian Space Transporter."

Something unsettling alarmed President Stockwell and he demanded to know, "You mean that's all we've got... just a defensive shield? Hubert, if those Zon devils fire on our Transporter, I want them incinerated!"

Hubert confidently continued with a sly grin, "The shields will be automatically turned on by the computers as soon as the Space Transporter is launched. If Zon ships fire on our Transporter or the Russian transporter, the powerful lasers on both orbiting platforms will also automatically return fire. They're aimed at the hovering Zon ships as we speak. In other words, Gentlemen, I think we have a fighting chance."

"Oh great!" interjected Judith annoyed. "You're all so proud of these destructive toys of yours. If this Sen Dar and the Zon threat hadn't come along, sooner or later, you'd probably have annihilated us all and perhaps all life on this planet. It shouldn't have taken those Zon maniacs out there to make us come to our senses."

"Get a hold on yourself, Judith!" shot back Sam. "I can't have you going off the deep end at a time like this. Look, if this works, you may yet be a key negotiator to arrange a complete dismantling of nuclear arms altogether between our two countries and likely China as well."

Sam patted her on the shoulder and smiled, and she calmed down, taking a deep breath. The Launch Control Director looked around at Harry and signaled him with one finger held up. Harry affirmatively nodded to the Director, and the Director began the countdown from ten.

"I hope Ra Mu knows what he's doing," quietly stated the President under his breath. "May God help us all."

The Launch Control Director continued, "T-minus ten seconds and counting. Nine... eight... seven... six..." and his voice faded to the background.

It was early morning just outside the Area 51 long launch runway, where the new Space Transporter's blue luminous surrounding antigravity light brightened, and the deep humming sound expanded.

The Launch Director's background voice continued, "three... two, one... we have a launch. All systems are in green. The Space Transporter is away."

Inside the control room, many launch personnel cheered as they got to their feet to intently gaze at the main view monitor, watching the Space Transporter dart straight up into the clear blue sky above the long runway, hangars, and surrounding Area 51 classified base in Nevada.

High in the nearby atmosphere hiding behind several clouds silently hovered a lone alien Zon Demon fighter with its slightly elongated triangular batwing-shaped hull. The alien anti-gravity craft with its faintly pulsing red glowing hull was poised to strike. The larger U.S. triangular Space Transporter darted up into view with its enshrouding luminous blue hull near the level of the hovering Zon ship. The Area 51 Air Force underground base, more than a mile below, rapidly receded far behind the speeding craft until it appeared as a speck on the ground. The Zon ship matched pace with the Transporter's upward speed heading to assume an orbital trajectory.

It was nighttime outside the Russian Plesetsk launch facility, as the turbofan fanjet and rocket-powered Russian Space Transporter's roaring jet engines went to full thrust. It traveled down the runway at an incredible speed but a short way, before it darted in a steep curved – almost straight up – trajectory into the night sky.

Vlasik was inside the facility, looking at their main viewscreen.

The Russian President and several Generals were standing behind him, clapping hands and yelling encouragement toward their second prototype Space Transporter with its powerful rocket engines igniting and its turbofan jet engines shutting off. No one could hear the jubilant yells over the loud roar of the powerful rocket engines being piped into the complex's loudspeaker system.

The fluffy clouds parted high in the atmosphere above Plesetsk, and the Russian launch site was revealed miles below them. The waiting Zon ship remained hovering behind several clouds as the Russian prototype Transporter sped upward toward its hidden location. The pale-red glow surrounding the sinister ship's hull was casting a shadowy silhouette on the surrounding clouds. The Russian Transporter swiftly approached the level of the Zon ship that instantly matched the Transporter's speed, following alongside as it continued to ascend into space toward its orbital trajectory.

It was early evening with clear skies in another area of the Russian wilderness north of Svobodniy. Another huge dish antenna, over five stories high, was pointing upward at a slight angle. A powerful green light beam suddenly emitted from the center of the dish antennae darted up into the starlit heavens, accompanied by a very low-frequency wavering hum.

And it was daytime in a hidden mountain valley somewhere in the Arizona desert. A similar huge dish antenna, also over five stories high, was also focused upward. A blue energy beam suddenly emitted from the center of the dish antennae darted up into the sky, accompanied by a very similar low-frequency wavering hum.

The view of space far above the Earth's atmosphere revealed the North Polar Region and the U.S. elongated triangular luminous Space Transporter flying in orbit - headed further east high over the Atlantic Ocean. The Russian Transporter prototype, now rocket-powered, was also entering orbit - headed from the east toward the west. The United States and Russian orbiting satellite weapons platforms were now in synchronous orbits traveling at the same speed, two miles apart, high over the same North Polar Region.

A green energy beam suddenly emitted from the ground area northeast of Plesetsk in Russia hit the reflective dish antennae on the Russian satellite platform, and it was instantly reflected back down toward the Space Transporter. At the same instant, a similar blue energy beam suddenly emitted from somewhere in the Florida everglades on the southern tip of Florida was projected toward the U.S. Space Transporter. Both beams simultaneously hit the Transporter, forming a transparent whirling energy shield that completely surrounded the hull's exterior.

An instant later, a blue energy beam emitted from the hidden Arizona dish antennae hit the Russian dish antennae on the Russian weapons satellite platform to be instantly reflected back down toward the Russian Transporter ascending into orbit. At the same moment, a green energy beam was sent from Russia's Svobodniy area to the Russian Transporter, and the two beams intersected on the hull, creating another transparent whirling protective energy shield that completely surrounded the prototype's exterior. Both unharmed Space Transporter vehicles continued on their way.

The U.S. anti-gravity powered Space Transport was now flying along its orbital trajectory, in a lower orbit below the satellites, with the radiant energy shield surrounding it. The Zon ship keeping pace with it, shot a red energy beam weapon at the Transporter that harmlessly bounced off the surrounding energy shield, headed directly back toward the enemy Scout fighter. The Zon ship skillfully moved aside just in time to avoid being hit by its own firepower.

The Russian rocket-powered prototype was now also flying in space along its orbital trajectory with the radiant energy shield clearly surrounding it. The Zon ship keeping pace with it, shot a red energy weapon at the hull that harmlessly bounced off the surrounding energy shield and was instantly reflected back toward the enemy Scout fighter. This Zon ship also skillfully moved aside just in time to avoid being hit by its own firepower.

Meanwhile, back at the secret Strategic Space Command Center, the President, Harry, and Judith were standing in front of the large viewscreen intently observing the computer graphics representation of the moment-by-moment events taking place in space. Hubert was standing in front of the console by the computer keyboard, shaking an encouraging fist toward the screen.

Orbiting in space, the long barrel-shaped laser cannon on the U.S. weapons satellite platform started moving to aim at something, and it stopped, then lit up along its length. Orbiting nearby, the laser cannon on the Russian weapons satellite platform also took aim and lit up, ready to fire.

At the Area 51 launch facility, Hubert very defiantly yelled out, "Ah... the bastards nearly destroyed themselves with their own weapons. I just knew it would work, and they won't be expecting a counter-attack."

"Hubert, I hope you're right," apprehensively stated Harry. "But we can't hold those shields up forever, and those two ships are bound to try something else."

"The lasers should kick in at any moment," confidently replied Hubert. "Then we'll know!"

The anti-gravity powered U.S. Space Transporter headed further along its orbital trajectory, as the Zon ship flying beside it began to glow deep violet - preparing to fire another type of powerful energy weapon.

The rocket powered Russian Transporter continued to speed in space headed along its orbital trajectory, while the second Zon ship flying beside it also started to glow deep violet – preparing to fire another powerful energy weapon.

From high above Earth's North Polar Region, both Earth prototype spacecraft now had a Zon ship flying alongside. The light surrounding the hulls of both Zon ships simultaneously brightly pulsed, but the laser cannons aboard both orbiting satellite platforms instantly fired powerful thick white energy beams at both Zon ships with deadly accuracy, instantly exploding them into rapidly disintegrating particles of brilliant molecular energy. The fiery energies quickly faded and vanished, leaving the U.S. Space Transporter and the Russian Space Transporter prototypes unharmed. They safely continued along their chosen parallel orbital trajectories.

At Area 51, exuberant cheers rang out from all personnel around the control room hidden below hangar complexes and the long runway. Harry took the cigar out of his mouth with a sigh of relief and triumphantly grinned. He smiled at Judith and President Sam Stockwell; wiping sweat from his forehead with a handkerchief. Then Judith sighed relief, just as Hubert slumped, emotionally exhausted, down into his chair in front of the keyboard, and he managed to pound his fist on the console.

He looked up and touched a button with a deep, relieved exhale, then asked, "Vlasik, are you still there?"

Vlasik's jovial voice answered back through the console's speakerphone with much happy shouting coming from the personnel in the background, "Yes, my friend. Fortunately, we are all still here."

Hubert added, self-amused, "Maybe now we can get them to listen to us, and we can start a real new era on this one little dust ball planet, huh Vlasik?"

"As you say, perhaps now the Politicians and the military men, they will listen. It would be good, yes?" cheerfully shot back Vlasik through the speaker system.

Overhearing their conversation, Harry sternly gazed down at Hubert and said, "You two can stop patting yourselves on the back now. Those two ships we destroyed are not the last of them we will be seeing. Sen Dar will be mad as hell, and he'll try something else on a larger scale. You two better get busy planning a counter-strategy. We've got to be ready for him."

Hubert moaned as he leaned forward, placed a hand on his forehead, and quietly shook his head.

It was very dark back on the spiral rock staircase that surrounded the hallow black obsidian cavern shaft. Kalem and Mayleena gazed further down its center toward the unknown and the mysterious cave of fears. They were breathing heavily with fatigue as they continued to feel their way along the cavern wall to cautiously take another step down the seemingly endless spiral rock staircase. A pinpoint of light far below them quickly grew larger until Etta appeared rapidly flying up the center of the cavern shaft, and he stopped to hover beside them, very much tired and panting out of breath.

"Well... well... well!" stated Kalem, tired and irritated at Etta. "So, the flying deserter is finally back, huh?"

Also tired and irritated, Mayleena shot back in defense of Etta, "Leave him alone! He's only trying to help find a way out of this foul place!"

Kalem rubbed both hands across his tired face. Then he gazed back at Etta with a friendly grin, "Yeah, you're right. Sorry, dear friend Etta. I didn't mean it. What did you find?"

Too tired to keep hovering, Etta flew over to Mayleena's shoulder and landed, then said, still breathing hard, "Almba dop bon dim! Bon dim!" ("There's just no end! No end!")

"Well, damn it, that does it!" stated Kalem, mad as a hornet. "I'm not taking another step down this pit. We're staying put until Ra Mu and Lumiera have had their fill of this sick joke!"

As the last words left his lips, the entire cavern lit up as the walls began to glow. The steps now clearly appeared to them to go on ever downward into infinity. Then a great rumbling began that shook the entire cavern. A moment later, the steps crumbled out from under Kalem and Mayleena, and they both screamed as they fell head-over-heels ever downward toward the bottomless void until they disappeared from Etta's sight. He was too shocked to move while he hovered in place for a moment.

Then his glowing tail mysteriously went out, and he grabbed it in both hands, gazed astonished at it, then back up to say mystified just in time, "Uh oh!"

And he fell screaming straight down head-over-heels after Kalem and Mayleena to quickly disappear in the dark void.

Far... far …far below, a huge pool of dark-brown, thick gooey bubbling liquid covered the bottom of the obsidian cavern. The last of the carved spiral stairs abruptly ended about ten feet above the oozing pool, but the chamber was also curiously softly luminous from phosphorescent minerals contained in the black obsidian rock walls.

Kalem's faint screaming from far away quickly grew louder, as if he was rapidly falling down toward the pool.

High above, he was still tumbling down head-over-heels with his arms wildly flailing. He closed his eyes and covered his face with an arm as his body approached just twenty feet above the pool - and then - everything mysteriously began to move in extreme slow motion, and his body abruptly stopped just one foot above the oozing, bubbling brown mud. Time just as mysteriously resumed its normal rate while he very cautiously removed his arm and opened his eyes. He grinned in relief, feeling his chest with both hands to make certain he was in one piece. He began to notice an intensely bad smell.

He grabbed his nose with a hand to close it off and angrily grumbled, "Dear God... what is that awful smell? That does it, damn it! I'm not taking any more of this crap!" And he yelled, "Ra-a-a Mu-u-u, get me out of this place!"

The mysterious force suspending his body above the pool quickly turned him over right side up, so his feet were below him, and then it just as mysteriously vanished.

"Wait!" he yelled out, terrified, and he plunged into the stinking stuff up to his neck.

He immediately began frantically wading in the oozing stinking stuff with his hands, struggling to hold his chin above the disgusting bubbling liquid.

"Alright, Ra Mu, you win!" he frantically yelled out. "Come on now; this isn't funny anymore. Get all of us out of this hell hole!"

Just then, some kind of creature swam past Kalem's body and brushed by his shoulder just under the liquid crud, revealing large spiked fins rising up on a scaly prehistoric-looking sharply curved backbone, and Kalem's eyes widened with terror.

"Great Ancient One, Prime Creator, please not that!" And he loudly yelled out, "Ra-a-a Mu-u-u! Come on, guys! I can't stand things lurking under my feet. I just can't stand it! Lumiera-a-a-a! Ra Mu-u-u-u!"

Kalem frantically gazed around for a way out and saw a sloping shelf on the other side of the pool that gently led out of the pool twenty feet, where it abruptly ended against the black cavern wall. As he began to turn his body around to make for the shelf, the spikes on the creature's back appeared again, rising above the surface of the ooze, followed by a huge head that slowly rose up above the surface.

Kalem looked around to see it was some kind of alien prehistoric-looking amphibian with a huge mouth, dozens of rows of razor-sharp teeth, and a long sticky tongue that lashed out three feet from its mouth every few seconds to loudly slap the surface of the slimy liquid pool. It had two dozen eyes arched in two parallel rows above its mouth, and it was making a terrifying shrill whining noise that grated on Kalem's nerves, and he winced. Then the huge mouth widened, revealing it could easily swallow a man whole, and Kalem's eyes bugged out. Repulsed by the horrible thing, he gasped and began to whip his arms through the thick ooze, desperately headed toward the shelf, and the creature plunged into the pool after him. Moments later, he was pulling himself up onto the rock shelf. He was covered with the stinking thick liquid, and he quickly dragged himself up to the back wall with the thing swimming around the pool in a circle, jabbing its spiked fins up above the surface every few seconds in search of its prey.

"Of course, dummy!" stated Kalem angry with himself in sudden recognition. "You had nightmares about that thing when you were a kid. This isn't real. Concentrate. Come on now... think!"

A moment later, the creature lunged out of the pool onto the rock shelf. Four sets of feet with claws on the end of each one were slowly inching the creature toward Kalem's scrambling feet, as he backed up against the wall as tightly as he could.

"Now... now... n-n-nice fishy!" stuttered Kalem, terrified.

"You don't want to eat me!" Then he bolstered up courage, mocked up anger, and shouted at it, "You aren't real. Back off, fish!"

The disgusting thing stopped a few feet from Kalem's feet and licked its lips with its long sticky tongue. Then it ferociously growled at him while drooling pools of saliva splattered at his feet. Kalem valiantly stepped toward the creature, raising both fisted hands up at chest level in mocked defiance, but the thing instantly slapped him back up against the wall with its tongue, knocking the wind out of him. Then in a flash, as he gasped for breath, the creature wrapped its sticky tongue around his waist, pinning his arms to his sides. The tongue then flipped him over onto his face, and it began to drag his body toward its gaping mouth. Fiercely struggling, Kalem managed to turn over face-up, but the creature's tongue yanked him closer to its razor-sharp rows of teeth, and he shut his eyes to concentrate with all his might on the point just above and between his eyebrows.

Gasping, he pleaded, "Ancient One, where is the omnipresent Sound? Ra-a-a Mu-u-u! Mayleena! Etta! Hear me, my friends." And he chanted louder, "Ra-a-a Mu-u-u!"

The creature suddenly stopped its advance for some inexplicable reason, and Kalem barely opened one eye to see why. The creature resumed its movement toward him again, and Kalem snapped his eye shut. Then he squinted both eyes to concentrate.

A huge spider web was laced across another black obsidian shaft five feet above its murky moss-covered bottom. Twelve-inch holes had been bored into hundreds of places around the walls of the chamber, and many hundreds of the thin white strands that made up the web disappeared in the holes, apparently attached to something further inside each one. Mayleena's faint screaming from far away quickly grew louder as if she was rapidly falling down toward the pool. High above, she appeared, falling straight down head first with her arms wildly flailing. As she approached twenty feet above the massive web, time mysteriously slowed down just as it had for Kalem, and she covered her face with her arms while she struggled to flip her body around. She just managed to turn her body parallel to the ground as her back hit the web, and it gave way downward about four feet like a trampoline before it bounced her body back up and down several times with her back, arms, and legs firmly stuck to it. As the web gradually came to rest, time mysterious resumed its normal rate of speed.

Terrified, she pleaded, "Dear Ancient One, no-o-o! Not spiders!

Let it be anything but spiders!"

Then she screamed upon seeing hundreds of hairy nine-inch-wide bodied, prehistoric black widow-like spiders scrambling out the numerous holes in the cavern walls along the thin web strands. They had three large red dots under their bellies and large dripping venomous fangs that looked like hooked prongs. They extended down from their rapidly moving feelers around their open mouths. Their eight legs had barbed hooks on the end of each one. All the spiders began to wildly hiss between shrill whistling sounds, and hundreds more of the nasty things appeared crawling down the walls. Then they all slowly began to move in unison along the web strands toward Mayleena. She frantically looked around herself in absolute hysteria, and her terrified screams echoed inside the shaft while she desperately tried to break the tight hold the web had on her body. Suddenly, she remembered something very important and struggled to control her fear.

She stated quietly to herself, "What was it he said? Oh, Ancient One, what was it? Of course, that's it! Concentrate on the point between my brows and call on The Ancient One's Omnipresent Sound presence to protect me."

The spiders were now drawing very close to her, and some of the creepy things had begun to crawl up her legs and arms. She began shaking with terror and then snapped her eyes shut and called out, "Ra-a-a-a Mu-u-u-u! Kalem! Etta! Oh, Ancient One, please hear me!"

The spiders mysteriously stopped, and she barely opened her eyes to peek at them, then tightly shut them again as a spider crawled across one of her breasts, headed toward her face.

Etta was dropping straight down a third black obsidian shaft, wildly waving his arms and repeatedly grabbing his tail to gaze, astonished at the fact that it wouldn't light up. He comically shook it each time to try and make it come to life, but to no avail, and his eyes finally bugged out in real terror. Far below, he could see that he was racing toward sharply pointed black rock spires that extended up three feet from the bottom of the shaft. As he covered his eyes with his little hands, time mysterious slowed down, and an invisible force abruptly stopped his fall only one inch from the razor-sharp point of one stone pinnacle that was right below his chest. Time resumed its normal speed just as Etta slowly removed his hands from his eyes to gaze at the pointed rock directly below him. He cautiously reached out with a finger and touched its razor-sharp point, then quickly yanked his hand back. Suddenly, the invisible force suspending him moved him a foot sideways, then vanished, and he dropped. He desperately threw both arms around the side of the rock pinnacle and slowly slid down it toward an unknown bottom. The bottom of the shaft was covered with thick green moss.

The large pinnacle he was sliding down gradually tapering upward above him, along with many other similar pinnacles that surrounded him as his rump hit the ground with a *thump*! This chamber was also curiously softly lit from a glowing self-luminous phosphorescent mineral that was laced throughout the black obsidian walls. Etta quickly stood up, quite indignantly grumbling under his breath to himself in Dren at the perceived injustice of it all, then he began to look around. He could see the spiral steps came to an end just ten feet above the tops of the pinnacles. Then he looked down to notice the moss formed a pathway between the pinnacles that led to the side of the bottom of the shaft's wall and through an opening into a larger self-luminous cavern. He dropped forward and cautiously began to walk on all fours to the cavern entrance. Then he peered in and went inside.

Etta looked around to see the moss-covered floor of the black obsidian pinnacled shaft through the opening in the rock wall behind him. Then he gazed around the much larger volcanic chamber that was more brilliantly self-luminous. A sixty-foot-high by a twenty-foot-wide moss-covered boulder was resting on the floor on the other side of the chamber near a thickly moss-covered rock wall. An old twisted tree with long dangling moss hanging all over it appeared to be rooted in the center of the chamber, reaching thirty feet upward. He slowly walked past the moss-covered boulder and up to the old tree and then sniffed it. A section of the boulder behind him silently extended itself like a telescoping rock foot, and it blocked off the exit into the black obsidian shaft chamber, making a soft rustling noise. Etta didn't pay attention to the sound at first, and then he slowly turned around and gasped when he saw the large rock had extended part of itself to block off the opening, and he raced over to investigate. The entire moss-covered boulder appeared to break away from the cavern floor and turned around toward Etta. It now revealed itself to really be a twenty-foot tall prehistoric-type of lizard with a snake-like head that had camouflaged itself as a rock like a chameleon; except this creature was able to change shape as well. Antennae, like those on a snail, were constantly receding and protruding from the top of its head, as a long snake-like tongue darted out of its mouth every few moments between large sets of fangs that extended in sharply arched curves from its upper and lower jaws. Its two long arms ended with twin-forked claws on each end that gradually curled to razor-sharp points. Then the thing began to hiss between its spoken words, sadistically talking with glee in a deep raspy voice.

"Welcome, little Dren... s-s-s-s-s…" it hissed and continued, "let me personally welcome you to my home... s-s-s-s!"

Etta was now frightened out of his wits because he realized what it was, and he shouted out, "Q Dalm chet, Morln! Drens boa chet toylma mon. Sep bavot!" ("I know you, Morln! Drens are your favorite food. Stay away!")

The Morln seductively replied, "Come now, my little Dren friend. I will make it quick and merciful with one tasty bite. No Dren ever escapes a Morln's lair once one has it trapped inside. You know this!"

"But you're an illusion," replied Etta, trembling. "I must get free of this nightmare."

And the Morln lumbered at Etta, but Etta ran around in circles and under its feet in various directions. The Morln was waving its two long arms in the air, trying to snag Etta as he ran by each time. Then its long snake-like tongue darted out of its mouth in an instant to wrap around Etta's midsection and snatched him off the ground. Terrified, Etta screeched, and his eyes bugged out as the tongue tightly wrapped around him very sadistically began to slowly withdraw back toward the Morln's gaping mouth. The Morln began to laugh in his raspy voice, then loudly hissed, and Etta gasped, terrified, snapping his eyes shut to concentrate. While he was being pulled within the Morln's gaping jaws, he opened one eye to see if things had changed, then snapped it shut. The Morln began to slowly close its jaws.

Suddenly, Etta yelled out, "Ra-a-a-a Mu-u-u-u! Kalem! Mayleena! Please hear me, my friends. Oh, Ancient One, hear me!" Then he remembered the connective sound word and loudly yelled, "Hu-u-u-u-u-u-u-u-u!"

The Ancient One's uplifting omnipresent Sound suddenly filled the chamber, and Etta's body began to emit a pale golden light glow, just as the razor-sharp fangs touched his midsection, pressed down and slowly began to penetrate the skin. Etta struggled with all his might not to scream and was about to when a whirling mass of blue-violet energy began to flow out from his palms, engulfing the Morln in fiery flames. Its tongue bubbled and blistered around Etta's unharmed body; then, it literally fell apart just as Etta's tail suddenly lit up, brightly glowing opalescent once again.

In shocking surprise, Etta comically glanced at his glowing tail and grinned wide, then darted up above the Morln screeching in terror, and it stood up like a tower in the small cavern. In hideous pain and choking, it clawed at its own throat while it slowly disintegrated into a puddle of smoldering goo on the cavern floor. The blue-violet energy coming from Etta's palms withdrew back inside his hands and vanished. Greatly surprised, Etta gazed at his palms in wonder, and his body slowly dissolved into the beautiful, radiant sphere of his true spherical Atma-self. Then it darted in a blur of light up through the cavern ceiling.

In her own obsidian shaft, Mayleena was still frantically concentrating hard with her eyes closed. She was chanting Master Ra Mu's name and calling on The Ancient One's Omnipresent Sound. The spiders had now crawled all over her body, and they were beginning to tear off her clothes. She was shaking, terrified to the core of her being, but she didn't give up her concentration. Then the spiders began to plunge their fangs into her exposed arms, legs, neck, and thighs, and she desperately struggled not to scream.

"Ra-a-a-a Mu-u-u-u!" she began to shakily chant under her gasps for air. "Ancient One! Kalem! Etta! My friends, please hear me!" Then she remembered the connecting sound and loudly sent out, "Hu-u-u-u-u-u-u!"

The Ancient One's Sound suddenly filled the shaft, and Mayleena's body began to glow with a pale golden light. As one spider began to crawl right into her mouth, her body began to sparkle around its exterior with silver-golden molecules. A blue-violet light suddenly radiated from her entire body, and the spider crawling on her tongue was instantly burnt to crisp, and it vaporized upward out of her mouth in a puff of smoke. The blue-violet energy quickly traveled away from her body up each of the spider web strands, dissolving each spider it touched like acid on metal. The remaining spiders, now screeching terrified, scurried up the walls and toward their holes, but none of them made it to safety before the energy destroyed them. Mayleena's hands and feet suddenly became free from the web, and she sat up startled. Amazed, she quickly touched her body all over to be sure it was really unharmed, and the blue-violet energy instantly withdrew back inside the silver-golden light surrounding her. Then her body slowly dissolved into the beautiful, radiant sphere of her true spherical Atma-self, and it darted in a blur of light back up the black obsidian shaft.

Kalem was only inches away from the sharp teeth of the amphibious alien prehistoric-looking creature. It was growling and slobbering as it continued to slowly drag him inside its gaping mouth, but he kept his eyes tightly shut, gritting his teeth.

Then he loudly yelled out, "Ra-a-a-a Mu-u-u-u! Ra-a-a-a Mu-u-u-u! Mayleena! Etta! Please hear me now, dear friends! Great Ancient One, please hear me! It's got to be now, or I'm fish food!" He remembered the connective sound word and loudly sent out, "Hu-u-u-u-u-u-u-u!"

The creature slowly closed its teeth over Kalem's head and shoulder, and the top teeth began to slowly puncture his back. Kalem struggled with all his might not to scream out as the Spirit Sound of The Ancient One filled the chamber, and Kalem's body began to glow with a pale golden light. The creature's long sticky tongue wrapped around Kalem's waist sizzled from the fiery light being emitted from Kalem's body, and it let him go, dropping him to the edge of the ledge by the sickly pool of smelly mud. Kalem was momentarily stunned, and then he reacted and stood up. Without knowing why, Kalem extended his arms, palms out, toward the creature. Blue-violet streams of fiery molecules poured from the palms of his hands to bombard the now screaming thing until it turned into a steaming and bubbling mass of melting flesh that quickly sank back into the now boiling pool, continuing to disintegrate. The blue-violet energy withdrew back into Kalem's palms, and he gazed amazed down at his own hands, turning them over several times to be sure they really belonged to him. His eyes widened, and he grinned like an imp.

"So that's what those two rascals meant by training," he stated delightedly to himself. He began to ponder the thought, just as a new cognition lit across his face. Then he softly asked himself, "I wonder... how powerful has Sen Dar become by now?"

As the words left his lips, Kalem's body slowly dissolved into the beautiful, radiant sphere of his true Atma-self, and it darted in a blur of light back up the black obsidian shaft.

Master Lumiera and Master Ra Mu were still standing with their arms out to their sides by their hips with their palms out. The Ancient One's Protective Spirit Sound and glowing golden light flowing down from the ceiling through them to their three adventuresome students sitting in the chairs was still spiraling around them in a transparent sphere of light. Both Kalem and Mayleena were sitting in the same position in the center of the pyramid sanctuary with their eyes closed; but Etta was now hovering, stretched out parallel to the floor just above his chair with closed eyes and his tail glowing. The Spirit Sounds of the high lilting, hauntingly beautiful flute melody predominated over the woodwinds, harps, and low-frequency mystical hum, as simultaneously, the radiant spheres of Kalem, Mayleena and Etta appeared coming up through the floor behind each of their chairs. The spheres moved just above each of their bodies; then, they entered them through the tops of their heads. The Ancient One's Sound and Light whirling around their bodies rapidly receded back through Ra Mu and Lumiera and backed up above the chamber.

"You are all safe at last!" stated Ra Mu with a pleased grin. "Each of you have returned successful from the tests."

Also pleased, Master Lumiera added, "You have nothing to fear. The illusion is now over. Each of you conquered your worst nightmares."

But the three students remained reluctant to open their eyes, and Ra Mu reassured them, "It's alright! You can each open your eyes. The cave of fears is permanently behind you."

Kalem snapped open one eye, looked at Ra Mu, then opened both eyes, and he jumped off the chair as if it would bite him in the rump. Mayleena then slowly opened her eyes, jumped out of the chair, and shrieked with pleasure at finding herself safe from the dreaded spiders. Etta finally opened his eyes, looked around the room, turned himself upright wearing a big satisfied grin, and proudly puffed out his chest.

Then he settled down on the chair and disappeared below the back while his tail slowly rose up waving with pleasure. Lumiera walked over to join Ra Mu, and they both happily grinned at their three successful students.

"You mean the whole time everything was just in our heads?" asked Kalem, puzzled.

Softly chuckling, Lumiera replied, "Let's just say that your deepest fears were manifested in your inner dream world for each one of you to conquer or be conquered by it. The way out of any negative influence is successfully accomplished by connecting to and relying upon the omnipresent Sound of The Ancient One or Prime Creator that is behind all life… and upon the loving trust and bond of friendship you have for each other."

"But you both saved us from those horrible things!" stated Mayleena, amazed.

"No, that is not correct, young one," kindly replied Ra Mu. "It was The Ancient One's Sound and Light behind all life you each contacted within yourselves by sending out the connecting 'HU' that saved you. What you each experienced came from the worst creations that you brought into existence during your former lifetimes. The ability to contact the Sound and Light was always there within you, but each of you had to first undo your former misuse of the creative imagination given you with the gift of life. Just a little nudging in the right direction was all that was necessary."

"Then, Sen Dar's spells can be defeated!" stated Kalem feeling courage well up inside.

Etta's tail brightened, and he flew up to eye level with Lumiera and Ra Mu. He put up his dukes, pretended to box the air, fiercely chomped his teeth, growled, and courageously stated, "Qui pak met gon nulie!" ("I'll bite him into submission!")

They all couldn't help but chuckle at Etta's antics.

Then Ra Mu commented with a chuckle, "Etta, my friend, I'm afraid you won't be able to bite Sen Dar into submission at all. You and Mayleena will better serve Kalem here with us. Remember, you were all in a higher inner true spherical energy form when you were in the cave of fears. You don't need to physically be with Kalem to assist him now. When the time comes, each of you must remember your experiences in the caves of illusion and draw upon what you have learned about your bond with The Ancient One, and each other or Sen Dar will win! If he does, we cannot intervene to save this world. The greatest test is yet to come!"

Not smiling, Master Lumiera added, "It appears that the United States and Russian militaries were successful. They joined forces together for the first time to use their own secret weapons to stop the Zon ships from destroying both prototype spacecraft launches. This marked a new era for planet Earth and every living thing on the surface. But Sen Dar will want revenge. He'll want to destroy everything he can, and we must move quickly before he accomplishes his perverted goal."

At the same moment, wise expressions appeared on Kalem's,

Mayleena's, and Etta's faces, and Kalem stated in wonder, "I understand many things now that previously alluded me. I believe we're ready for Sen Dar."

He respectfully nodded to Mayleena and to Etta, and they nodded their mutual understanding back at him. Mayleena stood up and walked toward Kalem as he stood up to tenderly embrace her. He fondly gazed into her radiant green eyes, then reached over and shook his courageous Dren friend's hand before proudly saluting him. Etta proudly saluted him back and flew up beside them.

"More Zon ships will likely be on their way to the United States and Russia very soon," stated Ra Mu to get their attention. "Admiral Starland informs us that Lieutenant Moreau's squadron will be waiting for them near Florida. Another squadron is in position to intercept any Zon ships headed toward Russia. You should know that it's likely Sen Dar will be with the Zon ships this time. If you hurry, Captain, you could join Lieutenant Moreau."

"If you succeed in stopping Sen Dar and safely return," added Lumiera grinning at Kalem, "I'll have a surprise waiting for both you and Mayleena. You may be married by The Ancient One itself if you both wish this. But remember, this kind of marriage is very rare, so don't be too late, Captain! Call on The Ancient One's radiant HU Sound and remember that your friends are always with you. You will not be alone. Farewell!"

Kalem smiled at Mayleena, and Etta hovered over next to her shoulder. Then all three respectfully looked at Master Lumiera and

Master Ra Mu, deeply grateful.

"We'll succeed at stopping him!" confidently stated Kalem.

Kalem tenderly hugged Mayleena again. Then he hugged Etta like a brother, and he briskly walked out of the pyramid chamber, followed close behind by Mayleena and Etta hovering behind her.

ESCAPE TO FIGHT AGAIN

It was dusk high above the Zon ceremonial pyramid, and stars were beginning to come out in the clear sky above this different parallel dimension on Earth. The deep orange-red and violet sunset faded to gray below the distant background horizon beyond the snow-capped volcanic mountain. Nearby loomed the Zon's black citadel fortress that had been built at the base and partially up the mountainside. Between them, nestled along the valley floor, was the strange city of charcoal-colored twisted minaret-like towers and small dome-shaped dwellings.

Sen Dar was standing next to the rectangular black obsidian pedestal topped with the bust of Zol Yul, positioned in the center of the flat-topped pyramid. Fourteen Zon Scout class fighters flew by overhead and slowed on the approach to the pyramid, aligned in two rows (seven in each), then stopped to hover several hundred feet directly above Sen Dar. Three of the ships hovered down and landed twenty feet away from him. The lead ship centered in the foreground between the other two ships had Sen Dar's personal symbol painted on the hull. High Commander Luboc quickly climbed down a ladder extended underneath the lead ship and walked toward Sen Dar at a brisk pace. Sen Dar began angrily pacing back and forth in front of the statue as Commander Luboc cautiously approached, bowed to one knee before him, then rose back to his feet and delivered reluctant news with downcast eyes.

"My Lord, it would appear their orbiting satellites were more powerful than estimated. My Demon Scout fighters fired at both rockets, but some kind of energy shield deflected their firepower back at them. Then both orbiting platforms disintegrated our two ships with some kind of powerful energy beam weapon."

"You fool," angrily shouted Sen Dar. "You call your cowardly men warriors? Your spineless Zon pilots have failed!"

And Sen Dar grabbed Luboc by the lapels of his uniform with one tightly closed fist, lifted him several feet off the ground, and threw him ten feet through the air to the platform floor. Luboc appeared unhurt as he slowly got up, angrily gazing back at Sen Dar. Then he restrained himself, suppressing his anger.

He humbly stated, "My Lord, we had no way of knowing that these backward humans had such weapons. You did not tell us anything about their weapons capabilities."

"Your Zon pilots were fools to allow themselves to be caught in such a simple trap," arrogantly snapped back Sen Dar, "and they deserved death, but it doesn't matter. We'll put an end to their orbiting platforms. You will personally instruct the pilots of one squadron to see to it this time. Send them to Russia and have them destroy Moscow, their capital city. Tell them to kill everything and everyone in it. Turn it to ashes! They can't defend against seven Zon Demon craft at the same time. I will personally command a second squadron to destroy the United States Capitol city first, and you will come with me as my personal fighter support protection. Then I will demand they turn their puny world over to me, their new Lord, to rule over them or quite simply... we will kill all of them! And High Commander Luboc," continued Sen Dar with an intimidating sneer, "do not fail me again!"

Luboc forced a phony smile and just managed to find enough reserved strength to hold back his anger. He saluted Sen Dar and then stiffly turned on his heels and briskly walked back to the Zon ship landed next to Sen Dar's personal Scout command ship. Sen Dar quickly followed behind him and headed over to the ship with his personal symbol on the hull's side. They both climbed up the ladders protruding from the center of the underside of each hull. Moments later, all three ships began to softly emit their high-pitched hum and pulsing pale-red auras, then lifted straight up to hover high above the pyramid.

One of the Zon ships moved into position in front of the rear six

Zon Demon ships still hovering above the pyramid. Luboc's support fighter and Sen Dar's personal ship moved to the front of the forward five Zon ships. Each group of ships then moved into V formations. The red glow around their hulls brightened, and both squadrons darted a high speed into the distant sky.

Numerous stars now spread across the heavens, as the two Zon squadrons stopped moments later, two-dozen miles away, to hover high in the night sky above a wide plateau at the opposite end of the valley. Soft glittering lights were coming from the towers and domed dwellings in the countryside around the pyramid and the tall spires of the Zon citadel were faintly outlined against the towering snow-crowned black volcanic mountain beyond it.

Sen Dar was gazing at the viewscreen, observing the distant background terrain and the other Zon squadron ships in two V formations hovering nearby. He was tightly holding The Ancient One's crystal in his right hand that was radiating pale-gold light through his clenched fingers. He walked over to the control console smirking and stopped, then arrogantly grinned as he touched the transceiver crystal control.

"This is Zol Yul, your Supreme Lord! I will now light up the invisible doorway between dimensions for you as I did before. Pass through quickly, and I'll follow behind you. We'll regroup on the other side."

He briefly closed his eyes and then snapped them back open. The light radiating from the crystal through his closed fist changed to wavering violet light, and a beam darted from it right through the ship's hull.

Sen Dar's ship was hovering in the lead position at the apex of the foreground Zon squadron with the wavering violet light coming from the ship's hull extending one hundred feet to disappear in the invisible vortex opening. A faint light began to appear whirling around the invisible widening center, making the opening increasingly visible until it was forty feet across. Then the wavering violet beam vanished, leaving behind an illuminated whirling energy tunnel.

Early morning light, blue sky, and a few clouds were visibly moving by the green molecular vortex opening, whirling clockwise, on the other side through the short twelve-foot-long by forty-foot-wide energy tunnel conduit. The blue molecules spinning around the vortex on the Zon's side of the energy tunnel were whirling counterclockwise at a slightly slower rate of speed. The two differing whirling energies came together in the center of the tunnel, briefly blended together to create a third rate of speed. One by one, the thirteen Zon ships that comprised both squadrons slowly moved through the opening, followed by Sen Dar's lead ship with his personal symbol on the hull.

Both Zon squadrons quickly regrouped in their two V formations on the other side of the whirling opening. The ships were now high above the ice and snow-covered Antarctica landscape near the ocean shoreline, pulsing with faint red auras as they hovered into parallel positions in the morning sunlight. Several fluffy white clouds floated by behind both squadrons. The sun had fully risen above the horizon over the ocean five thousand feet below the ships. Sunlight rays glittered like a vast field of diamonds off the frozen white wilderness nearby.

Inside his ship, Sen Dar was deviously grinning, wearing The Ancient One's stolen crystal on the chain around his neck, but he wasn't holding it as he touched the transceiver control again.

"This is your Lord, Zol Yul!" he arrogantly stated. "I have brought all you fortunate pilots into this parallel reality on our world again so that you may each take a proud part in what we are about to conquer. Behold! I will now make the vortex leading back into our domain invisible once again."

He stood back, grabbed The Ancient One's crystal, and it glowed with gold light as he closed his eyes and then mumbled something inaudible under his breath. The gold light changed to wavering violet light, and the crystal shot a beam through the ship's hull.

The violet light beam emanating from the hull of Sen Dar's ship penetrated the green molecular energy whirling around the vortex opening, and the clear view of the star-filled night sky on the other side rapidly faded into obscurity. The violet beam withdrew from the fading vortex to dissolve back inside Sen Dar's ship, and the vortex completely vanished from view, leaving the clear morning light background and a few passing clouds in its place.

Self-satisfied, Sen Dar grinned as he touched the transceiver's control again and stated with gusto, "My brave warriors, our new destiny awaits us. Now fly to victory!"

The pale-red anti-gravity luminance around the hulls of both squadrons pulsed at an increasing rate until they steadily glowed bright red. Then they darted across the sky over the coastline of Antarctica, headed far out to sea, and quickly vanished over the horizon.

Kalem walked out of the arched entryway leading from the huge domed city at the base of the tall snowed capped mountain in the parallel Lemuria dimension. The two-thousand-foot waterfall was gracefully dropping down its side in the distant background. He walked up to the ladder extended from the open hatch underneath his ship's hull. The other Galactic Alliance Scout ship and the huge Oceanan Spectrum Crystal ship were still parked on their adjacent landing pads to either side of his ship. Kalem looked back at the huge dome over the city and smiled. Then he climbed up the ladder. Moments later, the ship lit up - softly pulsing with pale-blue light, emitting the familiar low-frequency hum, and the ship hovered up a hundred feet. The pulsing light around the hull turned solid blue, and the ship flew in an arc up and over the top of the huge domed city to continue upward alongside the snow-capped mountainside. It stopped to hover just outside the oval cavern opening with the clear glass-like oval tunnel entrance leading inside the mountain. Then his ship slowly entered the oval tunnel, leaving behind the waterfall cascading out of the cavern opening, the sealed transport car tube below it, and the majestic domed city far below.

Some minutes later, a blue spot of light on the rock wall on the backside of Mt. Shasta appeared and widened as it spiraled open like a galaxy of tiny blue stars. into the sixty-by-hundred-and-twenty-foot oval clear glass-like tunnel opening leading out of the Guardian's secret base. Kalem's ship flew out of the lighted tunnel and headed upward in a spiraling arc until it stopped to momentarily hover several hundred feet above the surrounding forest treetops. The galaxy of stars whirling around the oval opening spiraled closed and vanished, leaving the flat gray rock wall behind. The ship flew up alongside the mountain, and it stopped again to hover just below the clouds that were once again mysteriously completely encircling the mountain summit.

Seated behind the control console, Kalem was gazing up at Admiral Starland on the main viewscreen, and the Admiral humorously stated, "Welcome back, son!"

"I didn't think I'd make it through that one!" Kalem agreeably replied.

"The Cave of Fears – is not easy to go through for any of us," continued Starland grinning. "But it is the fastest way to bring out one's latent abilities into conscious awareness for protection in a looming deadly situation, if you understand my meaning, Captain."

Starland chuckled at his own comment, reflecting on his own past experience, but Kalem was not amused by his father's cheerful attitude. Regardless, he forced a cheerful smile in return.

"Captain, we just tracked several Zon ships leaving the South Polar Interdimensional Transit Window," continued Starland more seriously. "Sen Dar must have discovered it through his abusive misuse of The Ancient One's crystal. A few minutes ago, their ships split up. One squadron is headed toward the eastern seaboard of The United States. I suspect Sen Dar is with them. Another group is headed along a trajectory toward Moscow in Russia. I've positioned one Galactic Scout squadron in the atmosphere high above the Russian launch site. Lieutenant Moreau's squadron is positioned high in Earth's atmosphere above the Transporter launch site at Area 51 in the state of Nevada. There's still time for you to join Moreau and command the squadron if you hurry. But this time, Captain, you're authorized to stop Sen Dar from embarking on another mission of destruction any way you can."

"I'm on my way," eagerly replied Kalem with renewed confident determination.

The viewscreen went blank. Kalem touched another crystal control, and then jammed his palms down into the guidance controls. The viewscreen lit back up, revealing a three-dimensional transparent map of California. A computer graphics representation of his ship above a red dot appeared moving at the end of a thin red line headed away from the large luminous letters – MOUNT SHASTA. This was clearly marked below them by a blue circle surrounding a black dot in northern California, while Kalem's ship continued to move above the red dot that swiftly crossed the United States. It slowed as it headed across the image of the Nevada state line.

At the same moment, Harry was still at the secret Strategic Space

Command center hidden underneath the hangar buildings at Area 51, nervously pacing back and forth again behind Hubert Griswald, who was standing in front of the control console keyboard intently monitoring the main viewscreen. Judith was standing to Harry's left, impatiently watching him pace back and forth, and President Sam Stockwell was standing next to Judith with his hands on his hips, intently watching the viewscreen.

Appearing a bit bored, the President frowned and stated, "Okay, General Faldwell, I've had enough of this. Call me as soon as anything else happens. I'm heading back to the White House."

Startled by something he had just witnessed on the viewscreen, Hubert jumped to the seat at the control console and furiously began typing on the keyboard.

"Mr. President, you'd better wait," he nervously yelled over his shoulder toward the President. "If I'm right, those Zon devils are headed up the coast on a trajectory that will take them right across..."

He paused to tap two more keys and then looked up, worried as he further studied the viewscreen. An image of the eastern seaboard of the United States appeared. Seven white dots were swiftly moving northward beyond the coast of Cuba. An arched trajectory line appeared being drawn moving from the bottom of the viewscreen northward. It passed right through the middle of the Zon represented ships and continued up the eastern seaboard to cut right through the middle of Washington, D.C.

"Oh my God!" blurted out Hubert, and he swung his chair around to urgently gaze at the President, stating astonished, "Mr. President, it's Washington, D.C. The bastards are heading on a trajectory that will bring them to the Capital!"

Sam blanched as he looked for answers from Harry. Harry angrily stuffed the unlit cigar into the corner of his mouth and bit down hard. Then he briskly walked over to the control console, picked up the phone handset, pressed a button, and grabbed the cigar back out his mouth.

"This is General Faldwell. I want the Air Defense Command in Washington at Devcon One ready for an enemy attack in one minute," he angrily commanded into the handset. "That's right, Colonel, scramble the stealth fighters. If they can catch up with the unidentified ships, I want them shot down as soon as they cross into U.S. air space. Is that clear? Good!"

He slammed down the handset, and then gazed with grim determination at the President. This time, Judith understandingly took his hand into hers. Harry's stern gaze vanished momentarily as he consolingly gazed into her worried eyes.

"Don't you worry, baby. We'll blast the bastards back to the dimensional hellhole they came from, and this time we'll have the help of the Guardians and Galactic Alliance ships."

Sam nervously approached Hubert and asked urgently, "Can't you realign the satellites and protect the city the same way you did both prototype Space Transporters?"

"There just isn't enough time, and we couldn't protect the whole city anyway," replied Hubert, worried with sweat beaded up on his brow. "The enemy ships will be over Washington, D.C. air space in minutes. Surface-to-air missiles and jet fighters can't defend against an entire squadron of those Zon devils. They're too fast and maneuverable. I mean... we might take two or three of them out with the Satellite laser before the rest attack the city, but I'm afraid that's it!"

Harry looked away to solemnly gaze around the control room at everyone there. With renewed confidence, he grinned at them all while they quietly stared back at him with bated breath, awaiting his next comment.

"Now, I guess it's up to our new Galactic Alliance friends to help us out. From all I've experienced about them so far, they keep their word."

He took a deep relaxing breath for all to see, confidently stuffed the cigar back into the corner of his mouth, and intently gazed at the main viewscreen monitor. Complete silence was inside the control room as all eyes followed his gaze to see what might next befall them.

Kalem had a wide panoramic view of the Area 51 launch facility in the distance through several white fluffy clouds several thousand feet below his ship.

Meanwhile, Sen Dar's ship with its symbol on the hull was flying several-thousand-feet above the ocean at the front of the squadron of six other Zon Demon ships in a V formation. The ships began to speed up as they passed over the last of the Florida Keys and then over the tip of Florida headed northward along the Eastern Seaboard.

Sen Dar was seated in a black leather chair with a high headboard at the top emblazoned with his symbol in gold and silver metal: the point of a vertical sword touched the middle of an upside-down pyramid with its apex positioned just above the north pole of a red world; two snakes wound up the blade above the handle with their heads facing toward each other and their forked tongues touching. Sen Dar was wearing a long black cape thrown over his left shoulder. The Zol Yul image was emblazoned on a thin gold crown that curved across his forehead. His hands were placed, palms down, with his spread fingers arched over the top of two luminous opalescent semispheric shaped guidance controls. They were set a-foot-apart in the center of a six-foot-long control console curved in a half-moon shape around his midsection. He was intently gazing at the oval-shaped viewscreen that was head-high directly across from him on the other side of the console. On it, the last of the Florida Keys swiftly passed into the distance toward the horizon as the ship continued northward further inland over Florida. A small semispherical crystal began to blink, and Sen Dar reacted with angry alarm as he touched it. The last of the Florida Keys passing over the distant horizon on the viewscreen telescoped forward, revealing two particular close together islands and Kalem's Galactic Alliance ship hovering in the position directly above one of them.

Sen Dar thought to himself with sadistic glee, gritting his teeth, *Ah, one lone Galactic Scout. How wonderful! Dare I dream it could be...?* He angrily grimaced as he touched the transceiver control and then forcefully commanded, "You will all lock onto the coordinates of that enemy ship I'm sending to you now. Spread out far and wide, above and below it. Go with stealth, or I will send you to your deaths. I want this one alive, if possible, but don't let him escape under any circumstances."

Kalem was gazing at his viewscreen, and Lieutenant Moreau appeared on it.

"Welcome back, Captain!" stated Moreau, quite upbeat. "I didn't expect to find you out here with us."

"You know I wouldn't miss this for the world!" cockily snapped back Kalem.

Moreau glanced down at his console, then looked back up alarmed, "Captain, seven Zon ships just appeared on my long-range sensors moving into positions to surround you. Watch your step, my friend. We're headed your way."

Kalem glanced over and touched a blue-faceted crystal control and focused on a panel readout.

"I see them now. I had my sensors on a short-range scan. Thanks for the warning, and Moreau, old buddy, don't be too late!"

Sen Dar's ship with its emblem emblazoned on its side was hovering in position several thousand feet above the ocean. The sun's rays were glittered like diamonds off the ocean waves crashing along the coastlines of two islands in the distance below his ship. The other six Zon ships were now spread out above, below, behind, and from each side, converging toward Kalem's one lone Scout ship. It was hovering a bit further west of the islands. Sen Dar's ship suddenly darted into position directly in front of the other Zon ships, effectively blocking off the last possible escape routes for the Galactic Alliance Scout interceptor.

Intently focusing on his viewscreen, Sen Dar angrily mumbled to himself, "I will soon vaporize this stupid slave of that Ancient One nonsense!" He touched the transceiver's control again and arrogantly commanded, "I want all of you prepared to fire on that ship on my signal. I will accept no excuses from any of you if you miss." He touched a control next to the transceiver control to arrogantly demand, "Galactic Alliance fool, whoever you are, this is Lord Zol Yul of the superior Zon attack squadron. You are trapped! Surrender yourself and your ship to me immediately or be destroyed. Reply!"

"Well, if it isn't the Master of all garbage himself," came back Kalem's unexpected confident, cocky reply through his transceiver. "I see you managed to crawl out from under the slimy rock you were hiding under. You can cut out that Zol Yul crap!"

Surprised, then with much disdain Sen Dar shot back, "It amazes me, Captain, how you seem to always manage to escape certain death. This time I will really enjoy blowing you to bits unless you surrender and bow before me, your new Master!"

Kalem replied just as he suddenly appeared on Sen Dar's viewscreen, grinning composed self-assurance.

"You don't have a poisoned crystal around my neck this time, cowardly Master of nothing! Come on then, bring it on!"

And Kalem promptly taunted Sen Dar by comically contorting his face. He stuck his thumbs in his ears, wiggling his fingers and flapping his tongue, and reached down. The screen went blank.

The childish taunting worked, and Sen Dar was instantly outraged.

He touched the transceiver control again to command, fuming, "All ships open fire on that Galactic Scout. I want the Pilot burnt to ashes. Destroy him, or I'll burn each of you alive in his place!"

He slammed his hand over the red dome-shaped fire control, and it lit up pulsing red.

All seven Zon ships simultaneously pulsed a white strobe-like light from around their hulls and shot a wavering fiery red energy beam toward Kalem's ship that quickly formed into an oval-shaped fireball as they rapidly closed the distance.

In sadistic glee, Sen Dar lustily watched his viewscreen to witness the oval fireballs converge on Kalem's ship from every direction. His grin widened as the fireballs were about to hit, but Kalem's ship instantly turned into silver-gold particles of light and vanished. The fireballs exploded against each other in the center of the space where the ship had just been, and Sen Dar was immediately beside himself with anger. He slammed his fists on the console.

Kalem's ship reappeared higher in the sky just a few hundred yards behind Sen Dar's ship, and the ship's hull instantly blurred through the spectrum, flashed white light, and a round blue Mazon fireball was shot from the hull toward Sen Dar's ship.

Now frantic, Sen Dar glanced over his instrument panels and then touched another small semispheric control. The viewscreen switched to a wide view directly behind his ship, revealing Kalem's Scout fighter in the near distance and a blue Mazon fireball almost at impact with his own ship.

"No-o," he blurted out, "I'll damn you to the fires of Enos!"

He slammed his palms over the dome-shaped guidance controls, and the ship suddenly lurched sharply to the left, nearly knocking him to the floor.

In the sky outside, Sen Dar's ship sharply veered away just in time at a curved forty-five-degree angle, and the blue fireball exploded near its side. The ship was sent spinning end-over-end but quickly righted itself before Kalem's ship darted away at high speed over the ocean, firing two more blue Mazon fireballs in the direction of the enemy ships. One of the Zon ships flying across his path that began to curve back toward Sen Dar's ship was just missed by one fireball, but the other fireball hit the second Zon ship flying beside it, brilliantly exploded it into vanishing energy particles. Sen Dar's ship had already fired two more oval red fireballs at Kalem's ship. But it darted upward, and both fireballs exploded below the hull, rocking the ship from side to side before it darted away over the ocean toward the horizon. The remaining five Zon ships moved behind Sen Dar's Demon fighter. Then they darted away in formation in pursuit of Kalem's fighter. Sen Dar's ship then raced considerably ahead of the rest of the Zon squadron. They appeared to close the gap as they rapidly receded into the far distant background over the horizon.

Two Galactic Alliance Scout fighters appeared zooming down from somewhere higher in the sky, firing on two Zon support ships as they passed below them, and another Zon ship trailing behind them exploded. Both Scout ships reappeared a moment later, leveling off before they sped toward the remaining two Zon ships. Four more Galactic fighters darted down from the overhead sky and raced after the other two Galactic Scouts firing on another nearby Zon ship squadron before they all disappeared over the horizon.

It was a full moonlit night high in the upper atmosphere above Moscow in Russia. Two Zon ships sped by and darted away into the distance, but they were both instantly destroyed by Mazon fireballs before they got very far. Three Galactic Alliance Scouts flew down into view, passing through their disintegrating atoms.

In the distance, another raging battle was taking place in the upper atmosphere over the Russian Capital. Six Russian ground-to-air missiles sped upward, but they harmlessly passed by several Zon ships that easily skirted around them. One lone Galactic Scout caught between the oval red fireballs coming from the two Zon ships was partially hit by one of the fireballs that exploded near the hull, tearing a large hole in its side. Moments later, the Scout ship exploded. Three more Scout Ships darted into view, passing through the dissipating molecules of their fellow Scout ship in hot pursuit of the two Zon ships. Both Zon ships attempted to dart away in a sharp curve in opposite directions; but two of the three blue fireballs shot from the three Galactic Scout pursuers hit one Zon ship exploding it. The other Zon Demon fighter darted away in a blur of light at greatly increased speed. The three Galactic Scout pursuers darted after it.

In the far distance, three more Zon ships flew across the sky, and three more pursuing Galactic Scouts darted away after them. Two more Galactic Scout ships flew down from the sky in a step curve and leveled off nearby to join them.

On the other side of the planet, Zon oval fireballs were exploding, rocking Kalem's ship, while it continued to speed further out over the ocean. His ship suddenly curved sharply upward in a loop to come back down behind Sen Dar's ship and four more Zon ships as they sped by below. A Galactic Scout ship quickly leveled out behind them, firing two more blue fireballs that quickly disintegrated the two nearest Zon ships. The two remaining Zon support fighters veered away in opposite directions to come around behind Kalem's ship. An instant later, one was destroyed by two more Mazon fireballs shot at them from two of five Galactic Scouts rapidly approaching from a distance. Sen Dar's remaining ship and Luboc's support fighter sped up, and then they darted away at much greater speed over the horizon. Kalem's ship darted away after it, closely followed by the six Galactic support fighters.

A transparent map appeared on the viewscreen inside Kalem's ship, revealing the last of the Florida Keys to the right of the ocean depicted on the right half of the map. A red dot moving across the map at the end of a thin red line extended itself from the Florida Keys far south and down over the Atlantic Ocean along the left side of South America to a coastline of snow and ice where it stopped on an X marked with luminous letters above it that read:

The South Polar Interdimensional Transit Window

The map faded away as Sen Dar's and Luboc's ships darted away from Kalem's ship in another increased speed jump. The enemy ships were headed across the distant sky, and Kalem grinned with determination. Then he jammed his hands into the palm guidance controls.

Outside, Kalem's ship was keeping pace behind the two enemy ships, firing several Mazon fireballs at them that exploded to each side of their hulls, severely rocking them from side to side. Both Enemy ships suddenly darted away again at greatly increased speed.

Sen Dar was watching Kalem's pursuing ship on his viewscreen, sitting down with his palms placed over the luminous semispheric guidance controls. Both controls were lit with a red glow passing between his spread fingers.

Yes... come to me, my little Captain, stated Sen Dar silently to himself, gleefully amused. ***I've got a surprise waiting for you. Feel how my power has grown, little Galactic fly! In one more moment, I'll have you in my grasp forever!***

And he touched his transceiver crystal.

"High Commander Luboc, head back through the invisible vortex. I'm sending you the coordinates. I wish to take this particular pilot to a special place and an unexpected surprise I have in store for him. Do it now!"

Luboc's ship suddenly veered away from Sen Dar's ship with increased speed, but Kalem ignored it and kept his ship close on the tail of Sen Dar's customized Zon craft.

Inside it, Sen Dar grabbed The Ancient One's green crystal hung on the gold chain from inside his shirt, and it lit up with emerald green light passing through his clenched fingers. A beam of green light instantly emanated from it right through the ship's hull, and he looked up at the viewscreen. He could see his ship was rapidly speeding over the coastline of snow and ice-covered landscape with the green beam extending out into the sky, opening a whirling interdimensional vortex directly in the path of his ship. He sadistically grinned with diabolical self-satisfaction.

A moment later, his ship darted through the forty-foot-wide whirling opening just as Kalem's ship, just several-hundred-feet directly behind, started to veer to the right to avoid entering the vortex, but it was too late, and his ship vanished through the opening, headed into another reality. The vortex whirled closed and faded from view, leaving only the snow and ice-laden landscape of Antarctica below to greet the six Galactic Scout support ships that appeared speeding over the frozen wilderness, and they instantly stopped to hover nearby.

Perplexed, Lieutenant Moreau gazed back and forth between his viewscreen and the crystal control console surrounding him. The viewscreen only revealed the cold, clear blue empty sky where Kalem's ship was moments before. He reached down and touched the transceiver control.

"Are any of you picking up anything?" he hesitantly asked.

The voice of another Galactic Alliance pilot answered back through the transceiver, quite puzzled, "They just vanished through that opening before it disappeared. I'm not picking them up on any of my instruments. We monitored the remaining Zon fighter darting further over the ice and snow toward the planet's South Pole."

Moreau shook his head, frowning, and replied, "Let it go. They're headed back to the Zon domain. This is not good because that area isn't the location of the South Polar Transit Window the Zon ships came through. Sen Dar has gone into some uncharted parallel dimension, and Kalem is in trouble again. Damn it... and we can't help him. Why doesn't he ever wait for reinforcements?" He thoughtfully hesitated and then reluctantly ordered, "We better get back and report this to the Admiral."

The blue anti-magnetic aura surrounding the hull of Moreau's Scout fighter brightened, and the ship darted in an arc up through the atmosphere heading out into space.

The luminous hulls of the five remaining Galactic Scout fighters brightened, and they too darted upward after it, leaving behind the ice and snow below the cold, deep blue sky.

Meanwhile, Luboc's ship slowed as it approached the coordinates of 'The South Polar Interdimensional Transit Window,' and the ship slowly vanished from view as it entered the invisible vortex opening.

CAN THERE BE PEACE?

*H*is mouth opened in surprise; Harry was watching the main viewscreen back at the secret Strategic Space Command hidden under the hangars located inside the mysterious, highly classified Area 51 base in the Nevada desert. Judith was standing next to him, grinning as she blew out a relieved breath.

"Whoa... that was too close!" and she looked at Hubert Griswald sitting at the control console and commented, "Hubert, correct me if I'm wrong, but it looks like the Zon ships have been destroyed."

Hubert stopped typing on the keyboard, turned around amazed, and excitedly stated, "They most certainly have been, by those Galactic Alliance ships. God bless them! Right now, they're headed back into space. There must be some kind of big command ship out there we can't see on radar, infrared, or from satellites. No Zon ships are currently being picked up by our military satellites circling the Earth." Relieved, he shook his head and curiously added, "Man, that must have been some battle!"

Harry stuffed his unlit cigar into the corner of his mouth, then yanked it out, and cockily grinned at the President to confidently state, "Mr. President, I told you they wouldn't let us down."

President Stockwell looked at Harry and Judith and apprehensively stated, "If we learn anything from this near disaster regarding what that knucklehead Sen Dar is capable of doing until he is permanently removed as a threat to our world, we'll have to somehow encourage the signing of some kind of a peace treaty with our new interdimensional space-faring Zon neighbors. We should do this before they get any more misdirected bright ideas to attack us."

"Mr. President, you'll need me now more than ever," eagerly stated Judith. "I could serve as a type of ambassador between our world and the Zon world in the parallel dimension. I can help get a treaty signed and some kind of beneficial interdimensional trade established. Cultures mutually dependent upon one another for growing abundance and advancement don't attack each other."

"That's just what I was thinking, Judith," he stated, grinning and raising his eyebrows. "But I want Harry to go with you on any mission to their government center to scope out their military capabilities. He could coordinate with you and Hubert to acquire any advanced scientific knowledge they may be willing to provide us, some of which we now know exceeds our own."

He gazed at Hubert for his expected support.

Hubert got up from the keyboard at the control console and hesitantly stated, "I...am uh... of course I'll help, anyway I can. We already have our own anti-gravity technology and weapons. If I'm not mistaken, we must understand more about the technology that powers their anti-gravity ships and weapons or we'll all be in serious jeopardy down the road."

"Of course... of course, Hubert," impatiently shot back the President. "We'll get to that, but right now, we have to ascertain the conflict is really over, and we'll need a peace treaty signed by them before anything else can happen."

Hubert reluctantly nodded his head at Sam's clear logic, and he sat back down in the chair.

"We better wait for word from Master Ra Mu before we proceed," Harry seriously interjected. "At this point, we know the Zon threat has been stopped for now, but we don't know what else this lunatic Sen Dar may be up to if he's still alive."

Sam thoughtfully rubbed his forehead and said to them, "Well, what in blazes do we do next?"

Admiral Starland was standing inside one of the huge clear observation domes near one end of his long oval flagship, looking up through it at Lieutenant Moreau's approaching Scout squadron. They soon entered the ship, one by one, through the open landing bay below the observation dome. He solemnly turned and stepped into the clear cylindrical glass-like elevator in the center of the wide round floor. The door closed, and the elevator slowly lowered out of view.

A short time later, Starland was standing at the back of the oval table in the flagship's conference room when Lieutenant Moreau walked in the room and over to him and saluted. Starland saluted him back, and Moreau raised his hands with his palms up, shrugging his shoulders.

"From what you told me on your way back to the ship, Lieutenant, I'd say my young son is in trouble once again. Tell me everything again. I want to know exactly what you witnessed."

"Well... as I told you before," somberly began Moreau, "we had destroyed all but one of Sen Dar's support Zon fighters when we maneuvered our ships to assist Kalem. We watched Sen Dar's ship open some kind of interdimensional vortex, and his ship shot through it. Kalem's ship was right behind it and couldn't swerve out of the way in time before his ship passed through it as well. The vortex whirled closed and vanished, and there simply wasn't anything left that we could detect. Admiral, what do you want me to do now?"

"All I can tell you is that Kalem has recently gone through a very special training to deal with Sen Dar," stated Starland. "He must come through this battle on his own. Let it be, for now, Lieutenant. Stand down your squadron and get some rest. I'll fill you in after I learn the outcome."

Starland grinned at Moreau and nodded. Moreau saluted the Admiral, then turned and walked out of the conference room.

Starland's grin dropped to concern as he closed his eyes to silently communicate with the omnipresent living energy known as The Ancient One or Prime Creator. Inside, he began to see a point of white light in the center of his inner vision that rapidly grew into a blinding sheet of radiant energy. It was accompanied by the uplifting blending of the mystic hauntingly beautiful high flute melody, a vibrant humming, and the subtle crashing ocean waves of The Ancient One's Sound.

You are the source of all life, and we exist as true individuals of the same exact living energy because of our collective great love for all life, and all that exists in the grand multidimensional creation, humbly stated Starland in the silent sanctity of his spherically shaped energy being or what people on Earth call Soul. He then sent out his secret communication into the Light and Sound with a long drawn out silent, ***Hu-u-u-u-u-u-u. May your care be with Kalem at this important crossroad in his awakening to this one great truth***.

Starland opened his eyes wide as if he could suddenly see into the far distance into another dimension to behold Kalem's situation and his mouth formed a slight grin. He casually walked out of the conference room.

Soon after, the Admiral was in his personal sleeping quarters aboard the ship sitting down with his legs crossed on a special large square blue pillow with his eyes closed. The Sound of The Ancient One was softly vibrating around the large room. Starland's true individual Atma or Soul-self sphere suddenly exited the body out of the top of the head and floated over to the center of the room. Another similar luminous sphere, surrounded by a faint golden aura, entered his quarters as it passed into it through the far metal wall. As it slowly approached, it transformed into Master Ra Mu's physical body with a faint golden aura around it. Starland's sphere quickly did the same, and they clasped forearms like the ancient friends that they were.

Ra Mu grinned and said, "As I mentioned on my way here, Kalem is now about to battle on Sen Dar's own terms in the ancient abandoned stronghold the Adepts know as 'The Isle of Banion.' You already know both Master Lumiera and I are doing everything we can to see to it that he survives the encounter."

Starland's smile dropped, and he asked, "Is he really ready to deal with Sen Dar's cunning negative power?"

"Just send your son all the goodwill and confidence you can," encouragingly continued Ra Mu. "You should know that Mayleena and Etta will be able to assist him due to the training they just received in 'The Cave of Fears,' if your hardheaded son remembers to call on The Ancient One."

Starland nodded his wise understanding agreement, cracked a little grin, and stated, "Now we must wait to behold the outcome. However, I do sense this will be a very close battle for my son's current temperament. We will see, Master Ra Mu. Yes, my friend, we will see. Now I must return to Master Lumiera in the domed city of the Adepts. I will have to be present there at any crucial moment to be of any help. Good bye, for now, Master Starland. For what it's worth,

I believe Kalem will return."

He gave Starland a wide, encouraging grin as his body transformed back into his luminous Atma or Soul sphere. It then darted out of Starland's sleeping quarters back through the wall. Starland's luminous physical appearing form transformed back into his hovering Atma sphere. Then it moved back above his body and vanished as it lowered down inside the head. The Admiral opened his eyes and let out a sigh. Then he stood up, walked over to the oval door, and passed a hand over the hand activator on the sidewall. The door silently slid inside the wall, and the Admiral turned back to briefly look inside his quarters, smiling at the memory of his encouraging meeting with Ra Mu. Then he walked out of the room, and the door silently closed behind him.

THE ISLE OF BANION

Sen Dar's ship was flying deeper into the vast twilight space in a higher parallel dimension of the physical universe. The ship harmlessly passed through beautifully unique vaporous sheets of violet clouds that kept appearing and disappearing in many places all around it. Then it faded into the far distance, just as Kalem's ship sped into view and just as quickly faded into the distance in pursuit.

Somewhere deeper in the eerie twilight void, Sen Dar's ship shot out of the thick vaporous clouds through a widening gap to continue its flight deep into a massive deep-blue atmospheric void of space with no apparent stars anywhere. In the distance, mysteriously balanced in the center of the void, was a wide floating mountainous island. Sen Dar's ship began to fly in a zigzag avoidance pattern as Kalem's ship, closing the gap behind it, fired several blue Mazon fireballs. Moments later, they both exploded in succession to each side of the hull, flipping Sen Dar's ship end-over-end. It quickly righted itself and darted at increased speed toward the island. Kalem's ship sped after it at increased speed. Both ships quickly dwindled into the distance as they neared the island, until they appeared like tiny specks against the gigantic landmass suspended in the exact center of the strange atmospheric void.

A golden halo above and behind the island coming from some kind of hidden sun or unknown light source was also creating a thin violet light aura that closely hugged the island's entire circumference.

Small black rock pinnacles gradually tapering upward from each end of the island rose to great mountainous heights at its center. A blue sand shoreline appeared to completely extend out of view around the entire base of the island.

Kalem was staring amazed at the viewscreen, observing the weird atmosphere and huge mysterious island looming ever larger, as his ship flew nearer to the blue sand shoreline in pursuit of Sen Dar's ship passing over the sand.

"Where in creation is this place?" he softly said to himself, mystified. ***Damn it all, I don't care if I enter demon fire itself***, he thought more determined. ***This time, Sen Dar, Lord of Madness, you won't escape me.***

He touched the fire control crystal again.

It appeared like soft twilight as Sen Dar's ship flew into view from the strange encompassing deep-blue space near the coastline along the central part of the floating landmass. It slowed as it passed low over the mysterious waterless, thin blue luminous sand shoreline bordering it that gently curved into the far distance. The ship continued over the tops of several rows of small pinnacles strewn along the other side of the sand. It was headed a little further inland toward a gap in a towering cluster of the giant black rock pinnacles.

A moment later, Kalem's Scout ship flew into view, just as another Mazon fireball was shot from the hull. It sped toward Sen Dar's ship flying in a curve through the gap in the giant pinnacles. The fireball exploded off the massive pinnacle's base on the right side of the gap, quickly dissipating black rock and dust off its surface. A moment later, Kalem's ship darted in a curve through the same gap.

The towering cluster of pinnacles were soon in the distance across the valley behind Sen Dar's ship, heading toward a tall mountain centered in the valley. Kalem's Scout fighter was in close pursuit. For some inexplicable reason, a wide celestial panorama overhead of alien stars, nebulae, and other stellar matter were now vividly visible all across the deep-blue heavens. Both ships speeding across the five-mile-wide oval valley continued to head toward the tall mountain towering in the center of the valley at the heart of the floating island landmass. It now appeared that the tallest rock pinnacles that had shielded the mountain from outside visibility completely surrounded the valley's outer circumference. Midway up the mountainside, just above a wide plateau, a shimmering turquoise-green waterfall was pouring out of a cavern. It was tumbling several-thousand-feet down to a long oval lake that stretched across the valley floor. Each side of the lake was lined with blue fir forest trees to its far end. There the lake water emptied into a river that split off in many directions, until the flowing waters dropped to unknown depths down open crevasses at the foot of many of the tallest pinnacles. The plateau ledge extended two hundred feet out of the side of the mountain halfway up from the base. As both ships approached, the thunderous waterfall a little further up the steep slope appeared to tumble out of a twenty-foot-wide by fifteen-foot-high cavern opening.

In the opposite direction across the valley, the distant gap through the tallest cluster of pinnacles was now far behind the two approaching ships. Sen Dar's ship soon hovered down and landed on the plateau, the pale-red aura around its hull shut off, and Sen Dar dropped to the ground out of the bottom hatch. He glanced toward Kalem's ship hovering down to land and deviously grinned. Then he ran up a wide set of carved blue-green granite steps that led in a gradual curve up twenty feet until they disappeared behind the waterfall roaring out of the cavern. He soon disappeared behind the shimmering cascade. Kalem's ship landed a moment later on the plateau next to Sen Dar's ship and the blue aura around the hull shut off. With his clear crystal laser gun drawn, Kalem exited the ship down through the bottom hatch crouching on one of the luminous blue-metal anti-gravity transport discs. He stood up just as soon as it cleared the underside of the hull, and he raced away upon it several feet above the wide carved steps to quickly disappear behind the roaring waterfall.

Inside the mountain, a thirty-foot-across flat plateau extended out from the sheer side of the interior cavern rock wall. Kalem appeared on his transport disc, slightly crouched down with his laser gun held in his hand pointed ahead of himself. He cautiously flew up the last of the carved granite stairs and stopped where the stairs abruptly ended at the beginning of the cavern floor. The waterfall loudly pouring down over the opening behind him was now completely covering the opening so that nothing outside could be seen. A pale light passing through the water into the cavern was eerily casting Kalem's shadow on the cavern floor and partially illuminating the ten-foot section of steps behind him. They led back down in a gentle curve to the left below the falling water. Additional light was filtering down over him from an unseen source high in the overhead cavern. He hovered on the disc further inside and landed it in the center of the plateau.

Then he looked around to behold that a huge natural cavern had been carved out of the inside the mountain. Large Grecian-style green marble pillars, left by a now extinct ancient race of beings, lined both sides of the cavern along the outer edges of the plateau. Carved into one of the pillars in a script that looked like ancient Greek letters was the single word *SERES*. The pillars extended a hundred feet up toward the cavern ceiling, as if they actually supported the chamber. An intricately carved marble bridge extended from the far edge of the plateau between two pillars in a long fifty-foot arch. It crossed a chasm to the other side of the chamber between two more pillars. There, it connected to another plateau that jutted out of the back of the sheer cavern rock wall with more of the pillars circling its outer edge. What appeared to Kalem to be molten lava was whirling in a pool at the bottom of a wide chasm located several hundred feet below the bridge. Large bursts of the fiery red liquid were being thrown up just below each side of the bridge every few seconds. Kalem noticed Sen Dar defiantly standing with his arms crossed on the far plateau across the bridge. Reflected light off the lava coming from below, was making his pupils appear to glow red. Kalem aimed his laser gun across the chasm at Sen Dar, just as Sen Dar's arrogant voice calling out to him ominously echoed in the chamber.

"Well... well... well," he began with a mocking chuckle, "if it isn't Captain Kalem all over again. Oh… that's right, you're one of the puppets of that mythical Ancient One nonsense, now, aren't you? As usual, the great Galactic Alliance fleet has sent its best little slave to do its dirty work for it."

With a pitiful shake of his head, Kalem called back, "Your twisted tongue can no longer influence me, Lord of all that is vile and yes… absurd. You can keep your foul-smelling words to yourself!"

"Hmm, that expected response is quite typical of your puny level of intelligence," calmly replied Sen Dar with taunting arrogance, and he motioned around with his arm as he continued, "Interesting place, isn't it? I found it quite by accident as the new Master of all the Zon worlds. An ancient race known as the Seres built this place millions of years ago, then simply vanished. They called this 'The Isle of

Banion.' Nice decor, wouldn't you say?"

"Yes, it fits you like a glove," replied Kalem, grimacing. "You know, dull and empty."

Sen Dar impatiently placed his hands on his hips and uproariously laughed before he continued, "Oh come now, my little insignificant Captain. I challenge you to fight me. That's why I brought you here. My powers have grown beyond what you could hope to understand. Fight me like a man on what the vanished alien race that once thrived here referred to as the bridge beyond time and space. The loser here loses his true self or what that Ancient One nonsense refers to as the Atma. The quite stupid people of Earth call it simply Soul, but they have no idea what that means any more than you do."

Sen Dar began to boldly walk over the bridge toward Kalem, and Kalem boldly began to hover on his disc over the bridge toward him.

Smiling delight, Sen Dar continued, "The liquid you see below you is not hot lava as you so stupidly thought! It's the Astral fire of this way station between here at the very edge of what is known as the Astral dimension or plane and many parallel dimensions of the physical worlds far below it. I learned this while studying the inscriptions on these walls put here by the long-vanished race of beings I just mentioned. That fiery liquid receives its energy from a dimension above this one. Then it pours down many similar strongholds to support worlds like Earth. This fire will destroy not only your physical body, my dear Captain, but also you as a being. I fondly look forward to throwing you into it!"

Kalem was now one-third of the way across the bridge, as was Sen Dar approaching from the opposite side. He suddenly fired the laser at Sen Dar, but Sen Dar grinning had waived his right hand and the laser beam was instantly diverted a few feet upward to blow a hole in the rock wall behind him.

"You won't be needing either of those anymore," he arrogantly stated, amusing himself.

With another sweep of his hand, Kalem's laser gun and his transport disc burst into flames. Kalem dropped the burning gun as he lunged off the burning disc onto the bridge. He watched the gun fall end-over-end into the flaming lava-like liquid below. Large red and purple flames enveloped it, then shot straight up toward the top of the cavern before they quickly died away. The transport disc burned into vapor and disappeared. Undaunted, Kalem angrily ran toward Sen Dar, but he was instantly stopped by a violet wall of fire that appeared in the middle of the bridge between them. Sen Dar waved his hand as he boldly walked right through the flames and grabbed the surprised Kalem by the throat with both hands.

Kalem ripped his hands away and hit Sen Dar hard with his fist squarely on the jaw, knocking him off his feet back through the wall of violet flames. He jumped through the flames and landed on top of Sen Dar, strangling him with all his pent-up anger, but Sen Dar's body began to glow with a red aura, and Kalem's hands around his neck were burned. Kalem backed away, stumbling in pain, while Sen Dar slowly rose to his feet, confidently grinning with hideous sadistic glee.

The wall of flames suddenly disappeared, and Kalem began to back up as Sen Dar approached him with outstretched flaming red hands.

Amused with his new toy, Sen Dar boldly stated, "You, little Captain, will now slowly painfully die, and I will laugh until your last miserable, pathetic breath escapes your useless carcass!"

"Kiss my..." Kalem angrily started to say as he suddenly leaped into the air feet first.

His feet bypassed Sen Dar's flaming outstretched hands and squarely landed the bottom of his heels on his chest, nocking Sen Dar backward head-over-heels right over the bridge. But Sen Dar just managed to grab onto the carved rock railing to stop his fall. He began to laugh again as a thin blue energy disc appeared under his feet. It quickly levitated him back up above the bridge, and he arrogantly gazed down, chuckling at his surprised prey.

He then extended his palms out toward Kalem. Searing beams of red light shot from them and instantly joined together a few feet past his hands to become a single thicker energy beam that hit Kalem, encircling his body in a fiery red aura. It lifted his body up to eye level and then threw him past the bridge across the far plateau, and he hit the side of the cavern wall hard. Kalem fell limp to the cavern floor, and Sen Dar began to triumphantly laugh as he levitated toward him. Kalem slowly regained consciousness, struggling to lift himself up on his hands, and looked up with blood trickling down the corner of his mouth to see Sen Dar approaching. Kalem was now more angrily determined than ever, and he stood up. Just as Sen Dar's feet touched the plateau floor, the blue energy disc under his feet vanished. Kalem was instantly hit with a green beam emitted from Sen Dar's palms that enveloped his body in an eerie aura of pulsating green light, and he clutched at his throat. He started to frantically gasp and quickly began to age as he dropped to his knees. His skin shriveled, his hair turned white, then fell out, leaving him completely bald. Then he began to appear extremely gaunt, and he extended a bony old finger out toward Sen Dar, who was now viciously grinning down at him.

Struggling to breathe, Kalem remembered, and he called out with a raspy breathless voice, "Ra Mu! Mayleena! Etta! Ancient One, where is your Spirit Sound? Hear me! Hu-u-u-u-u-u-u-u!"

He started to choke, gasping for breath. Now only a few feet away from Kalem, Sen Dar intensified the green beam hitting his body.

"Oh no, my Captain!" he stated with angry, vicious delight, "I want you to know what it's like. You won't die quickly, but you will be senile before the end. Finally... now I have you! Yes... call upon your stupid Ancient One!"

Master Lumiera and Master Ra Mu, with his staff, gripped in his right hand, were walking back into the central chamber of one of the three huge pyramids located in the domed city of the Adepts with Mayleena between them. Etta was slowly flying behind her with his tail glowing opalescent. Both Ra Mu and Lumiera appeared anxiously concerned. They quickly ushered Mayleena over by the three white chairs in the center of the pyramid chamber. Etta landed on another chair, disappearing for a moment behind its tall back, then he quickly popped his head up with his hands grasping the top of the chair, looking wide-eyed with concern at Master Ra Mu.

"There's no time to explain it to either of you now," urgently stated Ra Mu. "Kalem needs your help, or it will be too late for him. Both of you close your eyes and silently begin to send out the telepathic link HU sound to connect with The Ancient One's omnipresent living Sound. The Ancient One will then instruct you, and you will both know what to do. Now quickly, do as I say!"

Mayleena and Etta both closed their eyes and started concentrating. The Ancient One's Sound current instantly filled the chamber. A whirling gold light appeared through the top of the pyramid roof again that washed down over their bodies. Then it curved right out through the far wall of the pyramid chamber. The two Master Teachers compassionately looked on several feet away. Both Mayleena's and Etta's true radiant Atma or Soul-self spheres appeared emerging out of the top of the heads of their physical bodies. Both spheres darted right through the walls riding upon the gold light that rapidly receded behind them until it too disappeared through the chamber wall.

"The final test has come!" stated Master Lumiera gazing at Master Ra Mu. "They must not flinch in their trust of The Ancient One, or their lives will end, as will Earth and its people in the dimension on this Earth parallel to us here."

Ra Mu confidently encouraged, "Their love for each other is very strong. We will see!"

Just as the bald, shriveled old man that was now Kalem grabbed his heart and started to keel over in his final death throes, the Sound of The Ancient One began to fill the mountain cavern hidden in the bizarre, much higher parallel dimension of the physical universe. Sen Dar suddenly appeared stumped, and he very nervously glanced around himself while he kept pouring on the green light death beam around Kalem's succumbing body. Kalem doubled over on the ground, shaking. In the next instant, Kalem was enveloped in blue light, and Sen Dar's beam was reverted back toward him with such force it burned his hands and clothes before he could turn it off. He was momentarily stunned before he screamed out in pain and ran away from Kalem to the middle of the arched bridge. Kalem quickly reverted to his normal age and health with new hair, and he took several relieving deep breaths of fresh air before he gazed quite peeved in Sen Dar's direction.

But Sen Dar was quick on his mental feet, and he waved a spell from his right hand. A transparent Mayleena suddenly appeared right behind Kalem and lovingly called to him. Kalem spun around, and the false Mayleena embraced him before he could react. Kalem staggered on his feet while she began to kiss him passionately. His legs weakened as the blue light surrounding his body diminished intensity. The Spirit Sound dwindled, then vanished, and he fell to his knees, turning back into a shriveled old man again, and Sen Dar continued to drain his life force. Kalem was now too weak to break the spell, and Sen Dar straightened up. His burnt hands and clothes renewed themselves. Another blue light disc appeared under his feet, and he levitated up above the bridge. He began to grin wide in Kalem's direction with hideous glee, just as the false Mayleena began to choke Kalem with both hands, viciously laughing. Then a false Etta appeared next to Kalem and bit him hard on one of his shriveled hands. He struggled to pull his hand away and fell over on to an elbow. Sen Dar's palms emitted another more powerful burst of the green energy beam at Kalem, and Kalem's body began to dissolve while the beam slowly pushed him and the false Mayleena choking him to the edge of the plateau near the bridge. She released her chokehold on him and started to shove him over the edge. Just then, the true radiant light spheres of Mayleena and Etta appeared coming right out of the back wall of the cavern behind Kalem. They quickly materialized into luminous forms that looked identical to the false forms, but they were made of thousands of brighter radiant points of blue light than their false counterparts. Mayleena's form screamed with terror at seeing Kalem almost destroyed, and she raced up behind the false Mayleena, grabbed her by the back of the neck with great force, ripping her backward away from Kalem, spun her around, and pushed her backward over the edge of the plateau. As the false Mayleena tumbled down toward the molten red abyss, her terrified fading screams echoed throughout the cavern. She hit the fiery liquid and instantly burned into a twisted violet vapor that spiraled upward above the bridge and vanished.

The real Etta darted over to the false Etta, chomped down on the back of its neck, and violently shook it until its neck broke with a loud… CRACK. He tossed the false Etta's limp body over the plateau. It too plunged into the molten liquid and burned into a twisted violet vapor that spiraled upward above the bridge and vanished. The green beam coming from Sen Dar began to weaken drastically, and The Ancient One's Spirit Sound returned more powerfully, filling the cavern. Kalem's body quickly reverted to its normal healthy state again, and a brighter, more powerful blue aura reappeared around him. Kalem immediately extended his hands toward Sen Dar with his palms out, and powerful blue beams were emitted from them that joined together and pushed the green beam back. Sen Dar was now straining to hold his beam in place against Kalem's beam, then slipped to one knee as his strength began to give out. The blue beam increased intensity and disintegrated the green beam as it pushed it back toward Sen Dar until the blue beam enveloped his body and knocked him back away from the bridge to the opposite plateau wall. The disc vanished under his feet, and he dropped exhausted to the cavern floor with his clothes steaming. Yet, he appeared unhurt and quickly got up, then waved his hands again. Both Mayleena's and Etta's finer energy forms were instantly encased in transparent fiery walls of energy. They struggled to escape but remained trapped inside. In another instant, Sen Dar threw an energy fireball toward Kalem's feet, and it blew away the ledge out from under him. Kalem tumbled toward the molten abyss, and Sen Dar grinned, self-satisfied like a mad devil. But in the next instant, as he fell, Kalem threw a similar blue fireball at Sen Dar's plateau ledge, blowing it away, and Sen Dar screamed before he fell head-over-heels toward the molten liquid.

The fiery energy walls around Mayleena's and Etta's luminous forms vanished, and Mayleena screamed out, "Kalem, I love you! Trust us and The Ancient One with all your heart!"

Kalem's feet nearly hit the fiery lava when he suddenly stopped his fall with a blue luminous disc that appeared under his feet, and he levitated back up level with the bridge. Sen Dar almost hit the lava before he gathered his wits about him just in time, and he too levitated up level with the bridge on a blue disc of his own. He grinned at Kalem, took a big breath, and shot another green beam from his palms toward Kalem. It hit the transparent blue light field surrounding his body, weakening it once again.

"Great Ancient One, be with me. I trust you! I love you, Mayleena, and our dear friend, Etta. Hu-u-u-u-u-u-u…" and Kalem lifted his palms pointed toward Sen Dar.

Another powerful blue beam was instantly emitted from Kalem's palms that once again pushed Sen Dar's green beam back to the center point between them. Sen Dar's smile dropped to real worry. He gritted his teeth and struggled to push Kalem's blue beam back a few feet. The Sound intensified, and Kalem's beam strengthened, pushing Sen Dar's beam back until the green energy was splashing away from his body in every direction. He was now frightened out of his wits. Then his strength suddenly failed, and the blue light seared his hands, and he hunched over his energy disc, turning into a shriveled old man. His clothes began to smolder from the heat. The blue disc below him dissolved, and he screamed, then fell tumbling down toward the fiery molten abyss.

Time mysteriously slowed down for him as he continued to fall end-over-end. His face was a mask of terror while he raced to meet the molten liquid. Then he struggled to grab The Ancient One's crystal he still had hung on the gold chain around his neck inside his shirt, reached in, and pulled it out. The Crystal lit-up glowing green radiant light through his clenched fingers, and his body turned into particles of gold light that faded and vanished just inches from the bubbling molten liquid.

Time resumed its normal rate a moment later, just as he materialized inside his ship in front of the control console, clutching The Ancient One's glowing green crystal with a very shriveled bony right hand. Bent over, appearing to be a-hundred-and-fifty years old, he stumbled over to the control board and placed the palms of his two thin bony hands over the top of the semispheric guidance controls. He momentarily withdrew them, his eyes filled with rage, and his pupils actually began glowing red.

"Somehow..." he stated to himself in an old shaking raspy voice, and he coughed, gasping for air, "one day I'll return and destroy all of you! For now, Captain, I'll just leave you in this place to rot!"

He coughed again and began to chuckle weakly, but he stopped, grabbing his chest in pain, then placed his hands on the domed-shaped guidance controls, lighting them up.

Sen Dar's customized elongated triangular, slightly batwing shaped Zon ship, lit up with the pale-red light surrounding the hull, was emitting a faint high-pitched wining. It lifted off the plateau that extended out from the mountainside by the cascading luminous waterfall. As it stopped to hover sixty feet in the air, the hull pulsed, and a red oval fireball was shot from it down to Kalem's landed ship, blowing a gaping hole in its side, and the ship slowly tiled over smoldering. Sen Dar's ship then darted in an arc up into the strange deep-blue atmosphere that surrounded the mysterious - Isle of Banion. It stopped to briefly hover, and then darted high over the oval valley passing over the distant tall black pinnacles. It quickly faded into the far distant deep-blue atmosphere within the bizarre higher parallel dimension of the physical universe.

Impassioned, Mayleena's luminous physical form was crying as she stood by Etta's luminous physical form on the plateau next to the beginning of the arched bridge. Kalem hovered on the blue luminous energy disc supporting him to the plateau, and as the disc vanished, he landed on his feet next to them.

"I love you, my impractical Captain!" she lovingly stated.

Kalem reached out to take her hand; but his own hand passed right through hers. He reached out to touch Etta's head, but his hand also passed right through Etta's radiant transparent body. Kalem frowned just as both Mayleena's and Etta's forms turned back into their true Atma radiant spherical or Soul-self forms. He watched, disappointed, as they floated back over to the back cavern wall behind him and disappeared right into it. Kalem was now quite fatigued, but he managed a cheerful chuckle.

"So that's what Ra Mu and Lumiera meant," he curiously stated to himself. "Mayleena and Etta weren't really physically here at all." And he bowed his head, then silently thought to himself, *I thank you for these friends, great living sound of The Ancient One, the Source behind and supporting of all life.* He chuckled again and said aloud with a quirky grin, "Ra Mu, you rascal! How did you do it?"

He turned around and slowly walked up the arched bridge. He stopped in the middle to briefly gaze down at the dangerous molten abyss where he'd almost perished, then resumed his walk down the other side of the bridge and across the plateau on the other side. He stopped again by the carved steps to turn around and gaze one last time at the mysterious deserted alien cavern of the long-departed alien Seres race. Then he headed back down the carved steps that descended in a gentle curve to the left below the falling water.

Kalem was casually jogging down the carved stairs when he appeared coming out from behind the waterfall just below the waterfall's source, thundering out of the cavern opening. He continued down the twenty feet of stairs to the mountainside plateau ledge, and he stopped dismayed to gaze down at his wrecked ship still smoldering with a gaping hole in its side. He sat down on the last step, exhausted and breathing hard.

"The vial bastard!" he softly said to himself.

He placed his forehead on top of his hands as he crossed them across his knees and began to hear Ra Mu's chuckling telepathic voice.

Oh… don't lose heart now, Captain. Concentrate on your love for Mayleena, Etta, and The Ancient One's omnipresent living sound. Connect with it. That energy behind all matter is not nuclear in nature. It can then bring you home another way since, shall we say, your ride is retired for now.

And Kalem heard Master Ra Mu chuckle again as he lifted his head up from his crossed arms to take in a deep relieving breath, grinned, and said aloud, "That's the best news I've heard all day. I was beginning to imagine how long the walk back from this place would be."

He shook his tired head with a sigh and slowly stood up, rubbed his eyes with his fingers, closed his eyes, and slightly bowed his head. A whirling white light appeared above his head, along with The Ancient One's beautiful multilevel radiant Sound. The whirling light enveloped him, passing down over his entire body, transforming it into his true Atma or Soul-self energy sphere. It slowly vanished with the dissipating Light and Sound.

Ra Mu, Lumiera, and Mayleena were now all standing near the center of the pyramid chamber, and Etta was hovering above his chair near them. The clear quartz staff held in Ra Mu's right hand was glowing with white-golden light, and a beam of the light was emanating into the room from the round, oval opening in the Ankh symbol that crowned it. Mayleena and Etta were wide-eyed in anticipation of what was about to happen next. Tears ran down Mayleena's cheeks, and Etta began to nervously hover back and forth.

Knowingly smiling, Master Ra Mu and Master Lumiera watched as the beautiful uplifting Spirit Sound of The Ancient One began to loudly resound in the chamber. Kalem swiftly materializes near them with his eyes still closed, and head slightly bowed. The whirling light surrounding him dwindled, leaving him standing there. As he opened his eyes, the light whirling around him withdrew back into the Ankh symbol that crowned Ra Mu's staff, and the staff shut off. Master Ra Mu lowered the staff and grinned pleased at Kalem. Though weary, Kalem forced a haggard smile, and Mayleena jumped with delight into his tired arms. Etta flew over and hovered in front of him with a big relieved grin. Kalem smiled at him, then passionately hugged Mayleena with his own joyful eyes tearing. He let her go to proudly salute Etta, and Etta proudly saluted him back. Then he reached out and shook Etta's hand.

"Welcome back, Captain!" said Ra Mu upbeat. "You didn't think your friends would desert you at the last minute, did you?"

Kalem gratefully smiled at Ra Mu, then Lumiera, followed by Etta, and finally quite tenderly at Mayleena as he brushed away a tear from her cheek. To them, time seemed to stop as their eyes, now alive with delight, embraced one another in the timeless stillness of their silent loving communication. They could hear no sound now; except the gentle beating of two hearts that now beat in rhythmic harmony as one. Moments passed, then Kalem reached out his arm and tightly clasped forearms like a brother with Ra Mu and then Lumiera.

"I thank The Ancient One for all of you," he said, very relieved before he curiously added, "Something happened back there when it looked like I had no way out. The energy of you, my friends, entered me, and it made me fearless of death. Then the Spirit Sound of The Ancient One embraced me, and I wasn't angry at Sen Dar anymore. Instead, I began to pity him while he blindly continued to do battle because of the great anger he could not release. Now... I wonder what will become of him?"

Very pleased, Master Ra Mu replied, "You have overcome the largest part of the little self in man, Kalem. You have now become more like the loving omnipresent Sound and Light nature of - The Ancient One or Prime Creator – the 'Source' behind and supporting all that exists in the grand multidimensional creation. However, now a defeated, shriveled old man, Sen Dar is experiencing to some degree the repercussions of his own misuse of free will, power, and the gift of life. It will be a long time, if ever before he can cause any more mischief." He cheerfully grinned at Kalem and Mayleena and then said, changing the subject, "Well, come on, you two! Do you know what day this is?" He paused, but they seemed puzzled as he continued, "No? As I recall, a marriage is to take place before The Ancient One." He cheerfully looked at Etta and stated, "Etta, I believe you would serve nicely as best man. Are you up for it?"

Etta's big bulbous deep-blue eyes widened with joyful surprise, and he proudly flew around them several times. Then in one big excitement, he darted out of the triangular opening exit from the sacred pyramid chamber. They all chuckled at his naturally cute antics. Lumiera then nodded to Kalem and Mayleena. Kalem clasped her slender hand, and they casually walked together out of the pyramid chamber.

Master Ra Mu turned to the elder Master Lumiera and said, "Now I will make brief visits to General Faldwell, Judith, the President of The United States and to Master Starland, followed by the leaders of Russia and China. They will all want to know Earth will be safe from any further Zon threat and anyone like Sen Dar for the time being. I'll then pay a quick visit to the Zon High Commander Luboc to make certain he truly understands how he was controlled and manipulated against his will by Sen Dar. After that, I believe he will choose a new direction for his people. I will return soon to join the wedding couple before the time arrives. Farewell, for now, my dear former Master teacher."

Lumiera was already grinning wide as Ra Mu clasps his forearms with him with a nod of his head. Then Ra Mu simply faded into vaporous wisps of light that vanished, and Lumiera cheerfully turned and walked out of the sacred pyramid chamber.

CAN'T YOU KNOCK LIKE ANYONE ELSE?

*H*arry and Judith were asleep in their home in the suburbs outside of Washington, D.C., when Master Ra Mu arrived once again unannounced. A tiny blue six-pointed blue star appeared at the foot of their bed, with The Ancient One's uplifting Spirit Sound growing louder. The star whirling into the radiant sphere of his Atma-self, surrounded by a faint golden aura. Harry's snoring was so loud, Ra Mu's impish voice chuckled,

Oh... Har... ry. General Fald... well. Ju... dith. Judith? And he shouted, *Harry and Judith, wake up!* But they didn't stir, and he said to himself, *Oh well, I guess I'll have to do this the hard way... again.*

Harry was sleeping on his back on the far side of the bed, loudly snoring, and Judith was lying on her side by him facing the window, wearing a gentle smile. A pervasive glow appeared under the top sheet covering them with dozens of hand-like movements that started to massage both of their clueless sleeping bodies. They both startled awake and immediately backed up to the headboard pulling the sheet up around them with astonished groggy looks, just as the radiant sphere whirled and transformed into Ra Mu's physical body. He was surrounded by a faint golden aura, gripping the clear crystal staff in his right hand. Harry and Judith glanced at each other to be sure they weren't dreaming, rubbed their eyes, then stared, beginning to frown back at Ra Mu.

"Can't you knock like anyone else?" they simultaneously sputtered out.

Nodding with a chuckle, Ra Mu replied, "Like I said to you once before, Harry, your snoring is so loud an earthquake couldn't get through it, and I've been in some really big ones!"

"Oh gee... thanks, I guess!" shot back Harry, annoyed anyway.

Of course, Judith was also annoyed and embarrassed. She pulled the sheet up tighter under her neck, and she was about to give Ra Mu a piece of her mind when he wisely interrupted her.

"Judith, my dear, there isn't enough time for me to wait until morning to contact either of you, as I have other pressing matters to attend to. But I wanted you both to know the Zon attack has been thwarted. All of the Zon Scout fighters were destroyed in the battle, except for Sen Dar's ship, and he is on the run in another dimension far away from Earth with a fearless Galactic Alliance pilot on his tail. You can both rest easy for now. However, you must inform the President of these facts and encourage him to send a diplomatic mission to the Zon High Commander Luboc. He will be prepared to meet with you after I've met him first to make certain all of Sen Dar's influence upon him and the other Zon people are gone. When we're ready, Admiral Starland will contact you and send a Scout ship to pick you up in a discrete location at night. The pilot will escort you through the 'South Polar Interdimensional Transit Window' into their parallel dimension on this Earth. This will be the first of many diplomatic meetings you will likely both be attending."

Harry was already nodding his head and confirmed, "President Stockwell has already indicated he wants us to visit the new Zon leader and get a treaty signed a.s.a.p. I'm sure he'll authorize the journey once we inform him of your visit with us here tonight."

Judith politely confirmed, "I'll be going along with Harry as a diplomatic liaison between our own parallel dimension and the Zon domain. We hope to establish a United Nations embassy there and have the Zon people establish their embassy in Washington. After that, we can facilitate trade relations and sustain a lasting peace. Will that do, Master Ra Mu?"

"That will do nicely for now. You will be planet Earth's first official interdimensional representative, Diplomat Judith Cranston," cheerfully encouraged Ra Mu grinning wide.

Blushing, Judith replied elated, "Oh... I do like the sound of that!"

Harry winced at the sound of it and rolled his eyes just as she looked up at him, but he grinned at her upbeat and stated, "That would be ideal, dear!"

"General Faldwell," continued Ra Mu to get Harry's attention, "when the meeting between you two and Luboc has been arranged, I will meet you there to assure that a secret trust can exist between the people of Earth and the Zon race. The United Nations could represent the leaders of Earth, but I don't believe it is the right time just yet to let the masses on the planet know about the Zon or any other extraterrestrial races. Well, that is until they are first properly prepared for full-disclosure."

"Right, we'll keep this whole thing classified until it appears clear we can no longer keep it from them," enthusiastically shot back Harry. "They are being prepared for complete disclosure in that regard even now. Will that do?"

"That will do just fine, General. Eventually, the people of Earth should know they are not alone in the universe, but this can only happen when your world leaders can work together in harmony, especially in regards to ventures outside your own planet. Well, I wish you both the best and do forgive me for my unannounced visit, although I believe you will now both agree it was an important one."

Harry looked at Judith, and she grinned back up at him. Then they both gazed at Ra Mu and nodded their complete agreement.

"For now, farewell!" he kindly stated, smiling back at them.

His body then transformed back into his true spherical Atma-self that whirled back into a tiny six-pointed blue star. It faded away with The Ancient One's Sound.

Harry rubbed his chin and said, astonished, "I'd really like to know how on Earth he does that!"

He threw off the sheet, revealing his boxer shorts and white tee shirt underneath. Then Judith dropped the sheet held up in her hands under her neck, revealing her light-blue lacy pajamas, and they both stood up on each side of the bed. They walked around to the foot of the bed and briefly waved their arms through the air where Ra Mu had materialized. Amazed, they looked at each other and tightly embraced for a few moments before Harry let her go to walk over to the table at the head of his side of the bed.

He picked up a special phone, dialed three numbers, and said very enthusiastically, "Mr. President, this is General Faldwell. Yes... yes, I know it's late, but we just had a very special visitor in our bedroom. We now officially have Master Ra Mu on our side to bridge the gap between the Zon race and us. The game is on." Harry paused to listen and replied, "You bet your ass we're ready. I'll fill you in at the White House tomorrow morning." He listened again and then confirmed, "Right Sir, we'll be there at ten sharp. Goodnight, Mr. President, and pleasant dreams."

Harry hung up the phone and seriously gazed at his wife. She gazed back just as seriously, and they both headed for the bathroom.

A BRIDGE TO UNDERSTANDING

$\mathcal{M}$orning light was pouring through the overhead windows down into the sacred meeting chamber of Zol Yul over High Commander Luboc. The wide rectangular room was made out of green marble floors and walls with Greek-style blue granite pillars, spaced apart every four feet, that held up the ceiling made of highly polished, intricately carved dark wood. Luboc appeared to be asleep with his head on his crossed arms while he sat in an intricately carved high-backed, polished dark wooden chair. It was placed behind the shorter base of an elongated triangular, polished black obsidian table by the back wall. The two longer sides of the table came to a point facing the wall opposite him, focused toward two larger Greek-style blue granite pillars that adorned each side of a wide rectangular opening. A set of blue granite steps just beyond them led steeply upward below a large bust of Zol Yul carved into the arched header above the entryway. Four more tall backed, richly carved wooden chairs were positioned with two along each side of the longer triangular table. A single lamp attached to the center of the ceiling made from gold was shaped like a long flexible spiral tube that extended down six feet ending several feet above the table's center. Attached to the end was a pale-blue triangular glass shade that covered another smaller triangular-shaped, unlit glass light source.

At the back wall just to Luboc's left side was another smaller rectangular entryway and another set of narrower blue granite steps that lead steeply upward. Ra Mu's six-pointed blue star materialized in front of the desk and transformed into the radiant sphere of his true Atma-sphere, surrounded by a faint golden aura. The uplifting melody of The Ancient One's Sound began and gently increased in volume as the sphere transformed again into Ra Mu's physical self, surrounded by a golden aura. He was holding his clear quartz crystal staff clenched in his right hand. Luboc stirred awake, then slowly lifted his head to notice Ra Mu. He jumped frightened out of the chair, drawing his silver beam weapon, and immediately fired it. The thin red laser beam harmlessly bounced off the golden aura surrounding Ra Mu, and Luboc fired several more times with the same harmless effect.

Ra Mu smiled and kindly said, "High Commander Luboc, I am referred to as Master Ra Mu. I am not here to harm anyone, and you will not be harmed by me."

Luboc looked down at his weapon and slowly lowered the gun to his side.

"Are you a demon?" he fearfully demanded.

"No, High Commander!" Ra Mu forcefully replied. "I am part of a secret order of Adepts that assist individuals to reach higher states of awareness. We are stationed on this and many other worlds in the physical universe and in the higher dimensions beyond it, but that isn't important at this time. By now, you must have figured out that Sen Dar is not who he pretended to be. He is really a destructive renegade from another world that you know nothing about. He came here to try and gain back the power he had over many worlds that he lost due to his misuse of free will and the rights of others. His control over you is now gone, and he has fled away into an unusual cowardly retreat after your ships were defeated in their attempt to destroy people living in a parallel dimension on this Earth. You had no right to attack the Earth people, and they can now become your new friends. They will respect your right to your own domain in this parallel dimension much better than the disrespect you showed to them. What do you say, High Commander? Do you want to establish diplomatic relationships with them? Do you want peace between your two parallel dimension realities on this planet?"

Luboc sadly cast his head down and placed the silver gun on the tabletop. The golden aura around Ra Mu vanished as Luboc looked back up forlorn, and he slumped exhausted in the chair.

"What have we done?" he said, shaking his head. "I never trusted that vicious one! He was far more ruthless than we had been in our conquests of many worlds in our own domain in space. He had us all fooled with that crystal he wore. I don't think any of us would have ever cooperated with him in the first place if he had not used it, but he does look exactly like Lord Zol Yul, who disappeared from us so many generations ago. It was Lord Zol Yul that first assisted us to evolve our culture and science. We thought he had returned to fulfill the ancient prophecy - to take us to greater heights of awareness."

Ra Mu kindly replied, "Yes, they are very much alike; but it will take you a few years before you come to understand why that could be and how he came to be here in this lifetime. I can tell you there have been so many other lifetimes for Sen Dar, you, and your people. Trust me! One day, you will come to know the truth of this."

"I... I do not understand!" replied Luboc mystified.

"One day, my friend, you will, and you won't be alone," compassionately stated Ra Mu. "Would you like to know how you came to be in this life now and where you came from before you were born?"

Luboc thoughtfully lowered his tired head, then looked back up and answered, "When I look at the stars at night, I often wonder what life is all about and how I came to exist. Our endless conquering of other worlds came about for the most part without much bloodshed, for we always had superior technology and weaponry over those we came to dominate. In the end, all those civilizations in other worlds benefited from what we taught them. They have all become abundant, constructive civilizations. Yet, constant conquest has left me empty inside. Sen Dar killed the last High Priest that controlled our destiny right after he appeared here. Because of the way it happened, we naturally began to follow him as Zol Yul, but I knew something was not right. Now, what will we do?"

Ra Mu kindly replied, "You can head in a new direction. The people in the parallel dimension you attacked have something called Democracy. It isn't perfect by any means, but it allows all the people in those countries who practice it to have a say in who will rule their governments for them and how they wish to live. You could learn from them, especially the representatives I can send here from the country you and Sen Dar were about to attack called the United States. Would you like your people to rise to that higher level Zol Yul promised your people would come about one day?"

Luboc rose from his chair with renewed interest, and he walked around the triangular desk to stand in front of Ra Mu. He looked up at the windows and the morning sunlight streaming down into the room, and then he grinned at Ra Mu with a peacefully resolute gaze and nodded.

"I will have to consult with the other Commanders first, now that we have no head of our government. They may just find this new approach very refreshing since our way of life was wearing on us all. We have often talked about a need for change, but we had no idea what direction to take in order to bring about real change. Our Priest leaders would not listen, but I believe I could convince the others to receive the diplomats from the other parallel reality, and maybe... just maybe... it could work. Let me try."

Luboc humbly bowed to Ra Mu, and Ra Mu eloquently stated, "High Commander, there is no need to bow before me like you did to the tyrant Sen Dar. Only mutual respect is required."

Luboc looked relieved and cheerfully replied, "That... is exactly what we have all been looking for. We have wanted to grow more, but we are not able to do this under our current imperial system." He paused and then courageously stated, "Now something must change!" He thoughtfully looked away again, then back at Ra Mu with renewed enthusiasm and asked, "When I have the agreement from the other Commanders, how will I contact you?"

Ra Mu opened his hand, and the clear spherical crystal with a red ruby embedded in its center that he'd given to other beings at several points in the past appeared on his palm. He carefully reached his hand out to Luboc. The High Commander cautiously reached out and grasped the sphere, curiously looked it over, then gazed questioningly back at Master Ra Mu.

"When your people are ready," stated Ra Mu, "place this crystal on the floor when you are alone and call my name Ra Mu three times. Then I will come to assist you further. You and your people's actions in the next few days could result in great benefits for the Zon race and for all the people living in the parallel dimension that you can now access. Thank you, Commander Luboc, for trusting in what your heart tells you is the truth. Now I must leave you, for I have other pressing matters to attend to. Farewell, High Commander of the Zon people!"

Ra Mu reached out his arm, and Luboc clasped forearms with him, then he stepped back a few feet to hold his staff out at arm's length, and the golden glow reappeared around his body. He quickly transformed back into the radiant sphere of his true Atma-self, and it dwindled back into the small six-pointed blue star before it simply faded away with The Ancient One's uplifting omnipresent Sound.

Luboc stood there staring, amazed at the empty space where Master Ra Mu had just been. Then he slowly gazed down at the crystal sphere held in the palm of his hand, and a genuinely happy smile appeared on his face for the first time in many years. He cheerfully looked back up as he put the crystal sphere in his pocket. Then he turned around, walked at a brisk pace past the triangular table to the back of the room, through the smaller rectangular opening, and up the steep marble stairs toward the surface of the ceremonial landing pyramid.

CHAPTER TWENTY-ONE

TWO NEW DIPLOMATS HEAD SOUTH

An Air Force helicopter approached the mysterious backside of Mt. Shasta in northern California, high over the forest treetops. Then it hovered down and landed in a circular clearing on the first fresh winter snow a few days into the new year. The helicopter's side door swung open backward on rails, and General Harry Faldwell, wearing an Air Force winter coat with the fur-lined hood pulled back, was helped down the steps to the snow-covered ground by a man wearing shades and a dark suit. Then Judith appeared wearing the same type of winter coat, and Harry took her hand as she jumped off the last step to the ground. Harry waved goodbye to the suited man, and he closed the door. They stepped back as the helicopter lifted off the snow, and watched it slowly head up and over the tops of the surrounding forest trees, until it leveled off and sped away into the distant clear blue sky.

Harry hugged his wife and said upbeat, "Well, my dear, we've both stuck our feet deep in the thick of it now."

"Would you want it any other way?" she inquired, grinning and winking at him.

He just grinned back at her and took her hand as they began to trudge together through two feet of fresh powder snow, headed toward another larger clearing twenty feet further away they could see through a narrow gap in the forest trees.

Minutes later, they stopped at the center of the larger clearing near the base of the flat gray rock wall entrance that, when activated, opens a tunnel leading into the Guardians' secret Mt. Shasta base. They expectantly looked around themselves, then lifted their heads upward when they began to faintly hear a low frequency humming sound, gradually growing louder as if something was headed down toward them from high in the sky beside the glacial covered extinct volcanic mountain. A single much larger but less streamlined Scout class ship appeared hovering down through the donut-shaped cloud cover that hid the top of the mountain peak from view. It was soon lowering to land on the nearby snow. The thin blue aura around the hull faded, then went out, and an opening door appeared in the side of the hull where no seam had been apparent. As steps lowered from it to the ground, Master Ra Mu stood in the doorway with his crystal staff gripped in his right hand, and Lieutenant Moreau stood beside him, waving them aboard. Harry and Judith waved back and walked up the ramp as Ra Mu and Moreau stood aside to let them enter the ship. Then they walked inside behind them.

A moment later, the ramp withdrew, the door closed, and the seam vanished. The hull of the larger Scout class ship lit back up with a pale-blue aura, emitting the characteristic low-frequency humming, and the ship lifted off the ground. It momentarily stopped to hover fifty feet above the ground and then darted upward in a gradual arc, punching an upward whirling hole in the cloud cover surrounding the mountain summit.

Harry, and Judith were standing huddled around Lieutenant Moreau, who was just sitting down in the chair in front of the semicircular control console. Then he looked up at the wide holographic projected viewscreen behind the back of the control console.

"Welcome, you two," Ra Mu cordially stated, grinning wide at both of them. "I'm glad to see you here on time. Let me introduce our pilot, Lieutenant Moreau of The Galactic Interdimensional Alliance of Free Worlds."

Moreau turned his head and shook Harry's hand, then Judith's, and said smiling, "Welcome aboard. I've heard good things about you two from Master Ra Mu and Admiral Starland, the head of our space fleet. You should know it will take about a half-hour to pass through the South Polar Interdimensional Transit Window and arrive at our destination on the Zon landing pyramid. Until then, you can be seated for the ride, or if you like, I can leave the viewscreen on so you can observe our passage through the atmosphere around Earth to the South Pole area.

Harry curiously asked, "You're Captain Kalem's childhood friend. Am I right?"

"That's correct, General Faldwell. I think I know how you now understand that," jovially replied Moreau over his shoulder.

Harry looked at the viewscreen to see that the ship was already swiftly passing high over the ocean headed southward.

Glancing briefly over his shoulder, Moreau stated, "I experienced the record log of your entire journey here that started 100,000 years ago in your own parallel dimension. It was Master Ra Mu that gave me the experience when I was taken to the protected Parallel Lemuria dimension. General Faldwell, I believe you had the same experience, before I went through it."

And Harry looked appreciatively over at Ra Mu, who just nodded his head smiling, while Judith looked up at her husband with a curious expression.

"Harry, you never told me about that," she commented with greater respect for him than before.

Harry shrugged it off and replied, "Look, Judith, I didn't think you'd be ready to understand what I went through during that time. Hell, I barely comprehend it myself even now."

And he gazed expectantly at Ra Mu for some help, but Ra Mu cleverly changed the subject by turning his attention to Judith and he graciously smiled.

"Judith, please thank your President for his assistance with your United Nations representatives to write up and approve the treaty proposal for the Zon race. I also believe that he could not have succeeded without your assistance in drafting it in the first place. And General Faldwell, without the encouraging confidence you displayed for him that helped him overcome his fears, he wouldn't have had the courage to trust any Zon after what they did under Sen Dar's control."

Judith smiled and nodded at Ra Mu.

"Sam Stockwell is a hard nut to crack," jubilantly interjected Harry. "I'll grant you that; but once he's aboard, he'll stick to his guns and follow a decision through. Now it's up to both Judith and myself to see that the Zon race under Luboc's temporary command cooperate fully to sign the damned thing before something else happens to give them second thoughts, right Judith?"

She smiled up at her husband and then looked to Ra Mu, "From what you told us about your visit with Luboc, Master Ra Mu, I'd venture to guess he'll be looking forward to our arrival on their ceremonial landing pyramid. I, for one, am looking forward to meeting him."

Harry took the cigar from his mouth and added, "I only hope they'll be willing to share their technology with us, and there's a lot we can offer their people that could benefit them. To maintain lasting peace, we'll have to develop ships like they have, or we'll always be vulnerable to another attack from them or some other alien race."

"Relax your fears as a General for now and just offer them sincere friendship," patiently encouraged Master Ra Mu. "They have never known the concept of friendship with other races before, and it may be a key to obtaining what you're after."

Harry nodded, then stuffed his unlit cigar back into the corner of his mouth and bit down. Judith stuck her arm through his and appreciatively grinned up at him.

The larger Scout ship was soon flying over the coastline along the South Polar icecap, and it sped further inland then dramatically slowed and stopped to hover in front of the invisible 'South Polar Interdimensional Transit Window.' Then it slowly moved forward, disappearing a little at a time until it vanished inside, leaving a cold, crystal clear blue sky over the wide background of ice and snow that spread out to the horizon in every direction.

High in the atmosphere in the Zon domain, the larger Scout ship began to reappear a little at a time as it passed out of the other side of the invisible vortex. It continued another hundred feet before it stopped to hover in an alien late afternoon clear blue sky. The Zon ceremonial pyramid and the tall black volcanic glacial crowned mountain further behind it, with the massive Zon citadel built at the base, were twenty miles further away in the far background. The Zon city surrounding the base of the mountain and pyramid spread out below the ship for many miles, until the city dwindled into the rough rocky volcanic terrain. Wide plateaus receded one after the other away from the larger Scout spacecraft. The ship pulsed blue light and sped into the distance until it dwindled to a speck before it topped to hover above the landing pyramid.

Standing on the landing pyramid were High Commander Luboc and twelve other Zon warriors wearing weapons strapped at their sides. Two more Zon warriors dressed in Diplomatic attire were standing in a semicircle around the center of the landing pyramid as the larger Galactic Scout ship lowered and softy landed. The blue aura and low-frequency hum shut off. A seam appeared revealing the outline of a side hatch, and the hatch opened, then lowered stairs to the ground. Master Ra Mu, holding his crystal staff, gripped in his right hand, and some type of document under his left arm, and Lieutenant Moreau, wearing his clear crystal laser sidearm strapped in a holster at his side, walked through the opening and down the ramp first. Harry and Judith appeared, walking right behind him with Judith carrying a thick stack of bound treaty papers under her arm. The four of them walked toward High Commander Luboc and respectfully nodded to him and the other Zon commanders. They appeared pleased with the prospect of gaining new space-faring friends in an entirely separate parallel dimension of the physical universe, and a profound new destiny for the many billions of beings living in both parallel dimensions on Earth.

CHAPTER TWENTY-TWO

A RARE MARRIAGE AND A MISSION

$\mathcal{A}$ giant Oceanan Spectrum Crystal ship, with its many spires extended from its spherical cobalt-blue center, was landed at the edge of a lush two-foot-tall green grass field in the protected secret parallel Lemuria dimension on Earth. The clear domed city of the Guardians, covering the three giant white alabaster gold crowned and quartz-capped pyramids centered in the surrounding city, was several miles further away near the beginning base of the single snow-capped mountain. The massive ship was resting on the very gentle slope of a wide plateau just below an upper field filled with lovely flowers that looked like giant blue and violet orchids in full bloom that gradually climbed up the hillside. In the distance, as they gazed through the massive clear dome to the lower plateau, they could see a lush prehistoric-looking tropical jungle that extended several miles further away to a wide curved black sand dune beach cove.

Master Ra Mu, with his crystal staff in hand, and Master Lumiera were standing in the middle of the tall grass field. Etta was hovering between them with his tail glowing opalescent. Kalem was standing in front of them with his back to Mayleena, who was being lovingly embraced by her father, Oceanan leader Master Opellum.

"Be happy, dear daughter," he said to Mayleena, joyfully holding her at arm's length. "You and Kalem have a great destiny to fulfill together. Today you will both become complete within yourselves, with each other, and with The Ancient One. It is very rare for a man and a woman, or rather their two Atma-selves, to be married in this way. I know that it seems a riddle now, but you'll both understand what I've said at the right time. There is no hurry."

"Thank you, father," she gratefully replied in bliss.

Then she walked up to Kalem and tapped him on the shoulder. He turned around, threw his arms around her waist, and hugged her as he picked her up and spun her around, then set her back down. Master Ra Mu stepped in front of them and placed the Master Crystal Staff out in front of himself in the tall green grass, where it stood by itself held in place by an unseen power.

"This will be a marriage blessed before The Ancient One itself," he somberly stated and then grinned. "You both must honor this marriage as one born far beyond this world in the lofty home of your true Atma-selves on the Atma or Soul plane of being. You will be brought back together again as one and separate again to remain free individuals. Are you both ready?"

They solemnly nodded their approval, and Ra Mu folded his arms together across his chest, then slightly lowered his head. A wide golden vortex suddenly opened vertically, whirling in the sky far above them, and a white beam of white light shot down out of it that formed a white light cylinder around Ra Mu's body. Then the large luminous sphere of The Ancient One itself appeared coming down through the vortex opening. It appeared to be comprised of thousands of teardrops-shaped self-effulgent lights, built-in layers from a white central core through the color spectrum to a violet exterior, entirely surrounded by a pale-golden aura. Accompanying it was the omnipresent Sounds of its soft, soothing high, lilting flute melody mixed with the harmonious blending of full string harps, other stringed instruments, and woodwinds. Beautiful glass bells ringing from somewhere very far away were sounded as if they were coming closer with the intensifying Spirit Sound while The Ancient One moved closer.

Ra Mu raised his hands, palms out, toward Kalem and Mayleena, and beams of white light shot from his palms to painlessly enter their foreheads. Their bodies began to glow with the same light, and their two radiant Atma spheres appeared exactly like The Ancient One: except, much smaller, exited the tops of their heads and stopped to hover above their bodies. Opellum, Lumiera, and Etta had their heads respectfully bowed as The Ancient One moved down to hover a dozen feet above them. Then they all began to telepathically hear its deep melodious voice coming from the pulsating white light and gold-tinged center within its massive spherical radiance.

You are sanctified before the Source, the Center, or Prime Creator, also known as the all in all. You see before you the manifested eternal presence in all things, the life-sustaining omnipresent Sound or energy. What people call Divine Spirit or Divine Love is really this one life-sustaining Sound you hear and the Light you see within and without yourselves as the true individual spherically shaped living Atma or Soul. The true destiny of each Atma is not to worship the Source or The Ancient One, but rather to respect this Source, yourselves as true co-creative individuals with what you see before you, and all life in the multidimensional realities. You are each comprised of exactly the same eternal non-destructible living energy as Prime Creator. When the outer physical ears and eyes are closed and your inner world is calm, your true inner nature as the Sound and Light forever individualized surfaces in conscious awareness. The realization awakens that you are, in fact, the same identical nature as The Ancient One before you. Now you are beyond life and death and the temporal things of the lower worlds of time and space. Here in this moment of eternity, you are blended together again as one with each other and The Ancient One, as it was in the beginning. Do you know how many millions of lifetimes in many forms you each have lived on many worlds to come to this point? No? It matters not for now. However, you must live your lives freely and individually in true co-creative harmony and cooperation, one with the other and with The Ancient One before you. Gladly assist each other on your journey back to the true home of the Atma or Soul located in the lofty realm far above this Earth world. You are all now once again reminded of your long-forgotten original commission that was inherent within the center of each one of you. Remember to embrace each other in the new Ray of awareness in the HU, the Sound and Light of the omnipresent living energy presence that is behind and supporting all life and all that exists in the grand multidimensional creation. Then one day, you will journey back home to the higher realms, located far above the 'Void' known to some groups in the lower realities. There each of you will take your place as true co-creators with The Ancient One that you see before you - to be Master Teachers in your own right.

Kalem's and Mayleena's beautiful, radiant Atma spheres moved toward each other, then merged into one slightly larger, more energy-dense, and more brightly luminous sphere that began to sparkle like diamonds in bright sunlight. White light pulsed away from their joined sphere into the air in concentric circles for a few moments before the sphere moved up and merged inside The Ancient One itself. It was clearly hovering within it, appearing just as beautiful as the much larger Ancient One, but on a smaller scale. A moment passed, and their joined sphere came back out of The Ancient One to separate back into their individual Atma-self spheres. Then both spheres moved back above their physical bodies while The Ancient One continued to speak with its heart-moving heavenly benevolent voice.

Respect and cherish each other, The Ancient One before you, all life and all that exists in the grand multidimensional creation. Be of your own world regarding all life as a gift. Now you both know from personal experience the meaning of the ancient statement - I am always with you.

As Kalem's and Mayleena's true Atma energy spheres reentered their physical bodies through the tops of the heads, the beams of white light retracted from their foreheads back through Ra Mu's hands, and the cylinder of white light around his body retreated back up through the vortex opening high in the overhead sky. Ra Mu opened his eyes and looked up with the others to humbly observe The Ancient One as it swiftly flew back up into the heavens. It soon passed back through the opening to gradually dwindle to a speak of light high over the ethereal translucent crystalline towers and faceted crystal-like gem-studded domes. They spread across the heavenly realm on the other side of the vortex. Everyone gathered on the field continued to watch the rare vision in awe, as brilliant golden tiny atoms of light gently rained down upon them from the vortex opening, just before it whirled closed and faded from view.

Master Ra Mu looked down and keenly gazed with great joy into the blissfully tearing eyes of the just mystically married lovers.

"Now you know!" he stated, smiling wide from ear to ear. And he softly chuckled, then announced, "Master Opellum's Spectrum ship is awaiting."

But Kalem and Mayleena were still too transfixed, stunned with bliss, from the profound experience they just shared, and they didn't respond to him.

Then Ra Mu impishly grinned and said louder, "Hello in there! Is anybody home? I believe you two have a honeymoon to attend to on planet Oceana if I'm not mistaken."

Kalem and Mayleena both simultaneously blinked as they became aware of their surroundings once again. Master Opellum walked up to them with a joyful smile of his own. Master Lumiera was chuckling while Etta flew in front of their faces, excitedly chattering in Dren, very congratulatory, of course.

"Congratulations, you two!" cheerfully confirmed Opellum. "From the looks of it, you're both going to need a long honeymoon if you expect to be of any help to The Ancient One after that experience."

And he laughed loud and long at his own statement until everyone started to laugh with him.

Then Mayleena turned with Kalem toward Ra Mu, and Kalem gratefully said with a quirky grin, "You must have tremendous patience to believe in me. It couldn't have been easy."

A little embarrassed, Kalem looked at the ground and then back up with renewed courage to fondly gaze at Ra Mu, who continued to smile, apparently quite unaffected by what had just happened.

Then Kalem awkwardly approached Ra Mu, gave him a big bear hug, and let him go.

"You're welcome, Captain," delightfully chuckled Master Ra Mu.

Kalem shook his head, chuckling in response, and then he and Mayleena walked over to Master Lumiera. They began to thank him with respectful fond loving gazes and then followed it by gratefully embracing him.

Lumiera raised his right hand, palm up, in blessing and said with an encouraging smiling, glowing countenance, "Now, go in peace with the grace of - the Source, Prime Creator, or what you know as The Ancient One - that is now with both of you."

Grinning like children, Kalem and Mayleena walked up beside Master Opellum as he pointed to the huge waiting Oceanan Spectrum interdimensional spacecraft, and he cheerfully stated, "Newlyweds, your chariot awaits. May I be your personal guide?"

And the three of them began to walk away toward the waiting ship, but Opellum stopped to turn around and cheerfully gaze in Etta's direction, patiently hovering beside Ra Mu's side.

"Etta, my friend, have you forgotten yourself?" he loudly said with a cheerful grin. "Want to be left behind, or do you miss that lovely Dren bride of yours? I have a surprise for you too, my friend."

Etta was unconsciously smiling in his own state of bliss until Opellum spoke to him, and he shook his head. Then he screeched as a sudden realization hit him. He raced away from Ra Mu's side and up to Opellum to impatiently hover in front of him. Kalem and Mayleena looked toward the waiting spaceship as Opellum waved his hand toward it again. In the distance, a group of small specks coming toward them from the direction of the ship were rapidly growing larger as they approached, revealing Etta's wife Din with her long eyelashes and shapely feminine Dren characteristics. Beside her were their two playful male and female hovering Dren children – eleven and ten in Earth years. Etta's eyes bugged out excitedly, and he screeched again just before he raced past Opellum to hover beside Din and their children hovering at her side excitedly awaiting him. They all circled each other like happy bees hovering around a honey nest, and then Etta and Din tenderly rubbed noses together. The boy Dren climbed onto Etta's shoulders while Etta and Din both tightly cuddled their daughter between them. A few moments passed, and they separated. Din flew over to Opellum, hugged his neck with tears of joy streaming down her blushing red cheeks, and rubbed her nose on his. Etta turned toward the others and impishly wiggled his eyebrows up and down like the old comic actor Groucho Marks of the Mark's Brothers comic feature films, indicating some loving romance with his wife was in order. Then he spun back around and flew over to his two playful Dren children. Din joined them, and they flew as one very happy family toward the waiting Oceanan spaceship.

Pondering Etta's antics, Kalem grinned and stated, "Looks like Etta is in for a little quality second honeymoon vacation time himself. He's definitely earned it!"

Mayleena was standing with Opellum on her left side and Kalem on her right side as Kalem put his arm around her slender waist, and the three of them continued to walk toward the ship.

Kalem soon paused and curiously asked, "Um, Master Opellum, you mentioned your planet Oceana exists in a higher parallel dimension of the physical universe. Where exactly is that?"

Opellum paused to reflect and answered, "It's above, Captain, in a galaxy of stars within a finer dimensional reality than you understand at this point, but don't concern yourself with this for now. I'll explain it on the way. Shall we continue?"

And they casually continued their brisk walk together over the tall green grass field toward the massive Oceanan spaceship while Kalem continued to ponder Opellum's answer. Mayleena looked away with an impish grin, and Kalem glanced at her, then at Opellum with an inquiring gaze, but he didn't receive anything further from either of them. He shrugged his shoulders and cheerfully grinned anyway as they continued their walk. Mayleena turned around and waved goodbye to Ra Mu and Lumiera. Then Kalem waved goodbye, and both Masters waved goodbye in return.

A minute later, both Ra Mu and Lumiera were standing in the tall green field watching the massive Oceanan Spectrum Crystal ship light up. The twenty-four illumined crystalline spires protruding from its radiant cobalt-blue spherical center section, illumined with a different color of the spectrum – and each one emitting a different pure, harmonious humming tone. The huge ship lifted a hundred feet above the ground and rotated one-hundred-and-eighty-degrees. Then the huge spacecraft swiftly flew up into the sky. It climbed to five-thousand-feet, and then a beam of blue light was emitted from the top spire of the ship several hundred feet further upward to open a whirling interdimensional doorway.

On the other side, millions of clearly visible brightly shining stars and colorful radiant nebulae were located in a galaxy somewhere within a slightly higher parallel dimension of the physical universe. The crystalline ship continued its swift flight up through the vortex opening, and then it darted in a blur much beyond the speed of light, headed deep into the distant space of the hidden galaxy on the other side. The interdimensional opening whirled closed and vanished, leaving the crisp, clear deep-blue sky high over the countryside in the parallel Lemuria dimension.

CHAPTER TWENTY-THREE

RA MU AND LUMIERA RETURN HOME

*R*a Mu and Lumiera were grinning at each other as Ra Mu placed the palms of his hands together, as if in prayer in the East Indian manner of giving respect, and he bowed before Lumiera. In turn, Lumiera cheerfully returned the gesture, and Ra Mu grabbed the Master Crystal Staff that had been standing all this time by itself at his side, held up by some mystical force.

Then they both closed their eyes and began to sing out… HU-U-U-U-U-U-U… long and drawn out on the outgoing breath several times.

They knew quite well this most ancient connective sound or name is known to connect the true individual or Atma to the omnipresent living 1st Sound Source, Prime Creator, or The Ancient One – that is behind, supporting, and sustaining all that exists in the grand multidimensional creation. The sound was like a continuous round humming sound coming from their slightly parted puckered lips. A few moments passed, and golden light auras appeared around both of their bodies. They began to hear The Ancient One's Omnipresent Sound permeate the air around them: like the soft crashing of waves on a vast ocean; a low hum like millions of bees; and glass bells within a full orchestra arranged around a single hauntingly beautiful, and uplifting flute melody. Then they heard The Ancient One's deep melodious telepathic voice boom down from the sky above them.

Worthy Master Teachers, come with me now to rest and unfold further for a while in your true home beyond the lower worlds of time and space in the higher realms of pure Sound and Light.

The ancient Master Teachers gazed upward with grateful, humble, childlike smiles of the serenity of being. They could see the already open whirling golden vortex in the sky far above. Through it, they beheld the ethereally radiant crystalline towers and glittering gem-studded domes of The Ancient One's city that receded into an infinite horizon on the other side of the vortex. A cool-blue rarefied atmosphere in the faraway higher celestial dimension through the vortex was behind the brilliantly luminous sphere of The Ancient One, already moving down toward them. Then The Ancient One sent a radiant blue beam laced with gold light to their foreheads in one quick pulse, and their bodies turned silver-white. They transformed into glistening particles of gold light laced with blue light particles and turned into the radiant spheres of their true inner Atma selves, surrounded by bright golden auras. They appeared exactly like smaller versions of The Ancient One; except they were slightly larger and more luminous than Kalem's and Mayleena's Atma-selves. After all, they are known as Master Teachers.

The two Master Adepts then moved up to meet The Ancient One and slowly merged inside it, remaining clearly visible hovering within its twenty-foot-wide sphere of mystical radiant light. Then The Ancient One moved back up through the slowly closing vortex while golden atoms whirled down around its radiant sphere like falling snow. As it continued further into the distant background above the brilliant light coming from the celestial city below, it dwindled to a speck and vanished along with its mystical omnipresent Sound. The vortex faded from view, leaving the clear deep-blue sky over the protected secret higher parallel dimension of Lemuria on Earth.

A semitropical countryside paradise surrounded the tall green grass field, and in the distant background far below the mountain plateau to the west was the half-moon-shaped black sand cove. Sunlight passed through a large turquoise wave as it curled, then crashed along the glistening black sands. Exotic, colorful birds with long V-shaped split tails and twin sets of wings - one above the other - and sweet singing voices calling out the HU sound to each other, appeared circling over the green grass field.

Time mysteriously sped up while the sun quickly sank below the distant horizon over the ocean and a breathtaking array of sunset colors appeared through fleecy clouds.

Then time just as mysteriously resumed its normal rate, while the sound of another crashing ocean wave grew louder, and it crashed in another long curling wave along the glittering black sands of the distant half-moon cove.

A celestial symphonic orchestra and an unseen choir comprised of a thousand male and female voices singing… HU-U-U-U-U-U-U-U… in perfect melodic harmony on many levels grew louder, while the sound of the waves diminished to the background. The music swelled again and reached a tantalizing climax before it faded away altogether, leaving only a faint crashing ocean sound in the distant background below the plateau.

From high above the field, the wide panoramic view revealed a sky turning toward twilight with a few twinkling stars beginning to appear. The sky swiftly darkened to night, and the brilliant stars became fantastically numerous, spread across the celestial heavens among bright-multicolored nebulae laced between them. The spectacle above was richly beyond anything seen by human beings on Earth where the Unites States exists. The distant crashing ocean waves faded to absolute silence.

Moments passed, and a single happy cricket chirped. It was soon joined by a frog's merry croak. Then hundreds of crickets began to happily chirp with the merry croaks of many frogs in celebration of the sublime celestial night sky overhead. A shooting star, or one might assume now that it was something else entirely, appeared brightly burning across the thick star-filled heavens. It split into three separate shooting stars that transformed into brilliant violet disc-shaped fireballs. They continued across the far-flung star field and faded away in the mysterious galaxy above the well-protected, secret higher parallel dimension continent on Earth simply known as Lemuria.

The End
of
Guardian of The Ancient One

(The Parallel Time Trilogy – part two)

The Seres Agenda

(Special 5th edition published April, 2019)
(Larger 6 X 9 size - new original cover)
(Special techniques section added & hyperlinks in E-book)

Before they suddenly vanished long ago in galactic history, the mysterious eighteen to twenty-five-feet tall extraterrestrial human Seres race seeded humankind throughout the many galaxies. Then, they sponsored the creation of the entire Galactic Interdimensional Alliance of Free Worlds. Now, they have finally decided to return, and they will make their presence known by bringing about a permanent benevolent end to the experiment of evil on Earth.

The Emerald Doorway

(Book one of The Parallel Time Trilogy)

100,000 years ago, Earth's poles changed one hundred and eighty degrees overnight, destroying the lands as they sank beneath exploding lava in seething ocean waves. Rising from the sea floor, entirely different continents formed that we live on today, and there was a new beginning.

IT'S ABOUT TO HAPPEN AGAIN…
unless… they finally *INTERVENE*…

Journey to the Center of the Universe

(Coming book three of The Parallel Time Trilogy)

After the mystical experience of their marriage, the newlyweds Kalem and Mayleena arrive on her mysterious beautiful but mostly watered covered home world of Oceana for their honeymoon. Etta and his wife Din accompany them to celebrate a second honeymoon on their home world to spend quality time with their two Dren children.

All their lives are threatened in the midst of their romantic retreat when Sen Dar discovers their secret location through his greatly increasing occult powers. Their trust and reliance upon the one true Spirit Sound and Light coming from The Ancient One's highest realm beyond the physical worlds, and their bonds of loving friendship, are all that stands between their survival or complete annihilation.

The Adepts of The Ancient One decide to secretly combine their efforts with Kalem, Mayleena and Etta to give them a more powerful focus on the single struggle to keep Sen Dar's lust for power from destroying Earth. Our planet's total annihilation, along with all of us on its surface, is inexorably linked to the ongoing challenge to stop Sen Dar or perish, as we race forward through the mystic journey to the uplifting thrilling climax and Sen Dar's unexpected destiny, revealed on the other side of...

Journey to the Center of the Universe

GLOSSARY OF CHARACTERS AND TERMS

CHARACTERS:

Admiral Starland – This Admiral of the Galactic Interdimensional Alliance of Free Worlds is Captain Kalem's father and a Master Adept of The Ancient One. He is trim and well built, appearing to be in his early fifties by Earth standards, with short brown hair swept back at the sides. The hair is only streaked white at his temples and sideburns. His high forehead, squared jaw, smooth round chin, and blue eyes make him appear wise and stately in his uniform. His slim gray-blue pants have an oval gold buckle belting them at the waist that is identical to the one worn by his son, Captain Kalem. The GalacticAlliance symbol of three blue stars set in triangular formation above the apex of a gold pyramid, suspended above a silvery galaxy is also embossed over the left chest area of his long-sleeved shirt. Three gold bands encircle each cuff. The neck collar of the shirt that is open in front with a V-shape, gradually tapers to a point a few inches below the base of his neck.

Air Force Colonel – This seriously concerned officer approaches General Harry Faldwell to inform him that a Zon spy was detected on the launch runway outside the base hangars at Area 51 in Nevada.

Bronzed Bust of Zol Yul (Zohl-Uool) - Atop a four-foot-wide by two-foot-high black obsidian pedestal rests the bronzed bust of a man's head wearing a golden sun crown. The bust looks remarkably just like Sen Dar, when he first appeared coming through an opening interdimensional doorway behind the Zon High Priest.

Captain Kalem Starland – He is a six-foot-tall, ruggedly handsome, and courageous Caucasian Captain in the space fleet of the Galactic Interdimensional Alliance of Free Worlds. He's an extraterrestrial human in his late twenties, with blue eyes, short brown hair, and known as a renowned fighter pilot. He wears a single-piece formfitting body uniform made of a silvery-gray fabric. Two gold bands encircle the sleeves that widen slightly at the wrists. Three blue stars set in a triangular formation are embossed on the uniform's left chest area above the apex of a golden pyramid, positioned over the nucleus of a silvery galaxy.

Din – She is Etta's lovely female Dren wife, who has characteristic longer feminine eyelashes and a petite body. Her bulbous blue eyes are more feminine in expression, and her toes and thinner long fingers are similar to the five-fingered hands and toes of a trim human female woman. She and Etta are more lovingly bonded to each other, and to their two Dren children than most human beings on planet Earth ever experience. Like all Drens, she uses her hands and fingers in dexterous expressive ways.

Elder Guardian Council Member - A surprised elder Guardian Council member states to Master Ra Mu, referring to Sen Dar in the secret Mt. Shasta base, "But we thought he was killed in the fight at the Peruvian volcano."

Etta (Et-tuh) – This extraordinary benevolent and immediately endearing member of the extraterrestrial silica-based Dren race (not carbon-based like human beings) is very courageous. He is also telepathic with a photographic memory and has vocal cords. He is three-and-a-half feet long with smooth pale-green dry skin. Etta's large, bulbous, dark blue eyes are semispherical shaped, and his eyelids have short eyelashes that make his facial features appear more masculine. They are long and feminine on his wife, Din, and all other Dren females. Etta's six-inch-long jaw, squared off in front, has two flared nostrils about an inch apart, positioned on the front of each side of his nose. His mouth is a smiling crease around his jaw, which gives the impression he is amused about something when his mouth is closed. His arms are slightly shorter than his hind legs, but both are strongly contoured. Like all Drens, his tail glows like crystal opal in sunlight when activated, giving him antigravity levitating and flying abilities. He has a more loving, bonded dedication to his wife Din and to their two Dren children than most human beings on planet Earth ever experience.

General Harry Faldwell – This strongly built, no-nonsense, four-star Air Force General in his mid-fifties is a member of the President's cabinet, one of his top national security advisors, and the fiancé of Senator Judith Cranston.

Guardian Master Adepts of The Ancient One – The benevolent order of Master teacher guardians that are secretly stationed on Earth, many other world systems, and in parallel and higher dimensional realities, have been in existence for ages beyond the imagination of humankind on Earth. They do not normally interfere with the freewill choice of the people on any planet, unless there is an emergency that requires their direct intervention. When the people of a world system no longer have the freewill, they believe they have, to create a benevolent future, they are walking on the brink of destruction. At this point, the Guardian Adepts step in to prevent it.

Hubert Griswald (U.S. top scientist) - Hubert Griswald, a balding and slightly rotund man in his forties wearing thick glasses, wrinkled old slacks, and a worn cardigan sweater, appears quite irritated as he boldly walks up to Harry when he begins to take part in the unfolding story.

Lieutenant Marin – She is a petite Communications Officer about thirty years of age, stationed aboard Admiral Starland's

Galactic Interdimensional Alliance of Free Worlds flagship. She is usually seated a few feet away at the main control console on the bridge.

Lieutenant Moreau (Mor-rooh) – This Norbrian, in his late twenties from the planet Ulanim, is Captain Kalem's best friend. He is clean-shaven with and oval-shaped face, strong jaw, dark-brown skin, brown eyes, and short curly brown hair. He wears the Lieutenant's uniform of the Galactic Interdimensional Alliance of Free worlds that look identical to the one worn by Captain Kalem; except a single gold band surrounds the cuff of each sleeve instead of two.

Master Lumiera (Loom-e-air-ruh) – This Master Adept of The Ancient One is the guardian of the secret parallel dimension on Earth, where the continent of Lemuria never sinks beneath ocean waves because no polar shift takes place in this protected reality. He is a vibrant, healthy-looking elderly bald man, who wears a gold-colored silk robe tied with a matching sash at the waist and simple sandals. He emanates a subtle pastel gold light.

Master Opellum – Being over six feet, Opellum is tall for an Oceanan male. He appears to be in his late forties, according to Earth human comparisons. With strong limbs, his body is trim and precisely contoured. He is handsome in a most mature way beyond description, at least to his young daughter's perceptions. Like Mayleena, his nose is straight and slender. His jet-black hair flows gracefully straight back over the top of his pointed ears and down the back of his neck between his shoulder blades. Opellum's hair does not grow at the sides of his temples or directly above his ears. This makes his forehead appear to extend around the sides of his head, giving a powerful impression of silent strength and wisdom. He wears a very elegant blue, silken wraparound robe tied at his side by a smooth silken gold sash and matching tight-fitting slip-on shoes.

Master Ra Mu (Rah-Moo) – The six-foot-tall man with black curly hair and a short-cropped beard, wears a knee-length, maroon robe belted at the waist and simple sandals. Grasped in his right hand is a tall transparent crystal staff crested with a symbol similar to the ancient Egyptian Ankh – a vertical oval with a hollow center atop a cross. As a very advanced spiritual Master Teacher, he instructs and guides those individuals who want to return to their true nature as the Atma (eternal spherical energy being). He assists them to remember that their long-forgotten destiny is to become a fully conscious, trusted co-creator with the omnipresent source behind and supporting all that exists. He is also one of the Master Adepts of the Ancient One and Captain Kalem's, Mayleena's, and Etta's personal mentor and friend.

Mayleena (May-lee-nuh) – She is a humanoid extraterrestrial from the planet Oceana hidden in a higher parallel dimension of the physical universe. She spent her young and teenage years under the ocean in a domed city also named Oceana after their home world. The adult Mayleena is an exceptionally beautiful woman, even among other Oceanan women. Her long soft black hair is combed straight back over her head and behind her delicately pointed elf-like ears and down the middle of her back. Like all Oceanans, she can breathe underwater or on land, and she is telepathic - capable of sending the image of a blond Caucasian human woman into the minds of anyone that might capture her or see her as a threat when they meet.

Morln (Mor-ooln) – This twenty-foot tall prehistoric-type of lizard with a snake-like head camouflages itself as a rock like a chameleon; except this creature is able to change shape as well. Antennae, like those on a snail, constantly recede and protrude from the top of its head as a long snake-like tongue darts out of its mouth every few moments between large sets of fangs. They extend in sharply arched curves from its upper and lower jaws. Its two long arms that end in twin-forked claws gradually curl to razor-sharp points. The thing hisses between its spoken words, sadistically talking with glee to its prey in a deep raspy voice. Drens are a Morln's favorite food.

Norbrians (Nor-bree-uns) – This humanoid race is from the planet Ulanim. Captain Kalem's friend, Moreau, is a Norbrian. They have oval-shaped faces, round brown eyes, strong jaws, short curly brown hair and dark brown skin. The males are firmly built like Kalem. Note: In The Emerald Doorway (book one of the trilogy), during their training at the Academy on planet Telemadia (3), Moreau was always reminding Kalem of one appointment to keep or another. After all, Norbrians are like that. They grow up early with an innate sense of the responsible and sensible.

Prehistoric Alien-looking Amphibian – This alien prehistoric-looking amphibian with a huge mouth, dozens of rows of razor-sharp teeth, and a long sticky tongue that lashes out three feet from its mouth every few seconds to loudly slap the surface of the slimy liquid pool is Captain Kalem's worst nightmare. It has two dozen eyes arched in two parallel rows above its mouth and makes a terrifying shrill whining noise that grates on its prey's nerves. When the huge mouth widens, it reveals it can easily swallow a man whole.

Prehistoric Black Widow-like Spiders – Mayleena screams upon seeing hundreds of these hairy nine-inch-wide-bodied, prehistoric black widow-like spiders scrambling out of numerous holes in the cavern walls along thin web strands. They have three large red dots under their bellies, and large dripping venomous fangs that look like hooked prongs. They extend down from their rapidly moving feelers that surround their open mouths. Their eight legs have barbed hooks on the end of each one. All the spiders wildly hiss between shrill whistling sounds when hundreds more of the nasty things appear crawling down the walls. They are Mayleena's worst nightmare.

President's Aid – He's white-haired, trim, fortyish, and wears a blue suit and glasses.

President Sam Stockwell – This United States President is a ruggedly handsome man in his late fifties, with a full head of silver-streaked hair. He appears to be tough as nails when dealing with foreign leaders - and understanding if needed. He unexpectedly goes through the astonishing direct experience of finding out who and what he is that is not and never has been a physical body.

Russian President Nikolaev (Vladimir) – He is in his late fifties with thick white hair combed back, a rugged weather-worn face with a slightly large nose, and wears round spectacles. He is kind but can also be tough as nails.

Sen Dar – He is a diabolical, malevolent thirty-year-old slender man with high cheekbones, a long straight nose, and slightly wavy black hair that flows down to his shoulders. He usually wears a long black cape and a gray slip-on body uniform, belted at the waist with a gold buckle. Etched into the buckle, on the front of a thin gold metal band around his forehead, and on the right chest area of his body uniform is the symbol of a vertical sword superimposed over a red world. Two snakes are wound around and above the shaft of the handle with their heads pointed toward each other, and their extended forked tongues touching. The tip of the blade below the red world points to the middle of an upside-down black obsidian pyramid with its inverted apex touching the top of the star nucleus of a silvery galaxy. He wears The Ancient One's Transport Matrix crystal hung from a sturdy gold chain that he stole from Master Nim's dead body after he killed him.

Senator Judith Cranston – This United States Senator is trim and very attractive in her mid-forties with long black hair. She stands her own ground on important issues with her fiancé General Harry Faldwell.

Technical Maintenance – Etta darts around the corner and runs head-first into a cart being pushed by a young Mt. Shasta Base technical maintenance man, wearing gray overalls. He is knocked unconscious backward head over heels to the floor.

The Ancient One – This living presence or source behind and supporting all that exists is from a dimension far above the void known to certain religions on Earth. This mighty primordial living presence looks like a brilliant golden ball or sphere of luminous being more spectacular than anything witnessed by people on planet Earth or on most worlds of the physical universe. For the Atma or Soul – the true individual, after proper training or preparation, The Ancient One appears as a fifteen-feet-in-diameter radiant sphere: comprised of self-effulgent teardrop-shaped lights built in layers; from a radiant white lightcore; through the color spectrum to a shimmering violet outer layer, surrounded by a radiant golden aura.

The Dren Race – This highly evolved benevolent extraterrestrial race (silica-based – not carbon-based like human beings) looks similar to Earth's light-green salamanders but with smooth, dry skin, and they are much larger with distinct differences. They have longer snouts and expressive big bulbous dark blue eyes. From the tip of their thick tails to the end of their adorable faces, they range in size from two-and-half feet to over four feet in length. When any of them blink, a transparent set of inner eyelids closes down over their eyes just before their outer eyelids. They are telepathic and can speak with vocal cords, have photographic memories, and can levitate or fly through the air with a natural ability – developed over millions of years to defy gravity when their tails glow from the root to the tip like crystal opal in bright sunlight. Etta, in particular, is very courageously funny. He exemplifies the best qualities of human beings, but he is not human.

The Seres Race (Say-Rays) – These majestic, highly spiritually evolved, eighteen to twenty-five feet tall extraterrestrial human beings seeded human and humanoid races throughout the many galaxies long ago. Then they vanished from galactic history. They very recently decided to return to oversee the disastrous ways the younger space-faring races and humanity on Earth have headed in negative directions almost everything.

The Silent Observer – A mysterious visitor in a mysterious spaceship, hovers above Earth to continue to observe, as time is sped up, the phenomenal occurrence of entirely new continents, familiar today, rise up from the ocean depths between the massive vanishing continents of Lemuria and Atlantis. A remaining Atlantis Island then becomes situated in the ocean southeast of what is now Florida on the newly risen North American continent. A moment passes, and the tallest dormant volcano on the western coast of the remaining Atlantis Island violently erupts and explodes, ripping the land apart. Then it too sinks beneath boiling, churning waves.

The Zon Race (Zahn) – They are a humanoid race from a parallel dimension on Earth with dark tanned skin; but they have larger foreheads with higher cheekbones, and slightly larger oval eyes with deep-blue pupils. Their foot-long braided sideburns have various warrior symbolic jewelry woven into them. Except for the Priest, they are all dressed in violet-colored tunics with a laser-type silver metallic handgun belted at their sides.

Two Dren Children – These are Etta's and Din's playful Dren Children that appear to be about ten and eleven years old in comparison to Earth children. Often, they are observed frolicking on a floor, chasing each other through trees and up into the sky, or hovering beside Din. Etta's eyes bug out excitedly, and he screeches upon seeing them. Then he races over to hover beside her and their children. They also usually circle each other like happy bees hovering around a honey nest, and then Etta and Din tenderly rub noses together. Then the boy climbs onto Etta's shoulders while their loving parents tightly cuddle their daughter between them.

Vlasik (Velas-ick) – He's a thin, spectacled scientist-type in his forties, that sits at the computer console keyboard in front of the top Russian General in their classified space command launch facility. He's their top computer expert and the only one in the world capable of linking their equipment with similar equipment in the top classified Area 51 base with the top United States scientist Hubert Griswald.

Zon High Commander General Luboc (Loo-bahk) – This highest-ranking officer Sen Dar approaches after he kills the Zon High Priest, is a tough-looking muscular man. He suddenly bows to one knee before Sen Dar and the other Zon warriors immediately follow his example. Unknown to them, Sen Dar is misusing the Emerald

Doorway Crystal to hypnotize them.

Zon Warrior Priest Zol Yul – This High Priest of the entire Zon race stands in front of a pedestal wearing a rich red ceremonial robe with dark-blue arcane symbols embossed upon the surface. A gold headband with gold feathers spread upward out of the top like a fan sits on his forehead. Gripped in his right fist is an odd-looking spiral gray metal rod with a large ruby crystal set on top.

TERMS:

Admiral Starland's Flagship – A pale-blue antigravity light surrounds the hull of this over a mile in length elongated oval ship that emits a very low-frequency oscillating humming sound. It has a wide rectangular launch bay positioned on the upper curved surface of the front of each end of the ship, and a clear observation dome one hundred feet across positioned just above and behind them. City-sized crystalline structures built next to the observation dome gradually increase in height toward the oval central section of the ship. Thousands of human occupants appear tiny in comparison to their surroundings, as they move within the huge observation domes or stop to gaze through the many windows in the bridge towers that spiral higher toward the ship's massive middle section.

Antigravity Wave-Vector Pods – Three semispherical antigravity wave-vector pods, built in a triangular pattern on the bottom of each Scout ship's hull, are the power source for their antigravity drives. When activated, they project a balanced antigravity field around the ship's hull. Each pod contains twelve quartz crystal spires pointing downward in different directions.

Area 51 – Nevada Desert. – This highly classified U.S. Air Force base, known worldwide today as Area 51, has a very long runway in front of a series of aircraft hangars. Most of the building complexes are underground. The newly designed prototype triangular-shaped antigravity Space Transporter hovers a few feet above the runway, a dozen feet in front of its hangar by the very long launch runway before it takes off straight up.

Atlantis – This nearly independent colony continent two-thirds the size of the massive motherland Lemuria was located halfway around planet Earth 100,000 years ago, when it was destroyed during a cyclic polar shift: except for a surviving 500 square-mile volcanic Atlantis Island.

Atlantis Island – This is a five-hundred-square-mile volcanic island that survived the catastrophic sinking, 100,000 years ago on Earth, the massive Lemuria continent and its large Atlantis colony continent. The remaining mountainous volcanic Atlantis Island, centered in the infamous Bermuda Triangle, eventually became the new colonizing power on Earth, until it was destroyed 35,000 years ago through the misuse of science.

Bermuda Triangle Transit Window – This interdimensional doorway or portal is located in the atmosphere above and under the central ocean area of the infamous Bermuda Triangle. It can be accessed by advanced extraterrestrial spacecraft to travel between parallel dimensions. Many more interdimensional doorways exist in a geometric grid pattern on Earth in the atmosphere, at special land locations, or under various oceans and bodies of water.

Blue Transport Matrix Crystal – When an individual utilizes this crystal, for an instant, their body is suspended in the air before it's turned into brilliantly luminous rainbow-colored molecules that vanish with a great …*swish* and an echoing … *boom*. It transports the wearer any distance to any world across space or to any location they imagine. By collapsing time and space between the beginning location and the destination location, the wearer can instantly travel to a point on a planet or to a location on any other planet within the vastness of the galaxies. The Transport Matrix Crystal can only connect two points within the same physical dimension of the universe and open a brief corridor between them. It is one of two primary experiential aspects of the omnipresent living power or Spirit presence of The Ancient One. This is what advanced benevolent extraterrestrials refer to as 'Prime Creator.' This is the source of life within the individual. It supports them, and all that exists. Beautiful uplifting and enlightening light of many high color vibrations often accompany the experience of tuning in to it with the inner sight – what is known in certain esoteric circles as the proverbial third or inner eye of the 'Atma' or 'Soul.'

Blue Mazon Fireball Weapon (May-zohn) – This blue fireball energy projectile defensive weapon is used by the Galactic Interdimensional Alliance of Free Worlds starships, and by Scout class ships like the one piloted by Captain Kalem.

Deep-Blue Time-link Tunnel – This is an interdimensional energy tunnel created by one of the functions of the Emerald Doorway Crystal of The Ancient One. A radiant emerald beam forms into a whirling interdimensional vortex that opens to reveal Earth's distant future on the other side. Sen Dar escapes in his ship through it to avoid certain destruction.

Deep Star Cutter Class Spaceships – This fast-attack destroyer class ship, is shaped the same as one of the Emerald Star Galaxy Class Cruisers of the Galactic Alliance but only half the size.

Detection Device Green Faceted Crystal - This three-inch-long faceted green crystal that tapers to a rounded point, sent by Master Ra Mu, materialized on Harry's lap. It is used to detect a spy and glows when one is detected.

Diamond Tipped Gold Wire Headset – This thin gold wire headset with a faceted diamond-like crystal on each end, fits into the ear holes on each side of Etta's head. When activated, they light up, and it transmits whatever Etta sees or hears back to Captain Kalem's receiver aboard his ship, so he can monitor what is taking place around Etta.

Dren Extraterrestrial Race – This wondrous non-human alien race average to be about two-and-a-half feet long from the tip of their long thick tails to the end of their adorable snout noses. They are silica-based DNA creatures – not carbon-based like Earth humans, and they evolved with the ability to levitate (defy gravity) and fly through the air. They have photographic memories, are telepathic, and have vocal cords. They exemplify the most noble kind qualities of human beings. In fact, they excel at this beyond humans on Earth.

Emerald Doorway Crystal – This special crystal device of The Ancient One is capable of transporting a ship and anyone inside it across time and into parallel dimensions of the physical universe. It looks exactly the same size and shape as the Transport Matrix Crystal that Sen Dar stole from Master Nim on the planet Promintis – but it is green instead of blue.

Emerald Star Galaxy Class Cruisers – These massive starships of the Galactic Interdimensional Alliance of Free Worlds are surrounded by pale-blue antigravity luminosity and a subtle, very low frequency, oscillating humming sound. They have a wide rectangular launch bay positioned on the upper curved surface of the front of each end of the ship. A clear observation dome one hundred feet across is located just above and behind each launch bay. City-sized crystalline structures built next to the observation domes gradually increase in height from each end until they reach their height at the central hull area.

Etta's Diamond & Gold Wire Headset - He wears a thin curved gold wire headset across his head with a faceted diamond on each end that is placed into each ear hole. This tool allows him to telepathically transmit to Captain Kalem aboard his ship anything he sees and hears while on a mission.

Faceted Ruby Center Quartz Sphere – MasterRa Mu gives this clear crystal ball device with a faceted ruby embedded in its center to General Faldwell. It is a communication device that he places on the White House Oval Office floor in front of President Sam Stockwell. It provides him with direct contact but also has many other functions.

Galactic Alliance Scout Interceptor – This defensive Galactic Interdimensional Alliance of Free Worlds sleek disc-shaped, antigravity-powered spaceship is thirty-feet in diameter, made from a silver-blue composite metal. Three semispherical-shaped pods in a triangular pattern protrude downward from the curved bottom hull. When the alien craft flies, a pale-blue light surrounds the ship's circumference, making a soft humming sound.

Galactic Alliance Laser Gun – The sleek, smoothly polished, clear crystal laser gun of the Galactic Interdimensional Alliance of Free Worlds has clearly visible octagon-shaped green and red crystals extended down the length of the barrel inside the transparent shell.

Gravitic Suspension Transport Cars – After a double-ended transport car that looks similar to a double-terminated quartz crystal turns on, it hovers in front of the open end of a Gravitic Suspension Transport Tube and stops. Any passengers wishing to board it step from the loading dock down inside the car and then strap themselves into one of the two sets of seats that face each other. A six-inch-wide semispherical moonstone colored crystal control, set in the center of the flat-topped control monolith, activates when a hand passes over it. The transparent curved hatch of the transport car then swings down and locks with a... *whoosh*, sealing the car airtight. The car then levitates forward into the transport tube and stops after it clears the open end of the tube. The semispherical end swings down and closes with a quick ...s-s-s-sip, to vacuum seal the tube. The outer circumference of the tube illuminates radiant blue light along its entire length, and the transport car levitates up inside the tube with a foot to spare between it and the transport tube's inner wall. Both pointed ends of the car light up, changing colors from blue, then to green, and to red every few seconds, right before the car darts away at tremendous speed headed for the intended destination.

Gravitic Suspension Transport Tubes – The vacuum-sealed, antigravity, round transparent transport tubes are six feet wide and many miles long. They wind their way along the ground all throughout the city and countryside inside the ancient domed undersea city of Oceana. First revealed in The Emerald Doorway, they run along the bottom of Earth's ancient ocean. Gravitic Suspension Transport Cars travel in them at tremendous speed.

Guardians of The Ancient One – They are Master teachers that guide and protect students and guard one of three powerful consciousness transforming crystal devices. They are the Blue Transport Matrix crystal, the Green Emerald Doorway crystal, and the Master Crystal Staff. The Ancient One gave them to the Master Adept teachers eons ago to train their students in the right use of love, wisdom, and freedom. When a Master teacher guarding them is about to depart a particular lifetime, he passes the crystal device on to a selected student that is ready to accept the guardianship responsibility of being a Master Teacher.

Guardian's Research Foundation Patch - Two men and one woman are wearing parkas with a Guardian's Research Foundation patch on them in a conference room inside the secret Galactic Alliance Mt. Shasta base in northern California. Certain members wear this patch that represents a convenient cover, while they travel outside the base in case someone notices their activities.

Hidden Planet of Oceana – This emerald-green ocean-covered world, surrounded by light pink pastel clouds, has only two large equatorial islands protruding above the surface. It is located in a slightly higher parallel physical dimension of our Milky Way Galaxy. This is the home world of the Oceanans – the most advanced humanoid, pale-blue-skinned race that is telepathic, and can breathe on land or underwater. They established huge domed city colonies at the bottom of their vast ocean covered world that are connected to each other and to the domed cities on the two islands by vacuum-sealed transport tubes. They are not revealed in this hidden past disclosing adventure, but they are introduced in the hidden truth revealing 5th edition of *The Seres Agenda* book with a newly designed original cover.

HU (Hu-u-u-u-u…) – This is the first sound that emanated from the 'Source' behind all life (Prime Creator) that created the entire multidimensional universe. It is what the individual 'Atma' or 'Soul' travels upon to return home to attain a co-creative status with 'Prime Creator.' This is the primordial omnipresent living force behind all life. It is the first Sound often perceived or heard like celestial voices of an unseen choir, the single high note of a flute or a thousand male and female voices sending out the… 'HU.' This oldest, most dynamic life-transforming sound in the universe is hidden in plain sight in the first half of the word human.

Interdimensional Doorway Vortex Tunnel - Clearly visible in every detail, thousands of tiny light molecules whirl inward toward a center point between each end of a twelve-foot-long by six-foot-wide clear parallel time dimension tunnel opening. Rapidly vibrating blue light molecules spin counterclockwise at a slightly faster time rate on the far side of the vortex opening, and whirling green molecules spin clockwise at a slightly slower rate on Kalem's side of the opening. The two whirling energy fields rapidly slow their differing vibrations as they spin inward toward each other to join together, creating the twelve-foot-long whirling energy tunnel.

Lemuria (Leh-muur-ree-yah) – This is the continental name of the motherland of human beings on Earth. Also known as MU, this uniquely evolved culture lasted for 100,000 years before it sank beneath the ocean waves. This was caused when the physical and gravitational poles of planet Earth flipped over 180 degrees during the course of one night. This very advanced civilization began after the previous cyclic polar shift took place. Although the tallest mountain ranges had risen little more than seven thousand feet, each landmass extended more than halfway into the northern and southern hemispheres, surrounded by vast oceans. The original large colony continent of Atlantis, two-thirds the size of Lemuria centered over the equator on the opposite side of the planet, sank beneath the ocean waves: except for a remaining five hundred square-mile volcanic Atlantis Island.

Magnetic Blanket – When activated, this special Galactic

Alliance defensive weapon instantly projects a beam of violet light from the front end of each of the Galactic Alliance starships that converge in the center of the space between enemy vessels to form a transparent sphere of light. The beams then begin to pull the sphere of light back toward the Galactic ships, expanding and enlarging it, until it completely encloses all the enemy ships within a gigantic transparent sphere of light that cuts off their power.

Master Adepts of The Ancient One – Nine men and three women meet in this secret Mt. Shasta base in northern California, including Master Ra Mu and Mayleena, with Etta resting on the table next to her. Eight of the men and two women wear robes of various colors: each with slight design variations befitting the members of the mysterious, mystical order of The Ancient One's Master Adepts.

Master Crystal Staff - Master Ra Mu almost always holds this six-foot-tall, clear quartz Crystal staff of The Ancient One crested with the Ankh symbol. This is a cross topped with a vertical oval with a hole in the center. It is etched with mystical symbols. This is one of The Ancient One's three cosmic crystals. The other two are referred to as the Emerald Doorway Crystal and the Blue Matrix Crystal.

Master Opellum's Crystal Wand Device – This special device utilized by Master Opellum displays recorded past events, and it can transport or camouflage any being until they wish to reveal themself. To activate it, he holds this six-inch-long, octagon faceted blue-green crystal out a foot in front of his chest. It emits a pulsing and wavering blue-green light. Swirling particles of the gold and silver light are then projected from the crystal to form a holographic type recorded image or to unveil something stored in its memory.

Mt. Shasta – This is a solitary glacial-covered extinct volcanic mountain in Northern California in the United States. Contained within its hollowed-out interior is a secret Galactic Interdimensional Alliance of Free Worlds base established there in 1908. It is protected by operating in a slightly higher parallel dimension of the physical universe, so it is undetectable by radar or scans of any other kind, including detection equipment that exists on planet Earth.

Mt. Shasta Rock Wall Vortex Doorway – Kalem's ship passes over the forest trees, slows, and stops to assume a hovering position thirty feet above the ground and fifty yards away from the flat gray rock wall. The rock wall lights up, and the whirling tiny blue galaxy-like stars appear. They widen, revealing the one hundred twenty-foot-wide by sixty-foot-high smooth oval lighted tunnel, encircled by the rough-hewn cavern with a clear glass-like oval tunnel centered within it. The whirling stars widen more, revealing down the length of the oval tunnel several hundred yards further inside, a huge extraterrestrial spacecraft landing bay and base carved out of the inside of the mountain.

Oceana (O-shee-ann-nuh) – This mostly water-covered world in a slightly higher parallel dimension of our Milky Way Galaxy is the home world of the Oceanan humanoid race. Only two large island landmasses extend above the vast oceans. This is also the home world of the Dren race. They evolved inside huge extinct volcanic lava tubes that are located at the bottom of the ocean on planet Oceana.

Oceanan Crystalline Based Science – The programmable crystalline-based science of the Oceanan race from a higher parallel dimension of the physical universe is beyond any other known science in the galaxy. Their pure laboratory-grown crystal technology actually repairs Captain Kalem's mangled dead body and brings him back to life - after two Oceanan men pluck his body from the bottom of the ocean near the secret undersea domed city of Oceana. This science also powers the most advanced interdimensional spacecraft of the Oceanans known as Spectrum Crystal Ships.

Oceanan Spectrum Crystal Ships – They are gigantic spherical spaceships with multiple triangular spires extended from their surfaces. The dozen differently colored luminous crystal spires protrude outward to fine points from all around the spherical cobalt-blue main body of each ship. The rounded, pointed ends of three of the spires that protrude downward from the bottom half of the sphere to support the landed craft. This amazing spaceship can travel through space hundreds of times beyond the speed of light, into higher parallel dimensions of finer physical reality far beyond worlds like Earth, to other planets in our Milky Way Galaxy, and to or from Oceana – the home world of the Oceanan people.

Oceanan Race (O-shee-ann-nun) – The Oceanan humanoid extraterrestrial race look much like beautiful blue-skinned elves with slightly pointed ears. At first sight, any human being from Earth suddenly exposed to them would fall in love with them at first sight, for they emit an aura of very powerful uplifting energies. They originally evolved on a mostly water-covered world called Oceana in a hidden location within a higher physical parallel dimension of our Milky Way Galaxy - very far away from planet Earth. The Oceanans have small webs between the fingers on their hands and between their toes for the ease of swimming, and a second set of clear eyelids to see through while underwater. Three unobtrusive tiny gill slits located on each side of their necks underneath the backs of their chins open and close for breathing while underwater. There is a common ancestry, going back more than a billion years in galactic history, between human beings on Earth and other human and humanoid races like the far more advanced Oceanans. Therefore, human beings on Earth can mate with Oceanan humanoid beings if this kind of thing ever comes up.

Oval Red Energy Bolts - Kalem was seeing two-dozen Zon Scout Class charcoal-colored, slightly batwing-shaped triangular fighters on his viewscreen. Several had already fired red oval energy bolts headed toward his ship.

Personal Gravitic Transport Disc – The antigravity-powered metallic transport disc is an inch-thick and two feet in diameter. When activated, the disc hovers a foot above the ground surrounded by a luminous blue aura. A one-inch circumference of the disc's outer ring lowers to the surface like a step. After the rider steps upon the disk, a gravitational field anchors their legs to its smooth flat surface. The inner disc then rejoins the outer ring leaving no seam, and the rider then directs it with their imagination to fly through the air. When the rider wishes to stop the flight, the disc lowers to a foot above the ground, and the disc's outer ring lowers to the surface like a step. Once the person steps off the disc, the disc lowers to the ground and rejoins the one-inch outer circumference ring that molecularly rejoins with it, leaving no seam. The disc then shuts off.

Planet Earth's Cyclic Polar Shifts – Every 100,000 years, the solar system of planets containing planet Earth passes through an area of space that causes Earth's physical and gravitational poles to flip overnight. This event sinks most of the existing continental landmasses and raises from the seafloor entirely new contents like those we live on today. Fortunately, this past cyclic event that was due to happen again has recently been permanently ended by wondrous beings known as 'The Silent Mentors' – the mechanics of the grand multidimensional creation.

Plesetsk Launch Facility – This is Russia's secondary launch facility north of Moscow with a very long runway in the Guardians of The Ancient One story. It can launch payload rockets containing satellites and other experimental aircraft like the prototype Russian Space Transporter that takes off on a long runway. The primary facility to launch large rockets with astronauts is at Baikonur Cosmodrome in Kazakhstan.

Polished Chrome Timed Bomb - While Etta is in a storage room inside the secret Mt. Shasta Guardians' base, he jogs up to an open cabinet storage compartment carrying a six-inch-long by two-inch-wide polished chrome timed bomb device. His nimble fingers touch several crystal controls on the top of the cylinder, and they light up blinking. An LCD (liquid crystal display) window on its surface shows... 05:00 minutes, then... 04:59 as it begins to rapidly count down. He opens the metal door and places the device on the inside surface. It magnetically locked in place, and he closes the door. Etta has been hypnotized by Sen Dar's misuse of The Ancient One's stolen

Emerald Doorway Crystal.

Russian Prototype Space Transporter - Somewhere in Russia, fresh snow is on the ground surrounding one large background hangar. The distant sun beginning to rise up over the horizon in the crisp early morning air is reflecting light off the snow on the ground behind the silvery-gray hull of the new elongated sixty-foot Russian Space Transporter. In the rear, six jet engines positioned between four huge rocket nozzles are fired-up in preparation for launch. The sleek silver-gray metallic hull glistening with sunlight down the elongated triangular hull flashes off the opaque glass-like curved cockpit window. It is positioned behind and above the pointed triangular front end of the ship. The brakes are released, and the craft roars a short way down a long runway before it lifts upward at almost a ninety-degree angle and darts swiftly into the early morning sky.

Sefaris (Sef-far-res) – Earth astronomers call it the Andromeda Galaxy, the nearest galactic neighbor to our Milky Way Galaxy. However, the benevolent extraterrestrial Galactic Alliance planetary members and the Andromeda races call it Sefaris – the distant wonder.

Sen Dar's Customized Zon Scout Ship – this looks like a regular Zon Demon Scout class fighter, but it is customized to have a little more elegant elongated triangular appearance.

Sen Dar's Laser Pistol – This is a sleek silver laser type of handgun weapon Sen Dar took from the former Yalgull he temporarily controlled by misusing The Ancient One's stolen crystal he took from his former Master Nim's body after he killed him.

Sen Dar's Personal Symbol – This is the image of a red world set just above the square base of an upside-down black pyramid with the vertical point of a sword touching the top of the red world. Two snakes wrapped around the blade spiral above the handle until their heads turn inward toward each other with their forked tongues touching.

Spirit Sound Access Code Words – The Ancient One's map reveals and explains how to envision the planet or place you wish to go to. Then, by utilizing a specific command codeword sound, the Blue Matrix Crystal of The Ancient One will transport a being to the destination in a matter of seconds. In this way, certain precise sound frequencies woven into the omnipresent Spirit sound that supports and sustains all life are accessible.

The Ancient One's Parchment Half-Map – If the student can master the right use of the Blue Transport Matrix Crystal by learning to properly read and apply the instructions revealed in The Ancient One's cosmic map, training then begins with the other two mystic crystals. This eventually requires training from two

Master Adept teachers because only half of this special map is under the guardianship of one chosen Master Adept at a time. Sen Dar acquires half of the original map and seeks the other half. He eventually discovers the other part of the map located in a secret cavern on the planet called Maldec that once existed in ancient Earth's solar system between the planets Mars and Jupiter. Placing the two map halves side by side triggers them to mend themselves back together through an unknown mystical process. Then the locations of the other two mystic crystals of The Ancient One are revealed, along with the Master Guardian Adepts who wield them. In addition, also revealed are other ways to utilize the cosmic crystal devices.

The Ancient One's Spirit Light – This is the light anyone can experience, usually when the physical eyes are closed after they discover how to connect with it through the first omnipresent living energy. It sustains and supports the grand multidimensional creation. It is simply known as 'HU' – the first half of the word human. It is one of two primary experiential aspects of the omnipresent living power or Spirit presence of The Ancient One – what advanced benevolent extraterrestrials refer to as 'Prime Creator.' This is the source of life within the individual. It supports them, and all that exists. Beautiful uplifting and enlightening light of many high color vibrations often accompanies the experience of tuning in to it with the inner sight. The term inner sight is what is known in certain esoteric circles as the proverbial third or inner eye of the 'Atma' or 'Soul.'

The Ancient One's Spirit Sound – The enlightening Sound anyone can experience after the individual first discovers how to connect with it. Actually, this is one of two primary experiential aspects of the omnipresent living power. Also known as the living Spirit presence of The Ancient One – what advanced benevolent extraterrestrials refer to as 'Prime Creator' or the 'Source' of life within us - also sustains and supports all that exists in the grand multidimensional creation. A deep humming sound and the consistent high single note of a flute playing a hauntingly beautiful melody from far away, will often accompany the experience of perceiving it with the inner hearing. In certain esoteric circles, it is referred to as the proverbial third or inner ear of the Atma or Soul. This is one manifestation of the primordial omnipresent first sound or word behind all creation simply known as HU – sounds like the name Hugh when an individual sends it out aloud using their vocal cords to connect with it. To connect with the primordial HU, send out the HU sound with vocal cords or send it out silently through the creative imagination. An inspired, disciplined training is necessary to properly master its overall intended capabilities.

The Dren City of Onn (Ahhn) – This Dren habitat is located inside a large extinct tube-shaped volcanic lava flow at the bottom of planet Oceana's Ocean, runs along the seabed toward the largest island. Inside it, a gigantic air-filled volcanic cavern many miles in length and a half-mile high glow with a mineral lining the rock walls. It lights up the countryside as if normal sunlight were the source. Luminous blue-green algae that covers the ground, like closely cropped grass, adds to the illumination. Well-cultivated, palm-type fronds and flowers grow along many winding paths that lead from a two-hundred-foot-high waterfall cascading out of a cave opening down into an elongated oval blue-green lake. Four-foot-in-diameter dome-shaped windows curve outward from the rock walls along both sides of the falling water. Large growths of every gem crystal known, and many more unknown by the rest of the Galactic Alliance citizens, cover the volcanic rock surfaces between the windows. Near the city's outer borders, the crystals are dozens of feet high and over four feet wide. At a higher elevation, natural deep-water springs bubble up to feed tributary pools that run off in small streams that empty into the lake. The far end of the lake drops down a wide cavernous opening.

The Galactic Alliance Council – This is the central benevolent governing council that dates back to its beginning 500,000 years ago from present Earth time. The wisest individuals that represent hundreds of millions of advanced space-faring world systems comprise the governing council of the entire Galactic Interdimensional Alliance of Free Worlds.

The Galactic Alliance Planet Zetranami – This central benevolent governing world, four times larger than Earth with three moons Earth's size, is located near the Galactic core of the Milky Way Galaxy. The most advanced wise individuals that govern this world, represent hundreds of millions of advanced space-faring world systems that comprise the entire Galactic Interdimensional Alliance of Free Worlds – not yet revealed in published books.

The Law of Love – The good and bad experiences that beings receive from the repercussions of the benevolent or malevolent use of their imaginations is the way that each individual eventually learns self-Mastery, while living in the physical universe. This is also true up through the finer dimensions above the physical world. However, this is not so in the fifth dimension or the true realm of the Atma or Soul. From this glorious realm of joy and into the yet much higher pure dimensions that eventually lead to the realm of The Ancient One or what many benevolent extraterrestrial races refer to as Prime Creator, there is only one law that rules supreme over all others. It simply states, "Love and do as you will."

The Master Crystal Staff – This is the most important of the three mystic crystals given to the Master Adepts of The Ancient One so far back in galactic history that no race but the Silent

Mentors know when the event took place. This cosmic device is under the guardianship of Master Ra Mu – the Adept of The Ancient One entrusted to use it only for the benefit of all life. The cylindrical transparent pure quartz crystal staff is six-foot-tall, crested with a symbol similar to the ancient Earth Egyptian Ankh – a vertical oval with a hollow center atop a cross.

The Mythological Atlantis Known Today – When people today debate its past location, it is understandable if they believe it may have been located somewhere in the area of the Mediterranean Sea, the Indian Ocean, or perhaps near Central America. They are likely basing their belief on a glimpse they had into a life they once lived at some point along the past time-track. The most ancient Atlantis continent was destroyed 100,000 years ago at the same time the massive Lemuria motherland continent was destroyed. This event left behind a five-hundred-square-mile Atlantis Island. It is important to realize that the physical poles of the planet were in opposite positions back then, and those past continent locations cannot be pinpointed by placing them somewhere relative to present-day continental landmasses with the poles positioned as they are today. To understand where this more recent Atlantis Island was located, the individual must travel down the past time-track and witness it for themselves.

Three Mystic Crystals of The Ancient One – These three

special tools were given to certain Master Adepts in ancient Galactic history, so they could properly train chosen students in the right use of love, wisdom, and power or charity. Special guardians protect them because the longer that anyone possesses a mystic crystal of The Ancient One, the greater is the increase of occult powers that awakens within them. Therefore, it is important to put the three crystals together in a special way – a method given to only a properly trained and prepared student. When this is done, the student goes through a mystical experience to become enlightened when they personally meet with The Ancient One or the 'Source' behind all that exists – located in the highest pure dimensional realm very far beyond the lower worlds of creation. The student then becomes a God-conscious co-creator with the source behind all life and a Master Adept of The Ancient One in their own right.

Trans-light Speed – A very advanced extraterrestrial technology allows spaceships to leap past entire star systems in what is called multiple trans-light jumps. It is one of the biproducts experienced when using antigravity propulsion systems. In this way, the occupants discover they travel a great distance across the galaxy in a short time. Although one cannot calculate this in terms of speed, it means that a spaceship utilizing this function can leap through naturally occurring vortex openings in space, normally invisible to humans, that link parallel dimensions together. The ship then travels for a short time in the space of a parallel dimension before it pops out of another invisible opening back to its own reality.

True Atma or Soul Energy Spheres – This is the true self of all individual beings – what many benevolent extraterrestrial races refer to as the Atma or what the human inhabitants of planet Earth often refer to as the Soul. Like the Ancient One, but much smaller in size, the Atma is made of spherical light energy that extends in ever-widening concentric spherical levels. Each layer, from a white core through the spectrum to a violet exterior, is comprised of many luminous teardrop-shaped lights. A subtle blue-violet hue softly radiating between the layers culminates in the blue-violet exterior layer, surrounded by a pale-golden aura.

Two Dren Children – These are Etta's and Din's playful Dren Children that appear to be about ten and eleven years old in comparison to Earth children. Often, they are observed frolicking on a floor, chasing each other through trees and up into the sky, or hovering beside Din. Usually, Etta's eyes bug-out excitedly and he screeches upon seeing them just before he races over to her to hover beside her and their children. They usually circle each other like happy bees hovering around a honey nest, and then Etta and Din tenderly rub noses together. Then the boy climbs onto Etta's shoulders, while their loving parents tightly cuddle their daughter between them.

United States Prototype Space Transporter – The newly designed elongated triangular-shaped Space Transporter hovering above the long runway, a dozen feet in front of its hangar by the very long launch runway at Area 51, is ready for its first test flight. It has three semispherical pods located on the bottom hull pulsing with pale blue light. They are centered between each rounded triangular end, and a thin luminous antigravity light surrounds the entire hull that brilliantly flashes just before the Space Transporter shoots straight upward at tremendous speed to abruptly stop at 10,000 feet.

Zon Ceremonial Pyramid & Landing Pad – This is a huge flat-topped ceremonial pyramid and antigravity-powered Zon Demon Scout fighter landing pad. It is situated in the center of a surrounding city built in volcanic terrain. The nearby black volcanic snow-capped mountain and the multiple-tiered dark blue stone fortress that had been built at its base and partially up the side are in the background.

Zon Demon Scout Fighters – These are anti-gravity powered, charcoal-colored, Scout class-size attack fighters with slightly batwing-shaped hulls. An oval cockpit window is positioned at the front top of the apex of their distinctive sharp-edged, elongated triangular trailing hull edges. Three semispheric pods are set in a triangular position on the bottom of their hulls, and a thin pale-red aura surrounds the hull of each ship.

Zon Energy Discharge Weapons – This is a hand-held polished gray metal, normally holstered gun-shaped energy discharge weapon strapped to the sides of Zon warrior guards.

Photo by: Jungle Jim (Behrens)

After over forty years of extensive experiential research, R. Scott Lemriel has finally put forth his third book, ***Guardians of The Ancient One*** – the second book of ***The Parallel Time Trilogy***. The three-part episodic story that may appear fictional is actually entirely based upon the author's direct experience exploring the past time track for the last four decades. His experiential research uncovered a vast depth of deliberately hidden truth regarding a significant aspect of the true history of planet Earth and our solar system and the benevolent and malevolent extraterrestrial beings that have, in one way or another, directly influenced the condition of our world and the direction it is headed today. These journeys revealed a treasure far beyond any expectations. Written prior to ***The Seres Agenda's*** hidden truth revealing book, all three book manuscripts of the trilogy were created for the purpose of sharing the experiential benefits of this unique, uplifting life-transforming adventure with his current and future readers right here on planet Earth.

Lemriel was originally inspired to write ***The Emerald Doorway (Three Mystic Crystals)*** experiential truth-based adventure and ***The Seres Agenda*** hidden truth revealing book he first published that provides the inspiration and very special techniques for readers that want to have their own direct experiences with awakening deliberately hidden truth. Many awareness-expanding events occurred during his childhood and throughout the adult life that enabled him to bring these books to public awareness. They involved a series of experiences mostly with benevolent UFO phenomena events, extraterrestrial technology, and the kind spiritually advanced beings that wield it, journeys via out-of-body-travel into the parallel and higher dimensional realities, as well as numerous excursions along the past time track. These adventures eventually revealed a hidden history of Earth and our solar system that subsequently helped to confirm the depth of suppressed truth he was uncovering in his own life. In addition, the music compositions and productions he developed throughout his life from his early twenties continue to kindle the fire which drives his ongoing explorations into knowing ever deeper hidden truth by direct experience – in contrast, only believing or theorizing.

Today, his continuing journeys into the vast nature of the multidimensional universe and his unique, uplifting music continue to serve as an inner channel of inspiration to further explore and awaken ever so much more about our true nature as knowing eternal beings. Lemriel is genuinely passionate about sharing eye-opening, enlightening experiences and unusual encounters he gratefully received while uncovering cleverly hidden truth. For the first time, he discloses how our planet is about to be unexpectedly, benevolently transformed in the near future instead of destroyed because of a recent off-world decision that was finally made concerning changing Earth's current destructive destiny: he takes the reader on their own personal journey to discover the reality of the existence of UFOs or advanced alien spacecraft; extraterrestrials both benevolent and malevolent who fly them; the nature of our true spherical energy form the kindest advanced extraterrestrials refer to as the Atma or what people on Earth call Soul; and the reality of the existence of parallel and higher dimensions. He further reveals to his readers what he discovered about a most important part of planet Earth's missing ancient history and discloses how he experienced much about the depth of purposefully hidden truth from the guidance of masterful teachers the majority of human beings dwelling on earth today do not know existed at any time.

He gratefully acknowledges his mother for being the first person to read and experience the revealing depth of the transforming, truth-revealing pages that these books represent. She discovered, greatly surprised, much about her son she never knew or even imagined because he kept silent about his uplifting life-transforming experiences – until now.

Originally from Salt Lake City, Utah, where Lemriel spent the first six years of his life, he devotes a lot of his time to writing about his continuing explorations into uncovering deliberately hidden truth. He does this through ongoing out-of-body journeys and direct experiential explorations into the UFO and extraterrestrial phenomena with the great majority of kind beings that live in our vast multidimensional universe. He has a passion for writing books and screenplays, creating musical compositions, and has an ongoing dedication to bring into reality very special feature film and episodic TV story projects. This, coupled with a series of awakening lifetime events, provides him with the rare opportunity to serve as a co-creative conduit of the uplifting, life-transforming, omnipresent living energy that supports and sustains all that exists.

The changing destiny for grand new life-transforming adventures to be experienced is now opening up in a very definite protected manner for human beings worldwide, including the book-reading public. For your experiential benefit, explore the free YouTube.com videos of the author's personal presentations he conducted at International UFO/Extraterrestrial hidden truth disclosure conferences held around the world. If you wish, you can also explore many promotional videos about *The Seres Agenda* and *The Parallel Time Trilogy*, as well as listen to recordings of the author interviewed on many radio shows located inside Lemriel's unique uplifting and eye-opening main websites at www.ParallelTime.com. You can also explore various overviews of his feature film projects and listen to feature film-related music productions. Discover two uplifting recordings of his voice sending out the very special vibratory word simply known as HU that sounds like the name Hugh sent drawn out on the outgoing breath. It can safely connect each individual to the pure omnipresent 'Source' behind and support all that exists. All four of his interlinked websites & YouTube channel are located at:

www.ParallelTime.com (primary)

www.TotalSpectrumPublishing.com (supporting)

www.TotalSpectrumProductions.com (supporting) &

www.TotalSpectrumMedia.com (supporting)

https://www.youtube.com/user/LemrielT3691 (YouTube channel)

It is a wondrous adventure to experience the recovery or awakening of deliberately hidden truth on a grand cosmic multidimensional scale and discover the much greater knowing certainty of the vast love within it. The books, videos, radio interviews, music productions, and website links are also accessible through a search on Google by title, the author's official Washington, D.C. Library of Congress copyright pseudonym R. Scott Lemriel or his legal name R. Scott Rochek. Links to his very unique websites are also on Facebook, LinkedIn, and Twitter.

www.ingramcontent.com/pod-product-compliance
Lightning Source LLC
Chambersburg PA
CBHW020921110726
47900CB00001B/252